Forbidden Rescue

Book #2
The Blake Cutter Detective Series

By
E.T. Milligan

Copyright © Edward T. Milligan, 2020

Cover Design by Donika Mishineva
www.artofdonika.com

All rights reserved; no part of this publication may be reproduced or transmitted by any means, electronic, mechanical, photocopying or otherwise, without the prior permission of the publisher. This is a work of fiction. The events and characters portrayed are imaginary. Any resemblance to real-life people or locations is entirely coincidental.

The moral rights of the author have been asserted.

All rights reserved.

Acknowledgments

The author wishes to acknowledge the invaluable assistance of these people:

Robert Schobernd, Penny Glasgow Hutson, Donika Mishineva, and Jamie Austin.

Prologue (Excerpt from Book #1 – Past the Line)

Blake Cutter sat reminiscing through the events of his painful past. A car bomb, intended by an assassin for him, had killed his wife, Jenni. There was the murder of a prominent real estate couple, the Drummonds, in Bullet, Georgia. There was his encounter with Penelope Lane, a Jenni doppelganger, at the cemetery. Then Cutter made an unauthorized trip to the Cayman Islands with that same lady who had become a person of interest in the case. There was a strange and eerie discovery at Penelope's apartment before the woman he had become involved with took him hostage when her arrest was imminent. A sniper attack on the roof by an unknown assailant attempting to kill Penelope. Penelope's accidental fall from the roof to the ground which could have resulted in paralysis or her death, and then returned to surgery to resolve unexpected internal bleeding. The FBI was rushing to take control of the case involving Penelope by assigning an incompetent, rogue agent,

FORBIDDEN RESCUE

Ronaldo Kelly, to lead it. And finally, his time and effort being diverted to finding Olivess Norton, a young woman suspected of murdering Jimmy Delray, a known drug dealer, who may or may not be connected to the Drummond murder.

For Agent Blake Cutter, it all had become a nightmare, but was, in fact, his reality.

CHAPTER 1

On a crisp and cool late September morning, Georgia SBI Agent Blake Cutter walked into BPD headquarters for the morning briefing. His mind was preoccupied with figuring out a covert way to split time between the Jimmy Delray and Phillip Drummond murder cases without his SBI Chief Harry Ryker or any other police officials getting wind of it.

At that same moment, two unidentified men entered the front door of Bullet Regional Medical Center and walked into the ground floor lobby. They were dressed to look like the other hospital maintenance workers, in dark blue custodial pants, industrial stripe poplin work shirts, and nondescript black work boots, similar in design to military boots. They paused and viewed the atrium to verify they were not being noticed or followed. Then, they proceeded to walk across the atrium to a set of elevators located on the east end of the floor. One of the men was a skinny Caucasian male in his late thirties with thinning blonde hair, a scraggly goatee, and heavily tattooed arms. He went by the nickname Spector.

Spector carried two oversized, black canvas cargo bags, similar in size to military-style parachute bags. The bags had no identifiable markings and the bar codes had been torn off so the bags could not' be traced to any store purchase if someone happened to find them. The other man, Rico, was a tall, black, muscular-built man with dreadlocks down to his shoulders and several small facial scars along both cheeks and across his forehead.

Despite the oddity of wearing sunglasses inside a building in the early morning, the two surprisingly drew no attention from the crowd of workers and hospital staff passing through the lobby. Even the front entrance security guard who stood near the information desk saw them but did not give them a second thought as their falsified badges were visible on the pockets of their shirts. They managed to blend in with the normal cluster of hospital employees and staff passing the ground floor lobby every morning.

As they reached the elevators, they encountered another security guard who had not been on the ground floor when they conducted their dry run the day before. Spector was nervous as he reached for his badge with his left hand to reassure himself it was visible. He surmised the obvious; extra security had been put in place to defend the target they were commissioned to take out, the patient named Penelope Lane.

Rico, acting more composed, stepped in front of Spector as they approached the elevator furthest to the right. The security guard glanced at them from his post at the elevator on the far left. Luckily, the elevator that opened then was the one on the far right. Rico glanced back at the security guard for one second then turned to mimic talking to Spector. The young, newly hired security guard was preoccupied with reading the text messages on his cell phone.

"They've got more security in here than we expected," Spector pointed out. "Can we do this?"

"Do not wimp out, dog. I will take care of my end. You just make sure that thing goes off," Rico replied confidently.

"Where are you're going to be when it detonates." Spector asked.

"Do not worry, bro. I will find a safe place," Rico replied confidently.

"Good luck with that," Spector warned. "This is some bad shit about to go down."

Chapter 2

Rico entered the elevator and pressed the fourth-floor button. As the elevator door closed, Spector looked around the pavilion to ensure no one was observing as he waited for his ride. He glanced at the security guard who again was shirking his duties by rapping to a nurse and distracting her from her assigned duties. Despite the events of 9-11, the preponderance of active shooters, and the overall threat of terrorism at large crowded facilities, individual complacency was still the norm.

Sensing a general laxity in security, Spector heaved a sigh of relief as he stepped into the blue service elevator and punched the Level A button, the first of three below-ground floors. Level A housed the hospital's storage rooms and linen depository.

A few minutes after Rico and Spector had entered the lobby and then disappeared into the labyrinth of the facility, Cutter halted his vehicle at the parking lot in front of the main entrance of the hospital. As he got out, he noticed a nondescript, white panel van parked near the front atrium. He walked through the front double doors, looked back, and noticed the van pulling away. It left a subtle blip in his memory, but only a blip.

Moments later, when Cutter reached the ICU, he was buzzed in and found the ward at its usual early morning pace. Nurses scurried about with clipboards in hand as they made their rounds to dispense patients' morning medications. As he walked up to the nurses' station, he noticed Rico standing next to a water cooler near the end of the hall.

Cutter stared at him. Rico did not move but kept looking around as if he was waiting for something to happen. Although Rico wore a custodial worker's uniform, something about him did not seem right to Cutter.

Positioned behind the reception desk was a tall, slender African American female nurse in her mid-thirties. At that moment, she was speaking to an elderly couple who were visiting a patient on the ward.

"Excuse me," Cutter said as he stopped near her and interrupted her conversation with the couple.

The nurse stretched her lower lip to indicate her displeasure with the interruption.

"Can I help you?" she asked in an unpleasant tone.

"I'm Agent Cutter with the State Bureau of Investigation on assignment with Bullet Police Department."

"How do you do, sir," she responded respectfully. "Is there something I can help you with today?"

"That guy down the hall there," he said, gesturing with his head. "Is he one of the hospital staff?"

"I-I suppose so," she replied carelessly, glancing at the man. "I don't know these custodial people personally. They rotate so many through here. Why do you ask?"

"He just doesn't seem like a custodian type," Cutter remarked.

Her eyebrows rose. She looked over at the elderly couple and signaled with her hand for them to wait a minute, instinctively knowing that the inquiry by Cutter was a matter regarding security.

"What's a 'custodian type' supposed to look like?" she asked.

"I don't know. I thought a custodian usually had a mop or broom in their hand," he clarified. "He seems to be just hanging out at that water cooler doing nothing."

She lowered her eyes to the clipboard and then turned to speak to the elderly couple. "Mister Cooper is down in room seven, straight down that hallway on your right." She walked a few steps with the couple until she knew they were headed in the right direction, then returned to talk to Cutter.

As she approached Cutter, she peered down the hallway at the man. "He doesn't look like he's working," she agreed. She dropped her chart on the desk and stared down the hall at Rico again. "He's new. You think something's wrong?"

"I don't know," Cutter replied. "Do you know how long he's been up here?"

"We just buzzed him in maybe a few minutes ago. He had an ID badge," she replied, her tone now more serious. "Is there something wrong? I can see if anyone else on the staff recognizes him."

"No, that's okay," Cutter responded with an appreciative smile. He wasn't satisfied with her response but was cautious about causing a panic. "I'm just wondering if you keep a log on people who work on this ward."

FORBIDDEN RESCUE

She scoffed, "Look, sir. I prepare morning charts. If you've got some questions about this gentleman, you need to talk to my supervisor, Miss Pearl Simmons, and she can contact housekeeping. She'll be up here shortly."

"Thank you," he replied cordially. "Yes, I've met her before. I'll wait here and talk to her."

Meanwhile, Rico continued standing carelessly by the cooler. Cutter kept staring his way until Rico noticed him. Rico could smell a cop like fresh-brewed coffee. He turned his back to Cutter and began filling a paper cup with water from the dispenser. He swallowed rapidly, balled the cup in his fist, tossed it in the trashcan and walked toward the end of the hallway. Cutter had seen the reaction many times before by both drug dealers and terrorists.

At the end of the hallway on the right was an unlocked utility closet. As Cutter's attention was diverted by the arrival of the ward supervisor, Rico opened the utility closet door, stepped in, and locked the door from the inside.

Nurse Simmons walked up and spoke briefly to the desk clerk who informed her of Cutter's concern. She then approached Cutter. "My desk clerk said you have a question about one of our custodians," she said.

"There's a man down the hall who seems to be acting suspicious," Cutter informed her. "I just wanted to verify his identity. He......"

Cutter stopped talking as he looked down the hallway and no longer saw Rico. "Oh crap, where is he?" Cutter said softly.

As she furrowed her brow, Pearl replied, "There's an equipment room, medical room, and break room down there. He went into one of those rooms. What's going on?"

"Can you escort me down to those rooms, ma'am?" he asked. Cutter didn't want to be wandering around the ICU without authorization.

"Sure, we can go take a look," she responded cooperatively. They scurried down the hallway, glancing in patients' rooms as they passed. Miss Simmons opened the equipment room and medical room doors and Cutter glanced inside. There was no one there. They then looked inside the break room which was the last room on the left side of the hallway. There was one nurse sitting at the table, finishing a bagel and coffee.

"Good morning, Sarah!" Miss Simmons spoke. Then, Cutter noticed a room she hadn't mentioned, the last one on the right near the double doors.

"What's in that room," he asked pointing.

"That's just a utility closet where we keep cleaning supply and other stuff," she noted to Cutter. She paused a second expecting Cutter to tell her not to worry about it, but he didn't utter those words. Cutter could tell by the tone in her voice and her annoyed facial expression that she felt put out by having to open these various rooms for reasons unknown. Nevertheless, they walked over to the room together.

Exasperated she said harshly, "It's locked. I doubt anyone went in there."

Before Cutter could object, they overheard the ping sound as the ICU double-doors opened. A Caucasian male dressed in custodial attire walked in.

"Excuse me, but did you notice a tall Black man with dreadlocks pass by you, a man who looked around thirty years old?" Cutter asked him.

The man replied, "Just now? No sir."

"Who are you?" Cutter asked him.

With a furrowed brow, he answered, "I'm the ICU floor custodian. I'm just starting my shift." He noticed the concerned look in Pearl and Cutter's eyes. "Is there a problem?"

"Are you the only custodian working in the ICU?" Cutter asked.

"I'm the only one assigned to this entire wing of the hospital," he qualified the question. "What's going on?"

Cutter sighed heavily while thinking, then replied. "No worries. Thanks a lot for your information." Cutter nearly knocked the man off his feet as he pushed him aside and sprinted out the double doors into an empty hallway. Peering in both directions, he saw no one, then sighed heavily again, exhibiting frustration. He returned to the ICU front entrance.

As he stopped and shook his head in frustration, Pearl asked him, "Is everything okay? Did you see him?"

He paused for a moment and then said, "No, but just let me know if you see him return to the floor. I won't interrupt your work any longer for now. Here's my card. Call me if anything suspicious happens."

As he walked off the ward, he wondered whether he really had reason for suspicion or if he was becoming overly paranoid by his concern for Penelope's safety. Nevertheless, he clicked onto the radio net and called each security checkpoint within the hospital, giving a description and ordering a search of every nook and cranny of the facility for the mysterious fake janitor.

CHAPTER 3

Meanwhile, Spector had reached Level A, the first below-ground floor of the hospital. He surveyed the cavernous hallway until he located an inconspicuous spot in a far corner. He knelt and began unpacking the first black canvas bag.

Being a former U.S. Marine demolitions expert, Spector was the right man to bring into the crime world and for pulling off a bombing of a multi-floor building. He had fallen into the underworld's grasp after being dishonorably discharged from military service and spending a three-year prison stint at Ft. Leavenworth, Kansas Disciplinary Barracks. His prison time came because of a string of drug offenses while deployed and assigned to an Explosive Ordnance Disposal unit in Afghanistan. Spector honed his demolition skills and knowledge of constructing improvised explosive devices. He became self-taught on other incendiary devices through surfing the dark web at internet cafes. It didn't take long for the mafia kingpin Ransom Oliver, who needed a demolition expert, to get wind of Spector's talents and have his mob recruiters rein him.

When DeSalvo learned of his skills, he had his contacts on the street rein him in. Spector's life of small-time bomb making was officially over. For this assignment, he'd been dispatched to Bullet from Miami two days earlier. Upon arrival, he laid low in a seedy motel on the outskirts of town until he received DeSalvo's phone call to execute. Spector had no connections to anyone in the area. His materials had been stored in an abandoned warehouse on a remote dirt road outside Bullet. Rico Calderon, one of Oliver's trusted lieutenants, provided everything he needed.

Spector managed to fit everything he needed into the two black bags. The contents of the bags included several one-pound blocks of C-4 wrapped in pressure-sensitive adhesive tape, a container of ammonium nitrate, blasting caps, relay switches, timer-activated fuses, shaped charges, five hundred feet of detonation cord and a hammer drill and assorted sizes of drill bits.

After a visual scan of the floor to ensure privacy, Spector unloaded the bags and began using the hammer drill to systematically drill holes in concrete at various places along the exterior walls. He then inserted C-4 blocks inside the holes at every corner, stringing the blocks together in a daisy chain with detonation cords which were wrapped together at the ends with duct tape. Due to the low lighting and the fact the white color of the det cord matched the walls, Spector wasn't concerned about the wires being detected. He was more concerned about the C-4 being concealed inside the walls. Spector then fastened a blasting cap to each explosive and attached detonation cords to a relay switch which could be remotely activated by his cell phone. It took him less than an hour to get everything in place before he repacked the unused materials back into the two black bags. He then grabbed the bags, walked over, and punched the ground floor button of the elevator and took it to the lobby. The information he'd received regarding the arrival time of Level A employees for the day shift had been accurate. He now had plenty of time to casually make his way out from the hospital.

CHAPTER 4

As Spector was exiting the building, Cutter was about to enter the ICU. He encountered a middle-aged, red-headed hard nurse. He addressed her, "Good morning, Ma'am. I'm Agent Blake Cutter with the Special Bureau of Investigation. Can you tell me where I can find Miss Simmons?"

Speaking with a distinctive Southern drawl, she replied, "You just missed her, honey. She went to a morning meeting. I'm guessing she'll back in the next thirty minutes."

"Please tell her I'd like to see her and update her on information from our previous conversation," he requested politely. "I'll be in the waiting room."

"Sure, sweetie! Anything else I can do for you?" she asked, in her usual Southern politeness.

Cutter replied simply, "That's kind of you to offer, but no thanks."

Twenty minutes later, Cutter walked to the ICU waiting room. Meanwhile,

Pearl Simmons returned to the ward, was told an SBI investigator needed to see her, then proceeded there and found Cutter patiently waiting on the sofa. Cutter greeted her warmly due briefed her on the security situation. She immediately ordered all nurses to require visitors on the floor to sign in again with identification.

Meanwhile, Cutter scrambled back to the main reception desk in the pavilion where he confronted the security guard about the entry of the dark-skinned male. The guard drew a blank.

He then proceeded to the hospital video control room and reviewed the past three hours of security footage from the video surveillance tape. There was no one captured on the recording that fit the mysterious man's description.

Moments later, Michael Ryan, the hospital's chief of staff, joined Cutter at the front desk. After a short meeting with Cutter, Ryan called John Sanford, the hospital's human resource manager and ordered him to pull the files of all custodial employees. The HR department maintained a file on all past and present employees. The file included original job descriptions, employment contracts, copies of background investigations, and most importantly, identification photos.

Minutes later, Sanford arrived back at the front desk. He briefed them on the results of his screening of the personnel files. Amongst the twenty-five files maintained of custodial employees, Sanford stated that were only three identification photos that fit Cutter's visual description.

Sanford informed Cutter to rule out Oscar Smith, a 30-year-old African American assigned to the east wing. A telephone call to Smith's supervisor revealed Smith was currently on sick leave but when present, was a reliable and trustworthy employee. In Cutter's experience, Oscar Smith's name could certainly be an alias.

The other two Black males fitting his description were assigned to different outpatient clinics on the west wing of the hospital complex.

After Ryan slipped away from the conversation and headed back to his office, Cutter asked Sanford, "Can you, just for the record, verify the other two gentlemen?"

"What's the purpose?" Sanford asked, irritated by a further disruption of his busy morning schedule. "You said he didn't meet the height requirement."

"Maybe we need to take a second look at his physical features just to be sure," Cutter suggested. "You should want to eliminate all suspicions. I'm sure you understand the consequences if we've all miscalculated."

"Alright, if you insist, but I really think you may be wasting everybody's time."

"I don't think your boss would agree with that," Cutter shot back. Sanford frowned but did not challenge the request.

Suddenly, the elevator opened, and Pearl Simmons appeared. She scurried over to the desk.

"Agent Cutter, thank God, I found you," she said, out of breath. "I think I can clear this all up. I know the boys who work in the ICU. I look out for them. I don't want anybody racially profiling them."

"I take it you've had problems with that before?" Cutter inquired curiously.

"You're damn right," she replied, pulling Cutter to the side. "Somebody's got to look out for them. How many Black people do you think are in supervisor positions in this hospital?" she retorted.

"I see where you're going." he answered, rhetorically.

"That's right," she followed. "There might be Black custodians working here that fit the description of the man you're talking about, but I trust them. If we had somebody like that working up here, I would've had my eyes on him, and I'd be the first to know if something wrong was going on."

Cutter flashed a sympathetic grin.

"Okay, Miss Simmons," Cutter backed off. "I have one more thing to tell you, Agent Cutter."

"Yes?"

"Nobody's going to come in here and shoot up the place. I look out for my nurses and my patients; safety, also."

"I greatly appreciate that, Miss Simmons." Cutter acknowledged warmly. Though entertained by her candid and outspoken remarks, he excused himself from her and Sanford's presence and went outside to the quieter front entrance. There, he buzzed Ryan on his cell.

"Mr... Ryan, Ms. Simmons believes the man we're looking for is not one of the custodial workers for the ICU."

Ryan paused then responded, "Then we may have a security breach. I'll arrange reinforcement and put the staff on alert."

"I appreciate it," Cutter offered.

"Don't thank me. If you think we have a threat, that's enough for me. We take security seriously at this hospital."

"Glad we're in sync. Nevertheless, I don't want mass hysteria. There's one glitch."

"What' that?"

"I suggest you talk to your man, Sanford. It sounds like he's not playing ball or taking this as seriously as we are."

CHAPTER 5

During the next three hours, the entire hospital security staff ramped up to locate the intruder. Ryan requested the hospital security teams establish checkpoints on all exits and prepare for a hospital lockdown. BPD could only offer three additional officers due to the security requirement for a scheduled visit by a Georgia state senator.

Despite the resource shortfalls, Carruthers dispatched a sketch artist to the hospital, who met Cutter in the hospital cafeteria. From Cutter's description, the artist drew up what Cutter deemed a ninety-five percent composite. Cutter then had the composite faxed to each department head and each member of the makeshift security team.

At six thirty p.m., Cutter walked to the hospital human resource office. Sanford greeted him with an irreverent grin.

"I still don't see the need for all this," Sanford growled. "I think we're all overreacting."

"May I sit?" Cutter asked.

"Certainly," Sanford responded, gesturing Cutter to a couch.

"I'll level with you, Mr. Sanford. We were trying to keep information about this as discreetly as possible. We may be dealing with a paid assassin trying to either kidnap or murder a patient in ICU named Penelope Lane. She is also the suspect in two murder and is under police custody."

Sanford dropped his fountain pen on the desk and leaned back in his chair. "That sounds a bit of a stretch that someone would try to take out a patient in a hospital. I know there have been a couple of murders in the county lately, but an assassin targeting a patient in a hospital. It could happen, but c'mon!"

"I can understand your reason for doubt, Mr. Sanford. But you've been overruled. Law enforcement has authority when it comes to public safety, even in your hospital. You'd better talk to Ryan."

The comment annoyed Sanford, acknowledging he was being ordered in the politically correct way to 'shove it'. Sanford then stood abruptly and replied, "Okay, Agent Cutter. You'd better have a police official here when this story breaks out to the media. You're setting this hospital up for a PR nightmare. I'll follow orders but I'm hoping you can find a less intrusive way to deal with this. What comes next, the National Guard?"

Cutter rose, offered a crooked smile, and replied, "If it gets to that point, you'll be the first to know."

Sanford walked out of his office whispering expletives under his breath, yet fully realizing he was already outvoted.

During the time Cutter was meeting with Sanford, Rico was in the closet taking off the work shirt and pants. Underneath, he wore a set of blue hospital scrubs. He tucked his dreadlocks under a surgical cap before tossing the work clothes behind a wall locker. Then he checked the time and rechecked his 9mm pistol. He sent a text to Spector to confirm Spector's location. Rico was primed and ready to reward the first person to unlock and enter the closet with a bullet.

CHAPTER 6

The situation remained calm throughout the hospital during the evening hours. At nine p.m., Ryan, Sanford, and other key hospital officials departed for the day, convinced the threat of an intruder roaming the wards was a false alarm.

Cutter, still suspicious, decided to spend the evening on the ICE ward, slumped over the foot of Penelope's bed. At ten, she opened her eyes. She looked as one would expect a woman who'd been in the hospital recovering from several surgeries. Her lips were dry, her hair was a disheveled mess, her skin was ashen, dry, and flaky, and her body smelled of burnt hair from the surgeries. Nevertheless, Cutter wanted to divert her mind off her current state, so he invoked a poignant smile and said, "Good morning, Penelope."

"Blake, you're still here," she uttered, moaning as she raised her head from her pillow.

He noticed she was still heavily sedated, in pain, and drifting in and out of consciousness. "I'm not leaving you tonight," he replied with a smile. He was offended that she didn't respond, cognizant that she wasn't coherent enough to maintain constant communication.

She closed her eyes and then reopened them.

He was surprised she heard his voice.

"I guess I've made a fine mess of things, haven't I?" she asked rhetorically, tears welling in her eyes.

Her unexpected question left Cutter speechless. He could find no words to debate the obvious. She was a murder suspect and under medical arrest with charges pending.

She responded to his silent affirmation by lying back on her pillow. "I suppose I'll need an attorney," she declared.

Cutter desperately wanted to comfort her but knew comfort would only come with false promises. "I'll try to make sure you get the best public defender available or a good criminal defense attorney, if you can afford it," he offered, sounding like he was reading part of her Miranda rights.

Tears streamed down her face. She placed her palms over her face. "Why did this all have to happen? I didn't mean for either Dorothy or Phillip to die, honest I didn't."

"We shouldn't talk about this any further right now," he advised her. He sensed she was begging for him to embrace and comfort her, to offer her forgiveness. But the events of the last few days had reduced his level of vulnerability. She stared up at him confused and disheartened by his reluctance to appease her.

Dismissing the temptation, he wisely chose to lead the conversation in a different direction. "I'm afraid there's something urgent we have to deal with," he said.

"What is it?" she asked, wiping her eyes, and trying to compose herself.

He took a deep breath, then explained, "There was a man here on the floor this morning who we believe was posing as a custodial worker. We think he may have been surveilling our security setup. He could still be inside the hospital."

She began shivering. "My God, they're coming after me."

"I didn't say that," Cutter objected.

"What did he look like?" she asked.

"He's a tall, athletically built African American, with his hear in dreadlocks. He has a large scar down the left side of his face, and he was heavily tattooed on both arms."

She cupped her chin and thought for a moment. "I'm not sure but I think I might know somebody that looks like that," she revealed. "If it is who I think, he's a bodyguard for one of Phillip's business partners.

"What kind of business?" Cutter asked as his eyes lit up.

"I'm not sure, but I think he's one of the guys connected to the mob. They would meet Phillip at the Regal Room in the Devil Island Clubhouse and when they arrived, Phillip would ask me to leave."

"Do you know his name?"

She thought pensively for a moment and then answered, "If it's who I think it is, his name is Raphael, but he goes by Rico."

"Are you sure about this?"

"It all adds up," she concluded, her face paling with fear. "I knew if anything ever went wrong, they would try to kill anyone who could identify them."

FORBIDDEN RESCUE

Cutter clenched his teeth in anger, followed with a furrowed brow of concern. "Don't worry about it," he consoled her, deceptively. "We have extra security throughout this hospital and we're looking for him. We'll protect you here."

"Oh, Blake, cut the crap! You of all people know the mob doesn't give up until they get their target. They'll find a way to get to me . . . even in here."

"We can stop whoever it is, Penelope," he said, trying to reassure her. "But I need more than a name. I need to know what Phillip was doing, and all that you know about his contacts, friends, associates."

She paused before responding, indicating she knew much more.

"I know Phillip was planning a forgery scheme to gain property his wife owned. Since I worked in the building, he used me to spy on her . . . to pass information to him about what she knew and what she was planning to do with the land. He was hoping to learn the Real Estate's Commission's position on her bird habitat proposal. But then after a while, I realized he was just using me. He wouldn't call or see me for a while after I gave him information. Then, he would meet with me over dinner and time his questions. If it weren't on one outing, it would be the one shortly thereafter. He was very clever and deceptive. It became a predictable pattern for him. Every time he got the information from me, he'd shove me off. I felt like I was being disposed of like a soiled rag. I felt so insulted and betrayed."

"So, you went to the island that night to get revenge . . . to kill him?" Cutter prodded, inquisitively.

Avoiding a direct admission, she answered, "No! I just wanted to confront him about how I felt. What would you do if someone you care about and trusted used you and humiliated you?" Her conscience was now betraying her much more than Phillip ever did.

23

Penelope's voice began breaking, and she looked more exhausted by the moment from the strain of her admissions. But she continued. "I knew about the cruise. So, I went to the island, parked near the pier, and waited for him to return. I wasn't sure whether to extort him with my knowledge of his forgery fraud or just curse him out and end it. I just had to get even with him in some way for what he was doing to me. I was surprised when I saw him walking down the beach. I had no idea what he was doing, so I got out of the car and followed him. I figured I could catch up with him somewhere in a secluded area. I thought about how badly he'd hurt me. I was so angry. I wanted him to understand my pain."

"What did you do?" Cutter prodded, again. He noticed her looking faint but had to take the gamble that she would stay conscious and tell the whole story. *Who knows if I get another chance or if she'd be willing to talk so openly in the future, especially once she recovers?* he thought to himself.

She continued, "I followed him up to the pier at Moss Point. But then, I got scared. I figured someone would see me on the beach. So, I turned around and went back to my car. When I got there, I saw Dorothy walking down the beach. My first thought was that she was going to meet him. I became enraged by this. I even pictured him screwing her on the beach. Crazy thoughts entered my mind. Me . . . his mistress, jealous of his affair with his wife, right. I couldn't take it anymore. So, I decided to walk back to Moss Point pier and confront them."

She stopped talking, choked up and cried.

Though Cutter felt sympathy for her plight, he could not delay her from confessing. He had to hear the entire story. He glanced at the door to ensure no one was listening or nearby. He then turned back to her and remained silent momentarily until she was composed enough to continue.

Her voice broke further to the point it was barely audible, as she continued, "When I got to Moss Point, I saw him, sitting on a big boulder, staring out at the sea. But I was surprised he was alone. I didn't know where Dorothy was, and I really didn't care. I just knew they were conspiring against me . . . to get me out of their lives. I could not stand that thought, especially after I had written her an anonymous letter telling her how he'd deceived her."

"You didn't think for a minute that perhaps she was chasing him down the beach to confront him also?" he asked.

"I wasn't thinking logically, Blake. My rage and jealousy had overcome me. A rock lay next to where he was sitting. So, I snuck up behind him and hit him with it. Then, I hit him again. I noticed, the rock had blood on it, so I ran over to the shore and threw it in the sea."

As she wept, he asked, "I know this is painful, but what happened after that?"

Her face took on a demonic expression as she continued, "I wanted him to suffer just like he made me suffer. I was tired of being overlooked, getting the short end of the stick. Why was everyone like Dorothy getting it better than me?"

Cutter detected her beginning to ramble, getting off track of his intent for her tacit confession. So, he interrupted her. "I understand Penelope, but was he dead?"

She refocused and answered, "I noticed he wasn't moving. That's the first time I thought I might've killed him. For a moment, I was happy. That's what he deserved for how he treated me."

At that moment, Cutter saw a narcissistic, sadistic side of Penelope he'd never seen before. It shocked him but he internalized the emotion so as not to distract or scare her. Instead, he said, "I understand the feeling."

"Then, I stood there, and I got confused. I couldn't let myself believe he was dead. Phillip always seemed invincible. But as I stared at him, he didn't move an inch. So, I felt his pulse, listened for breathing and realized he was dead. "

Cutter accepted the lack of empathy in her expression. In those few short moments, he'd seen her emotions run full circle, from fear, to shame, to regret to justification, and to cold-hearted evil. But again, Cutter knew he had to keep silent, not to accuse or criticize her during a moment few detectives get—a confession without being coerced.

"I know you're getting tired, Penelope, so we can stop soon, but I need to know what finally happened on that beach."

"I just panicked. All I could think of was to drag his body into the bay and hope it would drift away and disappear."

Cutter's eyes widened with shock. "I guess you left the beach at that point," he inferred.

"Not then. I saw someone at the distance walking towards a hotel. I couldn't recognize the person, but I assumed it was Dorothy."

"What happened then?" he prompted.

"I followed her to the hotel. When she entered through the back, I ran to my car and left. I was going to drive home, but then I noticed how windy the night had become. That's when I realized the tide was coming in. I thought the body might be swept in by the tide and Dorothy might come back to the beach and discover his body on the shore. That damn tide would mess up everything. I had to take a chance and go back to make sure no one discovered his body.

"So, you rented a jet ski?"

"I found this rental shop near the main gate. This college kid who worked there rented me the jet ski and trailer and I had him hook the trailer to my car. He warned me it could damage my car, but I didn't care about that. I had to go back to make sure his body was gone. If it didn't wash up right after I left, I figured Dorothy would be blamed for his death. If someone other than me saw her walking down the beach that night, she would become the prime suspect. If there was an investigation, I would be in the clear. I couldn't help but think selfishly at the time. I'm sorry, Blake. I didn't mean to kill him."

Chapter 7

Cutter was tempted to let Penelope incriminate herself. But he knew he would be breaking a code of professionalism by allowing a suspect, even one he loved, to provide a detailed confession without being read the Miranda rights and have legal representation. He tried to pull himself back by warning her, "You shouldn't say anything else without legal counsel."

"No!' she shouted. "Don't stop me, Blake. I need to tell you everything."

"I don't advise it," he cautioned her again.

She grabbed his hand. "No, Blake. You must know the truth. I love you and care about what you think of me."

He could no longer resist the temptation, so he told her to continue, feeling that her next words might reveal extenuating circumstances. At least, that's what he hoped for.

She paused for a moment to wipe away tears. "I didn't go to Dorothy's home with intent to kill her," she said. "I thought she had someone spying on me, so I wanted to confront her about it, peacefully. I even thought I might confess to her about the affair and ask her for forgiveness. She'd already figured out that anonymous letter had come from me."

"How did it escalate?" he asked.

There was a pause as she again drifted in and out of consciousness. Cutter touched her forehead in an attempt for sensory stimulation. It seemed to work as she twitched strongly and regained consciousness.

"She seemed hospitable at first," she spoke coherently. "Then she asked me to come upstairs. When we got there, she showed me the hotel receipts from when Phillip and I stayed at the Ocean view on Devil Island. I could not believe Phillip had been that careless to leave them where they could be discovered. I could only guess he was such an arrogant prick that he wanted her to find out about the affair."

"Are you sure you feel well enough to continue?" he asked solemnly, remembering Caulsen's warning about her state of health. By now, her mouth was running on autopilot.

"I have to tell you the whole story," she said sniffling. "After she showed me the receipts, she became enraged, throwing them in my face, calling me a white trash whore. She even accused me of plotting with Phillip to steal her land. I could not take it. He screwed me and threw me away like garbage. I was tired of being treated like trash, Blake. It was more than I could take."

The uniformed officer standing outside the door overheard her voice becoming louder and stepped in. "Sir is everything alright?" he asked.

Cutter waved him back out the door. As the door shut, she sucked in a deep breath and winced from the discomfort of her chest contusions, but continued,

"I-I wanted to just walk out and leave the house at that point. But she grabbed my dress and put her hands around my throat and started choking me. Before I could break loose, she shoved me to the floor and spit on me. Then, as I rose from the floor, she slapped me and pushed me . . . like my dad did. That's when I lost it."

Cutter was tempted to ask her about that statement. Maybe she was priming him for support in a mental insanity plea. He made a mental note and allowed her to continue talking.

Suddenly, Penelope weakened and positioned her head back onto the pillow but continued talking. "Then, it all went to hell." she went on. "I managed to push her away from me. But when she laughed at me and said, *"You are nothing! Phillip would never want some lowlife like you for a wife."* That's when I struck her."

Cutter momentarily wondered if she was putting on a façade like she did in the Caymans. Needing a moment, he moved away from the bed and over to the door. He knew how clever killers could be, especially one who could get inside your head or worse, your heart. The ebb and flow of his emotions was unnerving. "This is too crazy to comprehend, Penelope. I don't know what to think."

Struggling to stay awake and coherent, she pleaded, "Blake, you've got to believe me. I never wanted to hurt anyone, but she pushed me to the breaking point."

"I believe you," he assured her.

"It doesn't matter what you believe at this point. Everyone will think I'm a cold-blooded murderer," she countered, prodding for sympathy.

"Nobody's rushing to judgment," he replied flatly, yet his face was creased with doubt. In his expression, she gleaned he held no magic wand to make her troubles go away. He walked back over to her bed and offered an obligatory smile.

"Let's not talk about this anymore today. You need to rest."

Cutter gently squeezed her hand. Mentally exhausted by the pain of her recollection, she closed her eyes and instantly fell asleep.

He left the room and the ICU ward, desperately needing space to come to terms with her confessions. It was shocking but most of all overwhelming. He had already been to the coffee dispenser several times that day, but another caffeine rush would offer some relief to his disappointment and shock. He needed a cup of coffee . . . and he needed it strong and black.

CHAPTER 8

Recharged by the black coffee, Cutter returned to the ICU waiting room. As he passed the front desk, his cell phone buzzed. It was McBain requesting a meeting with him at the hospital. He would bring along Lieutenant Tom Henderson, Chief of the BPD's Electronic Surveillance Division. He explained that for the past week, Henderson's team had been receiving backchannel information from an FBI field office in Miami about Bennie DeSalvo's activities. Miami law enforcement officers had been running wiretaps as well as surveilling several of DeSalvo's legitimate business establishments.

The meeting sounded important enough for Cutter to remain in the waiting room for McBain's and Henderson's arrival.

Thirty minutes later, Cutter received a call from McBain that he and Henderson had arrived at the hospital. Cutter gave them directions to the hospital cafeteria. Cutter found a vacant booth in the corner of the room. When the two arrived, McBain introduced Tom Henderson. "Blake, this is the man who may help get this case out of neutral. Let's get some coffee and talk."

After buying cups of coffee, they returned to the booth where Henderson started the conversation. "I'll cut to the chase. Blake. One of our contacts in Miami informed me DeSalvo has left his Miami operation in the hands of his trusted lieutenants. Through wiretaps, the bureau traced conversations between two syndicate members about an operation with a code name *White Shadow*. The boys in Miami don't have a clue what that means."

"*White Shadow*." Cutter repeated the words.

"You're familiar with it?" asked Henderson.

Cutter responded, "It's a syndicate code name for a kidnapping operation. I'm willing to bet Penelope Lane's their target."

Henderson interjected, "It's a long shot to think a big-timer like DeSalvo would risk exposure by ordering a contract on somebody this insignificant."

Cutter remarked, "Maybe there's something she knows that makes her a target . . . something that gives them a reason to want to take her out."

"We wouldn't get much support from the bureau on that theory," Henderson countered. "If we want an arrest warrant or even ground or air surveillance, we'd better establish something more concrete."

"We can start by locating that imposter that's running loose in this hospital," Cutter interjected. "If you really want to help us, Lieutenant, we need some backchannel communication with every investigator involved in this matter."

"That's unlikely," Henderson pointed out.

Frustrated, Cutter asked, "So why's there's such a problem?"

Henderson explained, "The problem is walls have ears, Agent Cutter. The bureau heads will make mincemeat out of anyone who blows their cover in

Miami. Forget about DeSalvo for now. It's best that you capture this intruder, see what you can get out of him and take it from there."

Though Cutter wanted to see pressure put on DeSalvo more than anything, he sensed a loss of focus. He asked, "So why is the bureau so bent on getting in on this case?"

Henderson leaned forward and whispered, "What I'm about to tell you is close hold. If this gets out, I'm screwed," he warned.

His eyes widening, Cutter replied, "You got it."

McBain nodded in consensus.

CHAPTER 9

Satisfied with their agreement of discretion, Henderson decided to reveal confidential information that would get him fired if leaked outside of BPD without authorization.

He briefed, "Two weeks ago, agents in Miami subpoenaed phone records of men suspected of being associates of DeSalvo. Most of the calls were pinged from cell towers near Devil Island, Georgia and one specially from an abandoned warehouse in South Miami. One of the phone transmissions from Devil Island was between DeSalvo and Phillip Drummond on the night of his death. We believe they were working out some details of a major forgery scheme. You'd better not bust DeSalvo unless you're sure you've got the smoking gun. The bureau has a surveillance operation ongoing. We're talking about the future of interagency cooperation if something gets screwed up. There's a lot more at stake here than protecting some young woman's ass.

If we don't nail DeSalvo clean, his operation will go completely underground, off the grid and it may be years before we get another shot at him."

"So, what does that mean for me?" Cutter asked, with a sudden incensed look on his face. "I've been trying to nail that son-of-a-bitch for over five years. This was my case in Miami . . . and I lost my wife in a car bomb intended for me because of it."

Henderson tightened his lips with a sympathetic stare. "I feel you, Blake, but here's the reality. It was never the intent of the bureau for BPD to do anything more than investigate a drowning and close the case. You weren't supposed to publicly tie the drowning investigation to anything . . . and I hope to this point you haven't done that. That's the feds' job when you have a mobster like DeSalvo who's on the FBI's most wanted list. Be careful not to get in over your head."

Cutter turned to McBain with an irreverent grin. "So, you knew about this?"

Cringing apologetically, Alex said, "Henderson filled me in a couple of days ago. I didn't want you to get in the crossfire unprepared."

Leaning back in his seat, Cutter replied sarcastically, "I don't know how to thank you, partner."

"You *should* thank him, Blake," Henderson noted. "This case was about to blow up in your face."

"My apologies, Tom," Cutter backed off. He realized his frustration with the situation was being misdirected. "I appreciate you looking out for me, but you didn't have to come over here to tell me this."

"No worries." Henderson replied as he stood. "I wanted you to hear it firsthand from me. You should take it more than as an advisory but as a warning. Just keep this conversation on close hold."

Cutter walked McBain and Henderson to the front entrance, while they continued their conversation. As they reached the front entrance, Cutter turned to Henderson and said, "Since you stuck your neck out for me, I'm about to break a promise of confidentiality. I figure I owe you the courtesy."

"Duly noted," Henderson pointed out.

"I've got a quasi-confession from Penelope Lane regarding the murders of both Phillip and Dorothy Drummond. She seems certain DeSalvo has put out a contract to have her silenced."

"She's been traumatized and she's highly medicated, Blake," Henderson argued. "I don't know if you can trust her confession while she's in that state. It won't be admissible in an indictment and may not even justify a warrant."

"I'll ask her to provide a deposition, once she's off the pain meds," Cutter countered. "I just need another day or two, that's all I need," Cutter pleaded.

Henderson paused in thought. "I'll ask Field Operations Command to include you in anything relating to White Shadow, but I can promise they'll read you in. You'd better move fast on finding that intruder. There's a lot of pressure to hand the entire case over to the bureau. Once that happens, you're done."

"I hear you," Cutter growled. "But this is more about politics than anything else."

Henderson replied bluntly, "I share your thoughts, Blake. But it amounts to nothing when it comes to an operation like White Shadow." The three exchanged handshakes as Henderson and McBain departed the hospital.

An hour later, Cutter received a call from Henderson.

"Good news, Blake. We may get lucky and have an ID on your intruder. I asked my contact from Miami Vice Squad to send you via e-mail some photos of an African American and a couple of dark complexion Caribbean males who have been on their watch list from previous syndicate activity. One of these might be your intruder."

Chapter 10

Five minutes later, Cutter received the text from Vice Squad, opened the attachments and viewed six photos of men associated with the Miami syndicate. *"I think that's him,* Cutter murmured. He then forwarded to Henderson the photo of a burly Black man with dreadlocks—the one which most closely resembled the man he observed on the ICU floor.

Henderson called Cutter immediately. "That description fits the bill," Henderson confirmed. "His name is Rico Calderon, a Cuban national. He's one of the guys we think has left Miami and is part of the Milano's crime family. We've heard he's running a chop shop on the outskirts of Bullet. According to what Vice passed on to FOC, his joint's been under surveillance for some time. They've observed a limo pulling in through the front fence on several occasions in the past week. I doubt the limo was there for bodywork. However, the bureau won't move in prematurely. They'll have to see some evidence of drugs, or shipping containers or something that would justify a search warrant."

"I'll show the photo to Miss Lane and see if she recognizes Calderon," Cutter said.

Then Henderson warned, "You must keep me in the loop step-by-step, Blake. The bureau didn't want those photos circulated but my contact in Miami took a risk and did us a favor. This gets out and you'll be handing our heads to Internal Affairs on a silver platter."

"I'll keep yours off the platter, but mine's already there." Cutter pointed out.

After hanging up with Henderson, Cutter headed back to Penelope's ICU room.

As he walked through the door, Penelope sensed by his cold steely stare it wasn't a casual visit. "Blake, what's going on? I didn't expect you to come back today?"

He hesitated, took a deep breath then said, "I have something I need you to look at." He pulled out his cell phone, clicked on the photo of Rico Calderon and handed her the phone. "Do you recognize that man?"

Her expression answered the question. Mortified, she handed the phone back to Cutter. Composing herself, she told him, "Several times when I was with Phillip, he would spot this man's car, pull over into the nearest parking lot and get into the other car and leave. He would always have me drive his car back to his office. Foolishly, I never asked about it or even complained."

"Are you sure it was the man in the photo?"

She hesitated momentarily, then confirmed, "Yes, that is the man. I couldn't mistake his face and those dreadlocks for anyone."

"What make and model of car did they leave in?"

"It was a black El Camino. Those cars are very distinctive so I'm sure about it. It was the same car every time."

Cutter took a deep breath and stared into her eyes. "Have you seen him on this ward since you've been here?"

Penelope scoffed, "I haven't seen anybody but you, the medical staff, and these four walls. What's going on, Blake?"

Cutter sighed for a moment, then informed her, "I think I saw this man on the floor."

Chapter 11

A half hour later, McBain arrived back at the hospital, to check on Cutter before heading home. Catching him dozing on a couch in the waiting room, he woke him saying, "You need a break, partner. Won't you go home?"

Yawning and stretching, he replied, "No. I'm all right. You didn't have to come by this late."

"I just happened to be in the neighborhood," McBain calmly joked.

Cutter sat upright giving his full attention. "I know you came here for a reason. Lay it on me."

"I got a call from Carruthers. He wants to see you and Ryker at his office in the morning."

"I can't leave the hospital right now, Alex," Cutter protested. "Penelope's starting to talk."

"You might want to break away, chap. Carruthers wants to talk with you and Ryker about a leak in the department. He thinks somebody's been tipped off about Penelope's whereabouts. He thinks it could be someone on the inside . . . or worse—it could be one of our own in SBI."

"That's worth me leaving here," Cutter acknowledged. "I hope it's a short meeting. I can't lose my chance to talk to her."

As they began to walk out, McBain said, "If we can find the leak, then you may not need to."

At ten thirty that evening, the BPD tip line received a call from a clerk in a Bullet southside convenience store.

The voice on the line stated, *"I overheard a woman fitting your description of Olivess Norton talking to another female inside our store about going out to some plantation home somewhere to retrieve her book bag and then leaving town. I had seen a news broadcast a few days before about a suspected homicide in which a thousand-dollar reward was offered by the BPD to anyone with information leading to the arrest of a suspect named Olivess Norton. I think this might be your person. I'm not leaving my contact information unless you're offering reward money."*

Within fifteen minutes of receiving the tip, BPD Chief Joe Carruthers was notified, and he had his deputy chief send the information to the field agents in that area as well as the BPD surveillance team. I took about an hour before one of the field agents reported back to Carruthers that he'd spotted two females in a late-model blue Toyota Tundra heading out towards the plantation site.

Carruthers immediately called SAC Harry Ryker at home. After a short strategy session, they decided to send an interagency task force out to the plantation with a standing arrest warrant Carruthers had initiated a week earlier from a magistrate. After a short consultation Ryker selected Agent McBain to lead the stakeout and apprehension.

Back at the hospital, a few minutes before midnight, a nondescript white van stopped at the front entrance of BRMC. It was the same van Cutter had noticed two days earlier. The driver of the van circled the facility several times casing it like a robber would a downtown bank.

Spector sat in the passenger seat. In his right hand he held a cellular phone he planned to use as a remote detonation device. His G3 Walter 9mm pistol was loaded and secured inside the unlocked glove compartment.

At the corner of the parking garage, the vehicle came to a stop, and Rico Calderon slid from the rear door, dressed in hospital scrubs. He no longer had dreadlocks and had changed his look by shaving his head. He always tried to be one step ahead of the cops. He walked parallel to the back side of the building to a side door to the interior stairwell. Rico used the stairway to carefully make it back to the ICU floor without being detected. If he'd encountered any law enforcement, he was prepared to engage them, given he carried a 9mm pistol and a sawed-off shotgun located in his backpack. He had two boxes containing twenty-five shotgun shells and ten magazines each holding fifteen 9mm shells. Along with the sidearm under his belt, he was armed with over two hundred rounds. Unobserved, he casually walked past the ICU entrance door and moved back into the utility room at the end of the hallway—the same room he'd hidden in two days before. Since the "All-Clear" notification had been given the night before, the utility room was again left unlocked as a cleaning crew had used it for storage of items that same day.

After dropping off Calderon, the white van made four passes around the hospital, to stall for Calderon to reach his destination. The driver stopped the van fifty yards west of the hospital entrance. He parked parallel to a set of tall shrubs, which hid the vehicle from view of people coming in and out of the entrance. After Spector killed the engine, he glanced at his watch, then punched a telephone number into the phone.

The detonator device was set to allow five rings before it triggered an explosion. That would give Spector time to disconnect the line and halt execution if something went awry. He wheeled the vehicle around to the side of the building.

At that moment, Cutter and McBain waited on the second floor for an elevator car.

McBain took a call from Ryker to meet at headquarters and command a team going after Olivess Norton. As Ryker's call ended, he and Cutter entered the elevator. "Looks like I'll be leaving you and be up all night—."

Suddenly, between the second and first floor, they heard a loud BOOM. The elevator compartment jolted violently then stopped abruptly. Both men fell to the floor. Simultaneously, the power in the entire hospital went out and the elevator compartment went dark. "What the bloody hell was that?" McBain asked, rising from the floor.

"I don't know," Cutter replied. "Felt like a small earthquake or maybe an explosion."

"I hope this isn't what I think is happening," McBain responded.

"Yeah! Me too."

As the hospital's backup generators kicked in, the service lights flicked on, and the compartment resumed its descent to the first floor.

Composing himself, McBain said, "That was definitely some kind of explosion." When the elevator reached the first floor, the door opened to plumes of smoke and debris rapidly enveloping the hallway. People were running and screaming in terror.

Someone shouted, "Somebody set off a bomb!"

The hallway and walls shook as another loud boom rang out from a second explosion. The glass doors at the end of the hall exploded from the overpressure. Shards of glass and metal knifed toward the floor. Ceiling tiles and metal frames collapsed. Veils of smoke billowed through the walls and enveloped the entire floor.

Through the screams, Cutter pointed up to McBain, "ICU!"

They rushed up the stairs fighting past people going down until they reached the fourth-floor stairwell doors. With the power off, nurses were frantically recovering patients off the floor. Confused, fearful patients and hospital staff rushed toward the nurse's station where the usual therapeutic silence of the late night had given way to screams of panic and chaos.

A nurse grabbed McBain's arms and asked him to help her with a bleeding patient and to push her wheelchair to the stairwell where an orderly needed help.

The below-ground floors and underground parking decks were instantly gutted by the blast, but the lobby and above-ground floor sustained moderate damage, which was enough to injure people from flying glass and debris. Most of the fifteen staff members in Levels A through C were injured from collapsing structures and falling debris. Walls buckled as the hallways became filled with smoke and a mixture of grey and white masonry dust. Those that escaped injury were expeditiously escorted through the chaos with singed eyebrows and faces covered in black soot.

Though the main back-up generator had momentarily restored limited power, it was only temporary as damage to the interior electrical lines quickly caused a loss of all auxiliary power within the hospital. Only battery powered emergency lights dimly illuminated the chaotic scene.

CHAPTER 12

Amid the chaos, Rico moved out of the small utility room. Though tossed about by the two blasts, he survived unscathed and was ready to execute his part of the operation. He took a moment to gather himself, and then retrieved his medium frame Beretta, semi-automatic handgun off the floor. He used the strings of his scrub pants to secure it to him and then gently opened the door and peered outside. He smiled, knowing that if anything went wrong, the gun would be untraceable, due to the serial number being shaved off.

He observed staff members frantically wheeling patients off the floor. Yet, no one made direct eye contact with him. So, Rico slipped into the hallway unnoticed, blending in with the crowd as he rushed to a spot behind a wall pillar only two rooms from Penelope's door. As he unobtrusively turned his back towards the wall, he waited for an opportunity to enter her room.

He observed the uniformed police officer standing guard by her door while looking unsure of what he should do.

The guard suddenly became caught up in the hysteria, leaving his post to aid one of the nurses having difficulty getting a wheelchair bound patient through the double door. He was then asked by another nurse to bring Penelope out of her room. He spotted a vacant wheelchair near the reception desk and pushed it toward Penelope's door.

As the officer moved the wheelchair inside Penelope's room and unfolded it, Rico snuck up behind him. Using a tactic, he had mastered as a commando in Cuba, Rico struck the officer across the back of his skull with the butt of his weapon. The officer clutched his head as he fell to the floor and lost consciousness.

Awakened by the explosions, Penelope painfully struggled to sit upright in her bed. As shock and fear encased her, she recognized Rico as the man with Phillip at the Devil Island Clubhouse, the man Cutter had showed her in the photo. She instantly surmised what he was there to do. She shouted at him, "What are you doing in my room? Get out, Rico!"

Rico rushed to the side of the bed and struck her pale, bloodless lips with a backhand smack from his massive, sweaty right hand. She fell backwards onto the pillow. With blood dribbling from her mouth, she attempted to rise but was knocked unconscious by a second blow, this one his knuckles against her temple.

He laughed with pleasure, mentally thanking her for the opportunity to unleash his unbridled rage. Rico purred from the adrenaline rush, thinking, *I wish time allowed for him to rape the bimbo.* He dismissed the thought as he surmised that engaging in a sexual assault might piss his boss off. *"But when the boss finishes with her . . ."* he growled under his breath.

At that moment, Cutter reached Penelope's door. He noticed the security guard on the floor as he rushed into Penelope's room while reaching for his gun. As the door closed behind him, he was paralyzed as a 9mm slug entered his left shoulder.

Cutter flinched and glanced at his bleeding shoulder. Rico responded by running up to him and executing a spinning sidekick, hitting the side of Cutter's head, and bouncing him off the wall. Cutter became Rico's next victim to fall unconscious. Rico took a brief second to savor his work before tucking his pistol back into the waistband of his scrubs.

Since DeSalvo explicitly said he wanted the woman alive and able to talk, Rico moved the wires from the nearby monitors and the I.V. needle from her arm. Gently, he lifted Penelope up and gingerly placed her into the wheelchair. He cautiously exited the room and pushed the wheelchair towards the double doors, as he blended in with other staff and patients.

Mission almost complete, he whispered under his breath.

CHAPTER 13

As Rico was exiting the ICU floor with Penelope, McBain bolted down the ICU hallway and into Penelope's room. He saw the fallen guard on the floor. He checked his pulse and confirmed that the guard was knocked unconscious but still alive. Then, he turned and saw Cutter struggling to his feet near Penelope's bed.

"Blake, what the bloody hell happened here?" McBain asked as Cutter stuttered and shook his head.

"I . . . I don't know" Cutter responded. Then, Cutter looked over at the empty bed. "Where's Penelope?" he exclaimed.

"Did someone take her?" McBain asked.

"I don't know. Check the bathroom!" he requested in a frantic tone.

"Blake, you're bleeding. What happened?"

Coughing and wincing, Cutter blurted, "Somebody shot me. I will be all right. Just check the bathroom!" he repeated as he struggled to recall what happened as the lighting fluttered to darkness.

McBain darted over and peered into the bathroom. "She's not there!" he announced as he turned back into the room.

Simultaneously, their faces went blank. The silent pause was heightened as smoke seeped into the room.

"Whoever shot me must've grabbed her." Cutter concluded. "I'm betting it was Rico Calderon."

Cutter stepped over the fallen officer and moved towards the door. "I've got to find them before they get out of the hospital."

McBain reached and grabbed Cutter's arm to stop him. "Wait a minute, Blake. What are you gonna do? You need medical attention."

With his right shoulder hanging low, he responded, "Let go of me, Alex. I am going after her."

McBain held onto his shirt sleeve and pulled him from near the door back into the room. "Look Blake. I will radio downstairs to get a search going for her. You have to get that treated."

Ignoring his warnings, Cutter broke loose from McBain and stumbled out the door and into the hallway, holding his left hand over his bleeding right shoulder.

"Wait, Blake!" McBain yelled, but it was too late. By the time McBain stepped over the guard and reached the hallway, Cutter was already through the entrance double doors.

McBain negotiated his way past debris and people screaming and running in different directions. He frantically made it through the pandemonium to go after Cutter. When he reached the double doors, he glanced out in both directions. He followed a trail of blood splatters leading to the stairway. *"Goddammit, Blake. You and this damned woman,"* he huffed. McBain switched on his handheld radio to the police and notified other officers.

"All stations, this is a security code one. We have a possible abducted patient. Look for a dark-skinned male wearing hospital scrubs and an incapacitated female patient with short black hair. She could be in a wheelchair. Guard all exits until further notice!

By then, flashing beacons from police cars and fire trucks and other first responder vehicles lit up the front grounds while news service helicopters filled the sky around the hospital complex. Through every exit door, terrified and confused patients and staff were herded by security guards to proceed into the main parking lot. Rico, pushing the unconscious Penelope in the wheelchair, blended in with other staff members who were wheeling patients out of the facility.

By sheer luck, the guard at the hospital's main entrance failed to hear the part of the radio transmission providing the identity of the abductor. He errantly cleared Rico through the exit with his unconscious patient in the wheelchair. Relieved, Rico peered across the lot and spotted the white van parked at the far west end of the building. He waved to Spector to approach him. He was acknowledged by the headlights flashing and the van proceeded forward, then stopped.

Scores of injured people blanketed the parking lot as medical teams set up makeshift triage points. Advantaging the crowds, Rico maneuvered the wheelchair to the drop-off point near the west entrance.

CHAPTER 14

One a.m.

As Cutter exited the main entrance, he recognized Penelope slumped over in the wheelchair as Rico and Spector were lifting her out of the chair and into the van.

"Penelope!" Cutter screamed.

Spector and Rico heard the scream and turned to see Cutter staring at them from the entrance doors.

"Stop!" Cutter yelled feebly, reaching to his side for his Glock. His holster was empty. He had fallen out of the holster when he fell to the floor in Penelope's room. Cutter frantically limped towards the van but to no avail. Spector and Rico hopped in the van and began driving away.

Rico pulled out his pistol and aimed it at Cutter. But Spector yelled, "Don't shoot! We don't need attention. The job is done!"

Seconds after the kidnappers sped away, a police SWAT van pulled up to the front entrance. As it plowed to a stop, the men dismounted to form a perimeter around the front of the hospital. Other police officers, firefighters and other first responders on the scene escorted the clustering herd of onlookers away from the building.

Battling blackout, Cutter caught the attention of one of the team members as Spector's van was temporarily stopped behind another exiting vehicle near the intersection to the main road. Cutter pointed at the van and yelled out to the man, "Stop that van! They've kidnapped a patient!"

As the SWAT team leader hesitated to react, the white van maneuvered around the vehicle in front of it, sped through the red light and veered left onto the main street. It would have been a perfect time for a traffic backup on the usually busy thoroughfare in front of the complex, but every move made by the kidnappers worked in their favor. A break opened in the traffic, and they easily drove through several intersections unabated.

Loss of blood had Cutter lingering on the edge of consciousness. A few steps later, he lost his balance and fell helplessly to the pavement.

McBain saw his friend collapse and ran to him. As a patient got out of a wheelchair, he grabbed it and the nurse with it and got Cutter seated.

Cutter momentarily gained consciousness. McBain took advantage of the moment by attempting to reassure him the captors would be located.

"They headed southbound. We've got several ALPRs along those routes." McBain informed him. He was referring to Automatic License

Plate Reader/Recognition units deployed in the South District due to a significant increase in car thefts in the last year.

Cutter grinned but then passed out. The nurse pushed Cutter to the parking lot where emergency care was being given.

McBain shook his head, looked at his watch, then jogged to his car to go to BPD headquarters as he had been previously ordered.

CHAPTER 15

Within a few hours after the bombing, national and local news teams had dispatched camera crews to the scene. Over ten different news teams surrounded the hospital complex with reporters clamoring for interviews with anyone having direct knowledge of or who had witnessed the incident. Police and news helicopters jockeyed for position as they hovered some 1500 feet overhead. The first reports indicated thirty-seven people were dead. Scores of injured were being triaged in the parking lots while others were transported to nearby hospitals. The uninjured patients were relocated to a local high school gymnasium. Satellite feeds hit regional and national networks in enough time for airing on every national and regional morning newscast.

Cutter remained hospitalized overnight at BRMC for observation. By morning, physicians determined the gunshot had not severed any major arteries or caused bone damage. At nine thirty a.m., Cutter was discharged and left the hospital with his arm in a sling. At the parking lot, he encountered a stream of reporters approaching the hospital front entrance to interview anyone connected with or having an interest in the incident—local law enforcement and ATF, hospital staff, and even victims. It was like a swarm of bees to an empty hive.

Through the infestation of media, Cutter looked to the distance and noticed SAC Harry Ryker's personal vehicle parked in the main lot. He waited at the entrance door as Ryker fought his way through the crowd and approached him.

"Are you okay, Cutter?" Ryker asked when he walked up to him.

"I've had better days," Cutter replied.

"What happened here?" Ryker asked, rhetorically.

"Where do you want me to start," Cutter replied as he winced in pain."

Ryker took note of Cutter's condition. "You can brief me later. You need to take the rest of the day off to recuperate."

"I can't afford to do that, "Cutter argued.

"That's not a request, by the way," Ryker replied, pulling rank.

Shifting, Cutter asked him, "What have you been told so far? You know as much as me."

Ryker briefed him, "We suspect that two mafia operatives connected with Bennie DeSalvo had some part in this. Rico Calderon for sure in the kidnapping of Ms. Lane. I spoke to both ATF and BPD by phone on the way here. No arrests have been made. Whoever perpetrated this attack got away clean. BPD's doing a trace on the make and model of the van to see if it has been reported stolen. I will have someone check to see what's on the hospital surveillance cameras. There is a briefing with the mayor later today."

"How'd you get through that mob?" Cutter asked, breaking a smile.

"I promised I would have someone give them an interview," Ryker said. "You don't get out of here quick, it's gonna be you."

Chapter 16

Ryker departed for the hospital entrance as Cutter decided to heed Ryker's advice and headed home to rest and recuperate. A few steps from the car, a female reporter and her sidekick camera operator approached him. Cutter caught sight of them and quickly stepped into his car to try and avoid them. Unfazed, she walked up to his driver's side door, knocked on the window and flashed her press credentials. "How about thirty-seconds about that bombing last night?" she asked in a muted sound.

"I have no comments at this time," Cutter replied, brushing her off. "You'll have to wait for an official press conference."

Her expression turned to chagrin as she pleaded, "C'mon, I've got to make a living too, y'know."

Cutter turned to face her, lowered the window halfway, and sighed, asking, "Okay, who are you?"

"Pamela Rutledge with Action 5 News," she answered proudly.

Impressed by her persistence, Cutter said, "I'll give you a minute and that's it."

"Go!" she urged.

"All we know so far is an explosive device went off in the lower deck of the hospital causing casualties. The hospital and local law enforcement are investigating. That's all I can tell you."

"Can you elaborate at all on the number of dead and injured?" she asked with a microphone pointed in his face.

"Sorry. I'm not providing any statistics," Cutter added simply. "You'll hear from us when we learn more." He started the engine, raised his window, and drove off.

Realizing she was being shoved off, she dropped her microphone to her side and murmured under her breath, "Prick!"

Chapter 17

The Stakeout

It was three in the morning. The task force consisting of two BPD Agents, McBain and veteran SBI Agent Lee Culver, a sniper from BPD SWAT and two members of the BPD special response unit arrived in two unmarked sedans and a van. They were staged at a location 250 yards short of the entrance to the plantation. After hiding the vehicles in the woods, they moved rapidly on foot to their assigned positions surrounding the plantation. Normally, BPD would utilize no less than 10 law enforcement officers to execute a search warrant or an arrest of that sort, but resources were strained due to other drug enforcement commitments. Thus, only one of the team members proceeded to the backside of the plantation to prevent an escape by that route. The sniper stationed himself on a small, concealed hill above the grave of

FORBIDDEN RESCUE

Olivess Norton's ancestor. McBain and Culver proceeded to a wooded spot fifty meters from the access road with a view of the dirt roadway that ran from the highway up to the plantation.

If the tips were legitimate, the task force anticipated Olivess Norton would arrive sometime during the early morning, from a drop-off point on the highway or in a vehicle delivering her to the front gate. In both scenarios, she would have to walk up the steps to the porch and enter the premises on foot, which would afford the team an opportunity to make the apprehension without entering the premises. What they couldn't predict was whether she would be arriving alone or accompanied by armed gang members. Although they were prepared for both scenarios, they preferred to not get into a gun battle with a bunch of youth.

The task force made up for their lack of manpower by dressing in black tactical outfits and face camouflage and carried high powered rifles with night scopes, tactical binoculars, multiple small firearms, and other accessories. If she'd enlisted the support of neighborhood gang members, they were prepared for a gun battle that could be problematic, especially in such a heavily wooded area that would be difficult to conduct a chase at night.

BPD had five assigned K-9s that normally accompanied a SWAT team with limited manpower for tracking and pursuit of suspects. The problem was the entire K-9 unit was tasked out to support the post bombing's search and rescue and hospital clearing operations. If Olivess wasn't wanted in connection with a murder, McBain's entire crew would have been assigned to the hospital bombing.

The night cloud cover and lack of moon illumination left the entire plantation area pitch black. A fog bank was forecast to blanket the area in the early morning hours, making it even more problematic to pursue a fleeing suspect through the woods. Fortunately, the police could use their portable battery powered lights to switch on when a human was confronted.

As they remained quietly in place, the only activity over the next hour was the noise of crickets chirping, wood frogs croaking and the occasional deer roaming through the woods. Over the next two hours, the task force remained patient and disciplined with minimal radio contact. They would wait as long as it took to secure the capture of a murder suspect.

CHAPTER 18

At approximately four in the morning, McBain picked up the humming of a motor close by. The team listened for footsteps as they assumed it was from a drop-off on the main road.

While McBain remained in his position, Agent Culver moved through the woods in the direction of the highway. After about a hundred yards of trekking through the bushes, he heard a loud roar of an engine as the vehicle accelerated until the sound slowly faded. It was apparent the vehicle had stopped near the entrance of the dirt road. Culver's mission was to move slowly through the woods towards the highway until he picked up the sound of footsteps and then take cover and radio back to McBain.

Two minutes later, Culver heard footsteps approaching in the middle of the road about fifty meters in front of him. Light from a flashlight illuminated a small area of the road. He could only observe shadows of two people, due to the overarching tree limbs causing complete darkness on the dirt road.

Culver radioed back to McBain, whispering, "Tango 1 this is Tango 2 over,"

"Tango 2 go ahead," answered McBain.

"Two individuals about fifty feet away approaching our direction."

"How far are you from my location?"

"About one hundred yards."

"Do you have a visual?"

"No. Only shadows and footsteps . . . but sounds like two or three people at the most."

McBain then ordered, "Maintain your position. When they're parallel to you or you have visual, click me."

Clicking the voice emitter had become law enforcement's latest method of short-range coded communication when voice or radio sounds risked detection. It was being used exclusively for team leaders to receive signals to proceed ahead with an assault.

Seconds later, Culver's night goggles picked up two heat signatures.

Culver radioed back, "Only picking up two. They just passed me walking, not talking, just footsteps. I can see them, but you have a clearing near you."

McBain pulled out his 9mm Glock from the leg of his black tactical pants, slowly rose, then brushed away damp leaves. "Roger. When I hear the footsteps, I'll call you back. Then you come up behind them. I'll step onto the road, and we'll make the apprehension."

"Roger, that!" Culver whispered.

Twenty seconds later, as the ground light and footsteps passed his area, he radioed back to McBain, "They're coming up on you." He then tiptoed onto the dirt road but a safe distance away from the walkers.

"Copy," McBain responded, indicating he could now hear the footsteps approaching his area. A few seconds later, McBain radioed back to Culver, "Go!"

Simultaneously, McBain and Culver flipped on their tactical lights mounted on their submachine guns and flashed onto the dirt road from opposite directions of the walkers.

McBain pointed his weapon at the female's face and shouted, "Stop where you are! Don't move!"

Her Black male companion, a dreadlock haired, low rise jeans wearing youth who was in his mid-teens, moved to reach at his bulging right pants pocket. From behind, Culver pointed his weapons at him and shouted, "Don't try it, son!"

The two halted any further movement. The male raised both hands, but the female raised her empty left hand only.

"Drop the bag, now!" Culver shouted to her, "Drop to your knees . . . both of you!"

The male knelt first as McBain shined his flashlight in his face. The female started to turn around, but Culver shouted, "Don't turn around. Just drop to your knees!"

She acknowledged and followed her companion to the ground. She dropped her head to the musty earth and uttered, "Okay, just don't shoot my cousin. He got nothin' to do with anything."

As McBain moved forward, he pointed his weapon with the light scope at the female.

"Let me see your face," McBain said loudly as Culver handcuffed the male.

She lifted her head, squinted from the light directly in her eyes and looked up at McBain. McBain reached into his jacket pocket, pulled out a printed computer photo, and gave it a prolonged stare. He then shook his head in frustration.

Culver asked him, "What's wrong Alex?

"It's not her," McBain dropped his weapon to his side, sighed heavily then responded. "This isn't Olivess Norton."

CHAPTER 19

Four forty-five a.m.

Forty-five minutes later, McBain and Culver arrived back at BPD headquarters with a uniformed officer and the two detainees in a police van with the other two vehicles following closely behind. The two detainees were brought into BPD through a side door to avoid any media attention. While they were taken to different rooms for interrogation, McBain phoned Ryker to brief him on the arrest.

"Her name is Lola Fields," McBain informed Ryker. "She stated she's a friend of Olivess Norton and claimed she came to the plantation to retrieve Olivess' book bag which contained some personal travel items. The young man's name who was with her is Richard Motley, a Bullet resident and who Olivess claims to be her cousin. She says he has nothing to do with Olivess

Norton's troubles and just agreed ride out to the plantation with her for company and protection.

Ryker instructed McBain to not call Cutter to participate in the interview, because had been admitted to the hospital for his injury. He directed McBain to conduct the interview of Lola Fields while Richard Motley, who went by the nickname Brickey would be questioned separately by another detective.

Brickey, whose father was a local construction worker and his mother a part-time substitute teacher at the local high school, was a handsome young teen, despite the stylish disheveled dreadlocks. When he turned twelve, he sought a nickname. African Americans males in Bullet rarely engaged in bullying in school but picked on him on the sandlot courts because of his name Richard. He had been teased frequently throughout middle school, called *Richard the Chicken Hearted, Richard Simmons and Good Golly Richard Motley,* amongst others whimsical references. None of them had any rhyme or reason for him, but they didn't need to in a small neighborhood where homies would pick on victims at any opportunity to get a laugh.

The way he sat upright in the chair rather than the way low life usually slouched, indicated to Culver he wasn't a troubled teen and not a felon or accomplice to murder. In the interview, he revealed he'd been a cousin companion of Lola Fields since elementary school. He stated that he met Olivess through Lola but knew nothing about her dealings with local thug, Jimmy Delray and certainly knew nothing regarding Phillip Drummond.

While Brickey was interviewed at Culver's desk, McBain had one of the uniforms look him up in the police database. His name came up in the database from several police interviews, but it revealed he had no priors, no rap sheet, and no outstanding warrants. So, he had a clean record and posed no reason for law enforcement to suspect he had any involvement with Olivess Norton or Lola Fields other than what was stated in his written deposition.

It was eight when Culver came to McBain's desk and informed him the interview with Brickey was complete and he was being released without further questioning.

Chapter 20

Eight a.m.

"Are you still letting Ms. Fields stew by herself?" Culver asked McBain.

McBain answered, "Yeah, but she should be softened enough by now. Let's see what she says."

They proceeded to Interrogation Room 1 and opened the door to the young African American female slouched in a chair on the opposite site of the table with her knees together and her legs shaking with nervousness. An empty can of Pepsi soda and bag of chips lay in front of her.

She knew they could charge her with aiding and abetting a suspected fugitive. She wasn't about to reveal any incriminating information unless she took an oath, or they strapped her to a lie detector. She took a deep breath and waited to see what was going to happen.

McBain walked into the interrogation room and Culver followed directly behind. They sat in the two chairs across the table.

"You've got about ten minutes to tell me why we shouldn't lock you up," Culver advised her, bluntly.

Lola placed her hands on the table, inched forward and professed, "Because I can tell you where Olivess is at."

Culver and McBain looked at each other with raised eyebrows.

"Keep talking," McBain prodded her.

She paused momentarily and then continued, "She sent us to retrieve her bag and bring it to her before she left town. She needed a few hours so she figured even if you caught us, the attention would be away from her till noon."

"While we go chasing our tails? Is that what you're trying to tell us?" Culver asked in a raised tone.

"Easy, Culver," McBain advised him, intervening.

"No!" she panted. "That's not what I'm saying. I was just hanging out on the corner with Brickey and his boys in Hopkins Glen when Olivess asked me and Brickey to take a taxi ride out to the plantation to get her bag. I did it as a favor. I didn't help her commit no crime if that's what you're leading into."

" So, where the hell is she now?" Culver asked.

"She at a motel on Highway 601."

"Is she's staying there?" McBain asked.

"No, she's just there waiting on somebody to pick her up."

Culver was about to lose it with the stalling tactic. "Stop playing games with me and spit out everything what you know."

Lola looked at both agents, slouched further down in the chair to relax and then declared, "She's waiting there for someone who's coming from Maryland to pick her up and take her out of state, to take her somewhere she can hide out. This guy gets paid to help felons and fugitive's escape justice. He knows Olivess ain't got much money so he's helping her with a small loan and some other favors that I won't mention."

"You mean he's a coyote."

She hesitated and did not respond.

Culver pressed, "Did you hear me? I repeat…is he acting as a coyote, taking people across the border for a fee?"

"Something like that!"

"How do you know this if you're not involved in it?" Culver asked her.

"I am not involved in her shit! She's just my friend and she asked me to do her a favor." Lola left eye began twitching, which Culver noticed.

"I think you're lying to me!" Culver shouted, slamming his fist on the table. "A man is dead, and you just participated in pulling a scam on the police."

"That's all I did!" Lola replied to admitting guilt through tears. "But I did it because I owe Olivess my life. She saved me from being bullied and risked her life to fight dudes and girls to defend me when I was young."

McBain and Culver looked at each other and both sighed while raising their eyebrows again. Neither was interested in a historical account of Olivess and Lola's relationship.

"Since you and her are friends, close enough for you to risk getting arrested, how about you tell me what you know about Olivess and the Drummond yacht cruise. We know you collaborated with her." Culver said. "I want to know everything you know about that night and then I'll decide if I believe anything you're saying."

Lola sat silently and stared straight ahead. Culver and McBain remained patient. "I swear to you, that's all I know."

Then why did your left eye start to twitch?" Culver asked her.

"I have Tourette's."

Culver and McBain immediately got up and left the room for the hallway to talk first.

McBain said, "I think we shouldn't push this kid with her medical problem. If she's telling the truth and gets sick on us, we're in for a lawsuit."

Culver debated, "You think that kid or her parents could afford a lawyer to sue us."

McBain stared at Culver silently, realizing Culver's comment was irrelevant.

Culver then said, "Okay, we'll let her go!"

About an hour later, Lola's parents arrived at the station and signed for release, pending a juvenile hearing to take place in a month.

CHAPTER 21

The night of the yacht cruise

At approximately ten p.m., a taxi carrying Olivess Norton pulled up to the side entrance of the Devil Island Clubhouse, which was on a side street adjacent to a narrowly wooded trail that led to the beach. During the day, it was a much- traveled route as customers would leave the clubhouse and take the short walk or job to the beach. But since the beach closed at nine p.m. it was now quiet and uninhabited.

Olivess exited the taxi, paid the driver the fee and a nice tip, and walked to the side door, which remained unlocked until midnight. She waited until the taxi departed and the engine sound faded, then took a moment to glance around in every direction. She didn't see anyone observing her. So, she pulled the door open and entered.

Clubhouse employees were instructed by management to only enter through the backdoor when coming to work since the biometric fingerprint employee check-in recorder for clocking-in was mounted on the back wall directly inside the door.

The side door led to the main kitchen, which was a prohibited area except for servers who would drop off their tickets and pick up their customer's meals.

Olivess scurried through the area on her way to the employee locker room. Several cooks glanced up at her with startled expressions as she passed them, but no one questioned her as to why she was passing through the kitchen area. They were too busy preparing meals for both the anticipated two hundred clubhouse guests and the catered appetizers for Drummond's yacht cruise.

Lola Fields was surprised when Olivess opened the door to the locker room. Olivess seemed just as surprised to see Lola changing into her server's clothes since it was supposed to be Lola's night off. There were a dozen lockers for use by employees who didn't want to wear their black pants and white blouse work outfits around town. Since, Devil Island Clubhouse was known to be an upscale operation, the club manager was gracious enough to allow them sufficient time to change after clocking in but warned them that any employee noted goofing off or loitering on company time would forfeit their locker room privileges.

As Olivess was removing her locker key from per purse, Lola noticed the brown paper bag Olivess had in her left hand.

"Hey girl! What you got in that bag?" Lola asked her.

Olivess didn't respond as she placed the paper bag in her locker.

Suddenly, Lola glanced down at the floor and noticed a plastic vial under the bench. It reminded her of the two-ounce baby bottle pop candy her and Olivess would buy, or sometimes steal, out of a corner grocery store in their neighborhood when they were kids. Lola reached down and picked it up and instantly discerned that it was not candy. She had seen those small containers before in the hands of drug dealers on the corners in the neighborhood.

"What is this stuff, Olivess?" she asked her. "Did this fall out of that paper bag you're trying to hide from me."

Olivess snatched the bottle from Lola's hand. "Mind your business, girl!" she barked, as she pulled the locker open and placed the vial into the paper bag.

"Are you dealing drugs?" Lola asked. "I hope you're not going to take some dope while you're at work here and get yourself fired."

Olivess slammed the locker closed and stared at Lola. She had never kept secrets from Lola, and they knew everything about each other; every time they skipped out of the house at night behind their parents' back, every time they'd lied to someone, every time they'd cheated on a test. They always confided in each other, and nothing was going to change on this occasion.

"I'm gonna drug that son-of-a-bitch racist Drummond with this shit," she declared to Lola.

Lola's heart nearly skipped a beat. "What are you talking about? We've done some stupid shit over the years, but this takes the cake, girl. Are you serious?"

Olivess changed her clothes without responding. Lola waited patiently for Olivess to answer her question. After buttoning her white blouse, Olivess put a hair band on her head and stomped towards the door.

Lola came up behind her and grabbed her arm. "Olivess, girl, you better tell me what you're up to. You're gonna get us all in trouble if you do something stupid tonight."

Olivess jerked her arm away and scoffed. "Stay out of this Lola. This is my business. This will be over tonight when the yacht cruise is finished. I am just gonna fuck up that man a bit for what is he's done to me."

Lola grabbed her arm again. "I wanna know what that shit is, Olivess. There's opiod's being laced with shit that can kill you. I ain't going down as no accessory to murder."

Olivess proceeded to shove Lola who tripped backgrounds and fell to the floor. "Stay out of this Lola and keep your mouth shut. I love you, girlfriend but this ain't your business okay. Nothing's gonna happen to us. Just trust me."

Lola was paralyzed with shock and fear. For a moment, her legs were so weak she couldn't rise from the floor. Lola's delay in rising to her feet, allowed Olivess enough time to exit the locker room without further interruption.

Olivess headed out to the main ballroom. The paper bag remained in her locker. She didn't talk to Lola the rest of the night and at ten thirty, she departed the ballroom and went out to the yacht for her duty for the cruise.

Lola was assigned to work at the clubhouse that night and was not on the yacht.

Chapter 22

Back at BRMC, the sound of sirens had dissipated as many of the first responders had departed BRMC. During the early morning, on-scene investigation continued with interviews throughout the hospital. Staff and building inspectors surveyed the damage to determine what parts of the hospital could be utilized to bring patients inside. Fortunately, because of the effective built-in fire suppression and standpipe systems, all fires had been rapidly extinguished, and damage was limited to the below ground and the first two floors of the hospital.

Despite one arm being in a sling, Cutter steered his vehicle back to BPD headquarters instead of heading home as Ryker ordered. As he walked up the front steps, Ryker buzzed him on his cell phone.

"Are you at home resting?" Ryker asked.

"Could not do it, Chief. I have too much work to do. I'm at BPD headquarters now, Cutter declared.

"Actually, that's good!" Ryker responded. "I want you to hang tight there. Olivess Norton's been apprehended. She is being transported back to Bullet as we speak."

"Olivess Norton?" he asked, having a momentary memory lapse.

"The Brick City murder case you're supposed to be investigating," Ryker reminded him harshly.

"Where'd she gets caught?" Cutter asked.

"She was apprehended at a motel on Highway 1. The arresting officers and a couple of sheriff's deputies should be arriving with her soon. I want you to sit in on the questioning."

"With all due respect sir, I couldn't give a rat's ass about the Jimmy Delray murder case right now," Cutter responded sharply. "Our primary double-murder suspect has been kidnapped and I need to stay hot on that case."

Ryker scoffed and replied, "May I remind you Cutter that the Delray murder investigation is *your* case, and this kidnapping isn't assigned to you, much less SBI."

Cutter paused in silent frustration.

Ryker continued, "Now that we are straight on this, I want you to close that case. See if you can get Ms. Norton to cop a plea in exchange for any information that may be useful in the Drummond murders. But do not make any promises until we can review the results of her interrogation. She worked at that beach club so she might know something useful to both."

The curiosity of a connection sparked Cutter's interest enough to withhold further debate. He assured Ryker he would fully engage in the interrogation. As he proceeded to his office to wait on the arresting team's arrival, he wondered what could be so revealing that it would warrant Ryker's interest in the Olivess Norton interrogation over the Penelope Lane kidnapping. It would not take long before he would learn the answer that would complicate his life even more.

CHAPTER 23

At eleven a.m., a black and white police cruiser, occupied by two sheriff deputies, the arresting officer, and a handcuffed Olivess Norton, pulled up to the front of BPD headquarters. That vehicle was followed by an unmarked white police sedan carrying an SBI agent and a homicide investigator from the Atlanta FBI Field Office.

The BPD Detention Officer met the party at the front door, signed for and took custody of the detainee, then walked her directly to the fingerprint room. From there, he escorted her to the personal effects holding area when he handed her to a custody officer. Meanwhile, the other officer took the elevator to the basement where a polygraph examiner and three uniformed police officers were waiting in a musty windowless interview room. Cutter was notified and immediately left his office to join them.

Olivess finished the personal effects processing, and the custody officer escorted her to the interrogation room. Once there, he unlatched her handcuffs and pointed her to a gray metal folding chair on the other middle portion of a long rectangular table. She squinted from the ceiling lamp that was tilted to shine directly into her face. Lacking a shower or change of clothes since the day she fled the murder scene, she reeked of body odor which trailed her across the room. Her head displayed an uncombed nest of disheveled braids. With her body odor seeping through her tank top, Cutter could taste his undigested breakfast backing up in his throat.

Hollis Smith, a bearded, paunchy African American interrogator, lumbered into the room and sat directly facing Olivess. Nicknamed Beacon, he was considered one of the more personable officers on the force, yet he was as feisty as a rattlesnake when interrogating a felony suspect. With the attendees remaining silent, Smith read to Olivess the charge sheet followed by the Miranda rights. Her look of indifference to the standard police procedure stretched to the far walls, but the tears welling in her eyes told a different story.

Smith was about to begin the interrogation when the door flew open. Elijah Combs, a court-appointed public defender, stormed in and immediately took a seat next to his client.

"Sorry I'm late," he announced.

"Actually, it's your lucky day," Beacon Smith whispered back, welcoming him with a less than cordial smile. "We've got a live one here that's going to need taming."

"There's no ventilation in here," Combs noted. "You guys sure go out of your way to make detainees feel uncomfortable, don't you?"

"Sorry we couldn't arrange a suite at Waldorf Astoria," Smith replied facetiously.

Combs was not amused or angered. He was determined to keep his cool, prepared for any onslaught of sarcasm or profiling that the interview might bring. He glanced at each of the room participants and then asked, "I'd like a moment with my client."

The group acknowledged Comb's request with a nod in unison and then left the room. "

As the door shut, Comb immediately noticed the fear in Olivess eyes. Her façade instantly faded.

"Ms. Norton, are you doing, okay? I hope they read you your rights."

"They did, and yes, I'm cool," she answered.

"So, what have you told them so far?"

"No—nothing!"

"Good. Keep it that way until I tell you to answer," he replied, breaking a crooked smile to try and ease her tension. "You have an attorney now and I'll be looking out for your best interest."

"I didn't ask for no attorney," she snapped back, eyeing Combs warily. It was obvious she didn't trust lawyers as much as she trust police officers.

"I can tell you are afraid and intimidated by all these people, but you can trust me. My job is to make sure your rights are protected."

She shrugged carelessly and then leaned back into her chair.

"I guess that means you're going to do as I've asked?" he inferred by her silence.

"I'm not going to sit here and say something stupid if that's what you mean," she declared. "I've seen my people clam up and get railroaded."

Combs, having watched his father on tape in the background of one of Dr. King's marches, suddenly found it difficult to counter her argument.

She continued, "There's only one thing I want, and that's to keep Jimmy D's boys from messing with my grandmother. I know what they'll do if they find out I'm a snitch. They want revenge against me anyway."

"I understand your concerns Miss Norton," he replied consoling. "When they come back in here, you can answer questions, but I'm going to ask you not to discuss Mister Delray's death until we've talked privately."

Clutching her palms in a prayer-like pose, she begged, "Please as long as you keep her safe, I won't cause any trouble."

Combs repeated, "You just remember not to incriminate yourself."

Combs went to the door and ushered the group back into the interrogation room.

Surrounded by a room full of watchful male eyes, Olivess tugged down to smooth her blue jean skirt and scooted forward. As she was preparing herself for the questioning, Vernon May, an assistant interrogation officer, whispered into Cutter's ear the plan of action. One of the officers moved over and flipped the switch on a video camera.

After he and the others sat again, Smith introduced himself. He laid the official charge sheet on the table in front of her and continued, "Miss Norton, you were placed under arrest on the suspicion of the stabbing death of Mister James Delray. If you'll be frank with us and tell the truth about your involvement, we may be able to talk about cutting you a deal."

"It depends on what you'll do for me," she remarked brazenly.

"I know a lot, but I want a deal up front, or I say nothing."

Combs stood up for a moment, then walked over to Cutter. He leaned close and whispered into Cutter's ear, "Sounds like she's been down this road before."

Cutter replied, "Be careful with both of them."

Chapter 24

Aware of the evidence already obtained, Smith decided to halt any notion that a police detainee was in the driver's seat of a negotiation. He replied to her bluntly, "Miss Norton, we've got a person who not only places you at the crime scene, but also witnessed you stab Mister Delray several times during an altercation before fleeing the scene. You're looking at a murder charge and fleeing the scene of the crime. That doesn't give you much leeway for being arrogant or making demands. I suggest you drop the badass routine and come clean."

She leaned back pensively, remembering a male classmate from junior high school who was sentenced to ten years in a state corrections facility after being apprehended during a botched robbery. To the best of her recollection, he still was not out. She glanced over at Combs, who nodded, giving her permission to tell her side of the story, but not admitting to murdering Delray.

"It was self-defense," she declared to Combs' surprise.

Quickly, Combs rebutted, "My client misspoke."

"The hell I did," Olivess countered. "I'm gonna tell the truth."

Combs dropped the pencil that was in his right hand onto the desk and leaned back in his chair in resignation.

"I guess you don't need me," he uttered in frustration.

Smith quickly seized the moment, as said, Keep talking, Miss Norton."

"I only confronted him because I didn't get some stuff I paid for. He attacked me so I defended myself."

"What stuff are you're talking about," Smith asked.

"A drug compound I need to take care of a personal matter. Only it wasn't lethal. So, I just wanted what I paid for, and I wasn't satisfied. He ripped me off and I wasn't gonna take that shit."

Smith's nose flared as he looked at Cutter in frustration. "Look Ms. Norton. You're talking in codes. You need to fill the gaps, or this interview is over, and you'll be going to prison for a long time. You're not my only case."

She sat upright, tugged again to smooth her skirt, and said, "If y'all promise me you'll protect my grandmother, I'll tell you the whole story from start to finish. And I'll tell you why I tried to poison that Drummond man."

Combs quickly interrupted, interjecting, "What she means if, she's only going to keep talking if we can talk about some kind of leniency in her prosecution."

"Very well, counselor," Smith said turning to look at Combs, "Let's first see if your client has something worth considering offering it."

CHAPTER 25

One year before the car bombing that killed Blake Cutter's wife.

Olivess Norton was working her normal ten to six-day shift at the Regal Room of the Devil Island Clubhouse. Suddenly, a tall, skinny Caucasian teenager with sandy blonde hair walked in and sat on the barstool located at the center of the bar. Olivess normally didn't take a liking to Caucasians, especially in Glynn County where racial tensions were always high. The population in the county was about seventy percent poor African American and thirty percent affluent Caucasian, further exacerbating the racial divides. But there was something different about this young man.

He was barely sixteen, two years below the state's legal drinking age. Yet, he ordered a shot of whiskey and downed it like a fifty-year old. She was impressed and curious at the same time. *How does a teenager get to order alcohol here?* she wondered. But then, he belched like a drunk sailor, and she knew he was just fronting for attention.

Suddenly, he glanced at her, and they made eye contact. He smiled and the dimple on his right cheek stretched wide. She swallowed a lump in her throat. There was an instant attraction. Guys with dimples always caught her attention. It was an unexplained magnetism. She could tell by his expression that he wanted to talk to her. But she was on duty and couldn't be caught lingering around the bar. He knew about servers' rules, so he slid off the stool and intercepted her as she was walking back to the kitchen.

"Don't I know you from somewhere?" he said to her with a wide grin.

"You couldn't think of a better pickup line than that?" she asked.

"Didn't mean to come across that way," he said apologetically. "I was just a little nervous approaching you. What's your name?"

"Olivess," she answered in an uncharacteristic sheepish tone. Her nervousness showed she already liked him. "And yours?"

"Jason – Jason Drummond!"

Her eyes opened wide, and she felt a sudden tightness in her stomach. "Is Phillip Drummond one of your relatives?

He paused for a moment.

She continued, "You know. The man who owns this hotel.""

"Yes, Phillip Drummond is my uncle."

She dropped a glass off her tray. He knew he had made her nervous. He figured it was because of her attraction to him. What he didn't know was she dropped the glass because she was disappointed to hear that he was related to the same man she'd heard rumors about being a racist.

"Let me clean that up," he offered, noticing the dropped glass spilled some liquid on the floor.

A good sign she thought to herself. *Courteous.* So, she decided to dismiss this revelation. *He seemed nothing like his uncle*, a good first impression she thought to herself. She didn't have time to engage in a conversation just then, but it was obvious by her smile as she walked away, that she had opened the possibility of a conversation if she ran into him again. Indeed, she did.

Chapter 26

Over the next three weeks, she encountered Jason several times, more frequently than she had seen anyone in the clubhouse over that period. She wondered if he had found out her work schedule and the encounters were more than just coincidental. They enjoyed playful banter and subtle flirtation, but no definitive date proposal was offered. She felt comfortable with him and was hoping he would ask her out. She wanted to get to know him on a personal level. On each occasion she came on shift that week, she stared at the entrance door as people walked in, hoping that she would see him . . . hoping he'd have the courage to ask her out.

On May 10th, Bullet Magnet School, the only private school in the Glynn County School District, rented the clubhouse for an end-of-school year party for their graduating senior class. Jason was valedictorian and part of the organizing committee. He came to the clubhouse with five other students and a teacher to organize the setup for the party that would take place that night.

Olivess was told about the event and asked to work that night and assist with the catering and meal set-up.

At eleven that morning, the party of seven walked into the clubhouse before making several trips to the school van to bring in flower arrangements, signage, and decorations. The contracted DJ was expected to arrive at six, two hours before the event.

Olivess and Jason made eye contact immediately when he entered the room. He waved from a distance, called out her name "Hey, Olivess," so she knew he acknowledged her in front of his classmates. She felt ecstatic to know he didn't pretend to not know her or was ashamed of his friendship with her. It was a good sign for her. It took another half hour before they both had a break and could meet and talk alone.

As he approached her, he said, "I thought we'd never get to talk, like something was trying to keep us apart."

"You think, right!" she responded, blushing.

Aware of her slight nervousness, he said, "Hey, let's grab a coke and we can talk."

For the next few moments, they sat outside on a garden bench and shared small talk about their backgrounds. It was pleasant and comforting to her. He was a nice guy, so she stopped by to chat with him several times as he was helping set up decorations and table settings. She was impressed he was not the type of guy that would be afraid to set a table. Then, she bravely told him she had dropped out of high school and had been working at the Regal Room for a year. It didn't seem to bother him or cause him to think less of her . . . at least to her it did not seem that way. After that confession, she shied up and went back into the kitchen, wanted to let her admission set into his head and to see if he wanted to keep talking to her.

As the group wrapped up their setup and prepared to depart, Olivess was cleaning up a table in the corner when he walked over to her.

"Do you have any plans for tonight?" he asked.

She was startled by the question but didn't want to show any fear or timidness, so she answered, "I have no plans. What did you have in mind?

"It's just I don't have a date for tonight's party. I would like you to be my date . . . if you don't think that's being too forward. I think you will have a good time. The only problem is I gotta be here an hour early to meet the DJ. The party starts at eight, so I will not be able to pick you up."

She stared at him momentarily, then turned away to think. She felt comfortable that he couldn't come to her residence, to know where she lived. It was too early for that.

"That's cool!" she said. "What should I wear," she asked.

"You can dress casual, no big deal," he said with a smile. He was not about to ask her to dress up on such short notice.

"Okay, I'll see you then," she said proudly.

"Fantastic! I will see you tonight."

She was further impressed that he walked away without doing something awkward like trying to kiss her. He seemed like the perfect gentleman, but she had seen it before. Yet, there was something she felt differently about him . . . that he had a great combination of charm, manners, intelligence, and daring. The question in her mind was, was it real. She was interested to find out. Nevertheless, she decided to bring pepper spray and a small pocketknife with her.

CHAPTER 27

At six that evening, Olivess arrived back at the Devil Island Clubhouse. She did not have time to get a dress laundered, nor did she prefer to wear one. She was a bit of a tomboy. Just wearing a pair of black jeans and a purple blouse was formal enough for her. She hoped Jason wouldn't mind or be embarrassed. But she really did not care. She never let anybody, including Clementine, tell her how to dress. She did balance her underdressed attire by neatly crimping her coarse black hair into a sawtooth, zig-zag style and adding a set of glitzy false eyelashes.

As she walked in the door, she looked toward the ballroom stage and saw Jason, conversing with the DJ while helping him unload equipment and move speakers to the two corners of the stage. That allowed the DJ to begin doing sound checks and prepping his music.

Jason was smiling and seemed in a cheerful mood. His blue blazer and a pair of tan dockers with a blue necktie and pinkish colored shirt was the typical pre-college preppy look.

As Olivess surreptitiously entered the ballroom and noticed well-dressed people milling about, she instantly froze and could not take another step muttering to herself *"What am I doing coming here* she muttered. *They are never gonna accept me here.* It was the type of negative thinking that had always held her back—that made her feel like a failure until she lost interest in completing high school.

As she changed her mind, she turned and started walking back towards the double doors to leave. She heard his voice.

"Hey, Olivess! Where are you going?" he yelled as if he thought she hadn't noticed him.

Her heart palpitated with nervousness. The sweet tone of his voice sent a chill through her spine. She was trapped in a state of confusion.

Jason walked briskly towards her as she turned around but did not move. "Hey, thanks for coming. You are early. You didn't have to be here until about six thirty."

Searching for words, she nervously pulled up, "I didn't have anywhere else to go. It is boring at home, so here I am."

"You look great!" he said.

"Thank you," she responded, sheepishly. She figured he was just being polite but appreciated the compliment just the same. She had only dated a total of four times in her life but had hung around boys a lot and never heard anyone compliment her.

"Well, since you are here, would you like to help me finish the decorations. There are only a few things left to put up, and I love your company."

"Better than sitting in here by myself." She responded acceptingly.

After they finished with the remaining decorations, Jason walked with her to the bar in the adjoining room and gave her a coke. They sat at a booth in the corner to kill the time until students would begin arriving in the ballroom for the social hour.

"So, where do you live?" he asked.

She stammered, "I-I live over on Jericho Island with my grandmother. My mom died when I was young, so my grandmother took me in."

"I'm so sorry to hear that," he offered politely.

"That's okay. My grandmother's great. You know the saying, if you cannot be with the one you love, then love the one you're with."

Jason chuckled, fascinated by her being so loose and open about her childhood plight. Reciprocally, she noted the empathetic look in his eyes, something that seemed true and uninhibited despite their lack of familiarity with each other.

They reentered the ballroom and sat at a round table with six other students. Four of the six were coupled up, while the other two hardly knew each other. Despite being the least familiar, Jason and Olivess were the most congenial throughout the night. They livened up the group as Jason told several whimsical jokes and stories and Olivess appeased his need for attention by chuckling with everyone.

"I'm glad you're having a good time," Jason remarked to Olivess.

"I didn't think I would," she replied. "I get nervous around white folk. I just came tonight because you asked me out."

He grabbed her hand under the table. She felt a chill through her body. Then suddenly, as he squeezed her palm, he abruptly let go. His attention instantly shifted to the entrance to the ballroom where he saw his uncle Phillip Drummond standing and glaring.

"Olivess, I want to introduce you to my uncle. He just walked in."

"What's he doing here?" she asked.

"He told me he'd come by and checked on the place. It is his country club."

She had only met Phillip Drummond once, but she remembered his face. It was the day she and several new employees were in training for their jobs as servers in the Regal Room. Phillip Drummond made it a point to meet Regal Room staff personally since country club management hosted several recurring state and local VIP events.

As Phillip caught the eyes of his nephew, Jason waved for his uncle to come over to their table to say hello. Once he arrived at their table, Jason walked Phillip around the table and introduced Phillip to every person at the table before Olivess. Olivess wondered if that was proper or some hidden sign of disrespect or shame. It was a feeling that was cemented in her consciousness from living in a city racially divided by county lines.

"Uncle, this is Olivess. We just met a few weeks ago. She lives on Jericho Island."

Olivess' eyes widened. She was always a detailed person who noticed everything in a person's speech . . . what they said and what they did not say. She noticed that Jason did not state her last name to Phillip as he had with each of the other students he introduced. Neither did he say that Olivess was his date.

Phillip stared at her wearily. He did not offer a handshake as he had just done with the other guests at the table.

"What's your classification, Olivess?" Drummond asked.

"My what, sir?"

"Are you a graduating senior?" he asked, clarifying.

Olivess hesitated pensively, not sure how to respond. She felt embarrassed for a moment, but then realized that no one at the table was paying attention to the conversation, especially with the loud music from the band in the background.

"I-I'm not in high school but I have my G.E.D.," she said to him proudly.

Phillip's disapproval instantly registered on his face as he furrowed his brow, as if he were studying her to judge if she measured up as a person who should be attending the event.

"Where'd you meet this girl?" Phillip asked his nephew, bluntly. Olivess overheard the question but the others around the table did not.

Jason's jaw dropped as he stared at his uncle momentarily speechless. Phillip was Jason's only uncle, but Jason felt as close to Phillip as if he were his own father, particularly since Jason's parents divorced when he was only five and he had since lived in Bullet with his mother.

Olivess did not like being called a girl in any context. She was eighteen and considered herself a grown woman. She took the question as a personal insult to not only her race but her character. She dropped her head and stared down at the table.

Finally, Jason responded saying, "We met a few weeks ago . . . right here in the clubhouse. Olivess works here." His tone sounded to her like he was defending her honor, for which she was pleased.

Phillip Drummond then walked away without saying goodbye to either of them or began circling the ballroom to greet other students.

"Why didn't you say I was your date?" Olivess asked Jason.

"I didn't know you wanted me to call it a date," Jason stammered, feeling put on the spot.

"Of course, it's a date . . . unless you think it's not a date and I'm just here." she jostled.

His eyebrows raised as he said, "No – no. It is a date. It is as much of a date as any date I have had. I am sorry if I offended you."

Olivess broke a wry grin. Again, she had never heard a boy apologize to her in any way. She was extremely impressed with his sense of caring. So, she decided to drop the matter and enjoy the remainder of their evening together.

"I get the impression your uncle doesn't approve of you dating me."

"Who cares what he thinks," Jason said to console her; but unintentionally he confirmed her suspicion by the inflection of his voice.

Chapter 28

At eight thirty, after a few roast-type presentations and short speeches concluded, Jason decided to locate his uncle before he left. Olivess leveraged the moment to take a bathroom break and freshen makeup.

Moments later, as she exited the bathroom, she glanced to her left and noticed Jason and Phillip standing and talking near the entrance to another room. She slipped behind a middle pillar and listened in.

"Why did you act that way towards Olivess?" Jason angrily asked Drummond. "She might have been offended. She's a nice girl and is becoming a good friend."

There is that word 'girl' again, I swear Olivess murmured to herself, but then maintained her focus on the conversation.

"I don't know why you're resorting to hanging out with girls who aren't suitable for you," Phillip whined, bluntly. "You're known by the company you keep."

Jason's eyes watered as his face strained. He looked torn at hearing Phillip's comments; torn between his loyal respect for his uncle's advice and dislike of the racist overtone. "What are you trying to say?"

Phillip looked deep in his nephew's eyes, "It's like you are in some type of rebellion, dating a high school dropout and someone like her. You know your mother would not approve of her. You can do better."

"You mean someone not black!" Jason replied bluntly.

Phillip hesitated before answering, then he stammered deceptively, "Well-well son, I just thought you'd bring a more suitable date to your senior party, frankly…someone on your level."

Overhearing those words, blood rushed to Olivess head, and she suddenly became dizzy with shock and hurt. Her knees buckled and she felt faint. But she composed herself and proceeded back into the ballroom and sat at the table. She did not blame Jason for her uncle's prejudice. Phillip Drummond was a racist and a bigot, who had nothing to do with her being hired as a server at the Devil Island Clubhouse. She liked Jason to this point, and she was determined to see how or if the newfound relationship would progress beyond the evening's event.

CHAPTER 29

Two days later, Jason called her. She agreed to another date, this time, a more private one. That Friday, he met her at a local cinema, and they enjoyed a movie. Afterwards, they went to a karaoke bar. There, Jason sang the John Legend song, *All of Me* and even boldly announced to the crowd that it was a dedication to her. He was pushing all the right buttons. Despite their racial difference, which was an issue in a segregated town like Bullet, Olivess Norton had found a friend, a nice and charming guy who had the potential to become a soulmate.

A special date occurred two weeks later when he invited her to be his +1 for the annual Glynn County Realtors Association Annual Reception, an event hosted by Phillip Drummond at the Devil Island Clubhouse Ballroom. There were only a handful of young men under twenty-one that were invited to attend. Since Jason had shown an interest in training to become a realtor,

Phillip had invited his nephew to attend. Little did he know Jason would be enlisting Phillip's limo driver for the night as payment for a favor that he owed him for Jason using his tech skills to repair the driver's personal computer and restore his hard drive.

At six that evening, a black stretch limo pulled up in front of Olivess' grand-aunt Clementine's house. Jason stepped out of the limo wearing a blue tailored suit and carrying a calla lily wrist corsage encased in a translucent flower box. Olivess was so shy of Clementine's meager home furnishings that she rushed to the front door to prevent him from entering the home. Clementine followed behind her in a near cadence step. She had not moved that fast in years.

After a respectful conversation with Clementine, Jason slipped the corsage over Olivess' tattooed wrist. The arm markings cheapened the look she'd tried to offset with the marooned-colored, strapless, tight-fitting short cocktail dress and four-inch black heels.

Clementine flashed a big, proud smile as they walked down the steps to the waiting limo. It was like a Cinderella fantasy for a redbone who had never liked anything fancy before.

Twenty minutes later they arrived at the reception. While Jason and Olivess sat at their assigned table, Phillip Drummond finished his introductory remarks at the podium and then approached them. Phillip shot an acerbic look at Olivess, then asked Jason, "Can you come out in the hall with me. I need to speak to you?"

Jason followed Phillip into the hallway. Olivess stayed at the table but craned her neck to follow them with her eyes. She read the menacing scowl on Phillip face. She could not read his lips, but she put two and two together.

She knew they would be talking about her, and Phillip would be questioning Jason's date choice. It made her so uncomfortable, she felt like walking out at that moment. ere talking about her. But she decided it was more important to hold her ground and not being intimidated by Phillip.

"I don't want you seeing that girl," Phillip demanded strongly. "She is not good enough for you. You are going to an Ivy League college for Christ's sake. What are you going to do…take a college dropout with you? I am not paying four years tuition on behalf of your mom to see you start making bad choices now."

"What are you trying to say, uncle?"

"If you see her again you will not see any of my money," Phillip declared. I don't take risks with my money son. Is she your girlfriend, now?"

Jason paused before answering, his eyes watering. "No, she is not, but I like her. She is a nice girl and I plan to continue seeing her," he continued, defiantly.

"Then that'll make my decision very easy," Phillip said then walked away.

"What is that supposed to mean?" Jason asked, shouting at Phillip's back as he walked away.

Phillip heard Jason's question but decided not to answer as he proceeded over to a group of businesspeople for a conversation. Phillip was never one to reveal his actions to Jason. He held out hope that Jason would discontinue the relationship with Olivess based on his threat. Phillip's arrogance left him confident that a breakup would happen soon.

CHAPTER 30

Over the next week, Olivess did not hear from Jason . . . not a call, not a text, nothing. That Saturday, she called him. He did not answer. She called ten times and left ten messages until his voice mail was full. She thought for a moment that he had gotten a different cell phone, but then she concluded that he was intentionally avoiding her phone calls.

On Monday morning, she walked to Jason's high school and waited in the parking lot until students came out for the break after first period. She was lucky that he was outside. . . at least she thought she was lucky to see him. Then she did what was stupid, unanticipated. He was standing with four other males, members of Future Business Leaders of America.

She proudly walked up to him, boldly, unafraid, and unintimidated by the crowd. Olivess was never afraid of a group, but she thought Jason would walk away with her to talk in private . . . but he didn't. He didn't move or even react to her approach. That beautiful smile that had surrounded her warmed her like a blanket was gone; replaced with cold, steely eyes, telling her she was not welcome around him or his friends. He stood between the four other males, two on each side of him.

"What's going on, Jason," she asked. "We had a wonderful time. What is your problem, now?"

Jason did not respond . . . so the 'wanna-be' attorneys to the right of him decided to speak on his behalf. "Listen, half breed! Jason ain't blowing his college tuition for you. He ain't jeopardizing his relationship with his uncle Phillip over some school dropout."

Olivess lunged at one of the boys, who stepped back to avoid being struck. Two of the other boys pushed her to the ground, then the three of them ran, leaving Jason standing over her. Other students in the area froze in place, some stared in shock, other more dutiful ones videoed her on their cell phones.

Jason grabbed her hand and helped her to her feet. She wiped away the single tear straining its way out of her right eye. She wanted him to see the anger and disgust on her face, but no tears.

"I am sorry, Olivess. My uncle does not want me to see you," he said to her. "He is like my father and he's paying for my college." She saw the conflict on his face. She knew it was the mask of Phillip Drummond behind the cold face that had changed everything . . . had changed the expectations of their relationship."

"You son-of-a-bitch," she shouted, angrily. "Fuck you! Why did you mess with me in the first place if you were going to wimp out like this?"

"I'm sorry," Jason repeated, and then he turned his back and walked away.

He did not look back as he rushed past the campus main gate and onto the street. As she looked back towards the school, she noticed Jason walking into the side door. She overheard the door slam as he disappeared from her sight . . . and from her life.

Chapter 31

The Interrogation Room

"Miss Norton... Miss. Norton?" Elijah Combs uttered, trying to divert Olivess from her daydream. Suddenly, the door she overheard slam shut was not the side door of Jason's private school, but the entrance door to the interrogation room. Cutter was the last of the group of law enforcement officers who reentered the room. He had just been a party to the discussion in which the assistant district attorney agreed on a positive plea bargain if Olivess Norton revealed information that would lead to the arrest of the syndicate leaders who had infiltrated Bullet, Georgia. But they were not about to play their hand until Combs played his.

As the door closed, Olivess' heart felt like it dropped to her knees. The memory of her experiences with Phillip and Jason Drummond was chilling, especially considering her current state of mind.

As Cutter sat across the table directly in front of Combs, Ryker and Smith stood at the side of the table momentarily and stared at the two.

"Okay, Mister Combs. What are we gonna do here?" Beacon Smith prodded. "Go ahead and read her rights and get her booked. We got other cases to work."

After Combs read her rights, Olivess slid closer to Combs and whispered in his ear a full thirty seconds. Combs' eyebrows slowly raised as she spoke. He then nodded his head at Olivess as a gesture to move back to her position. Then Combs looked up, stared at Ryker and Smith, and cleared his throat before speaking. "My client has some information regarding some illegal activity that's been going on at Devil Island."

Smith chuckled and looked at Ryker with curiosity. He then looked back at Combs and declared, "Look, we have your client on a murder charge so this better be worth our time. What is she trying to do?

Olivess interrupted and spoke softly, "Sir, I have some stuff to tell you about the men who are dealing drugs and guns here in Bullet. I will talk if you're willing to cut me a deal."

The three men stared at each other in a momentary silence then shrugged.

Smith then said, "Okay, let's hear it."

At that moment, Smith and Ryker moved over to sit across the table and folded their arms. Combs took a yellow legal pad out of his folder and placed it in the center of the table but did not give Olivess direction to start writing anything. It was pre-positioned in case she revealed something significant.

Olivess glanced over into Combs' eyes.

"Go ahead," he said in a calm, fatherly-type tone.

She inhaled a deep breath before speaking, "I used to serve food and drinks to Phillip Drummond in the Regal Room during his lunch business meetings with some mob men."

Smith pursed his lips and glanced at Cutter and Ryker then turned to Olivess. "How did you know they were mob men?" Smith asked.

"Think about it," Olivess said, "A group of men in suits walked in together, scattered around the room while two of them sit at a booth and start talking. A couple of others wearing suits with bulges in the jackets, positioning themselves by the door the whole time. What does that tell you?"

Smith looked at the other officers, shrugged, grinned, and then said to Olivess, "Okay. You might be on to something. Keep talking."

She went on, "Well, I remember hearing Drummond referring to another man he called Bennie. I thought it would be fun to eavesdrop. So, I did and overheard them talking about some document they were going to forge."

Cutter scooted forward in his chair and stared in Olivess' eyes, asking, "So why didn't you tell someone about this conversation you supposedly overheard?"

"It was not my business at the time. I see drug dealers in my neighborhood do terrible things to anyone who snitch, y'know what I am saying."

Smith urged her on. "What else do you remember about these men?"

Olivess looked up at the whirring ceiling fan for a moment, then shifted her eyes to the overhead fluorescent lights in a semi-hypnotic state. Smith and Combs didn't know what to make of her movement . . . if she was stalling to further fabricate her story or just pausing to release nervous energy. Then, she lowered her head and continued, "Over the next few weeks, they came in several times, and I waited their tables, hoping I'd catch more of what they were planning."

"How often did they meet?" Smith asked.

"I would say about twice a week. It was hard for me to believe these dudes would be having that kind of conversation over lunch. They just thought I was just a dumb server. . . a dumb Black server they could talk about crimes in front of . . . like I didn't mind hearing about that type of shit!"

"Something bugging you, Miss Norton?" Smith asked her. "Otherwise, we'd prefer you check your language.

"I just don't like racists," she followed, fidgety and in a lower tone, then folding her arms to calm her nerves.

"Wait a minute, Miss Norton," he interrupted, motioning over to the uniformed jail guards, "Ask Mister May to step in here."

"Who's he?" Olivess asked.

"He's the assistant district attorney."

"No!" she bellowed out, angrily. "I don't want to be telling this shit to no committee. There are too many of you in here already. Y'all making me nervous."

"Fair enough," Smith agreed, gesturing to the uniform officer to withdraw his request.

"Okay, Ms. Norton," Smith relented. "Nobody else is coming in. But the officers in here right now will stay. So, don't get uptight."

Olivess continued, "Well I remember that man's name was Bennie DeSalvo."

"Wait," Cutter interrupted her as he furrowed his brow. "Are you sure you heard him say the name Bennie DeSalvo?"

She paused momentarily in thought, then answered, "Yeah. He introduced him to several other men."

"I only have a few more minutes, so I'm going to ask you just one more question," Cutter said. "Did either of these men mention the name Penelope Lane?"

"I heard them say the name Penelope, yeah," she confirmed, confidently.

Cutter dropped his pen in the middle of the desk and leaned back in his chair silently.

"Something wrong with what I said?" she asked, twitching.

Smith glanced over at Cutter inquisitively and then replied, "Nothing at all Miss Norton, as long as you're telling us the truth."

"I swear," she said, placing her right hand over her heart in a childish but an apparent sincere gesture.

"So, would you be willing to testify in court?"

"Yeah, I would," she said, sheepishly.

"Would you be willing to provide a deposition? Cutter asked.

She suddenly lashed out, "I ain't stupid, man. I'll give you whatever you want if you give me your word that you're going to protect my grandmother from those guys," she prodded, leaning back arrogantly. "If you ain't doing that, then I ain't writing shit."

Chapter 32

Smith intervened, "Look, Miss Norton. Allow me to give you a reality check. We don't even discuss what we can do for you until you write that statement. You've been implicated in a felony that can send you in prison for a long time. You agree to our terms and then we'll consider your concerns."

Suddenly, she broke down from the stress of the interrogation as tears trickled down her face.

Respecting police protocol, Cutter warned, "I think we should switch gears. Give her a little time to settle down."

Interrupting the diversion, she blurted out, "Well, I did stab Jimmy D. But it was self-defense."

"How could it have been in self-defense when there were half a dozen stab wounds?" Smith questioned.

Combs immediately intervened, "Don't say anything else, Miss Norton."

She countered, "No, I want to say this while I got witnesses here."

Combs shrugged in frustration.

She continued, "It wasn't my fault. I just confronted Jimmy D about the stuff I ordered not being what I wanted. One thing led to another and then he just went crazy on me."

"Would this 'stuff you ordered' happen to be the same drugs you 'perhaps' slipped into Phillip Drummond's drink the night of the boat cruise?" Smith asked, catching her and everyone else in the room completely off guard.

She flashed a crooked, nervous smile. "Well, that ain't what I'm talking about right now."

"Okay, Miss Norton. "We will not go there," Smith said, backing off to keep her from shutting down.

"Then he tried to like, pistol whip me right there in the streets. Imagine that! A boy I used to call my homie. I had to defend myself, y'know what I am saying?"

Smith leaned forward, saying, "That story might get you off on manslaughter. But that is only if you can find someone to corroborate your account of what happened. That is not what an eyewitness told us. Besides, we have suspicions you also tried to poison Phillip Drummond. Was that self-defense also?"

"Back off, Beacon!" Cutter warned, afraid that Smith's badgering could affect her willingness to further cooperate.

Hoping for sympathy, she asked rhetorically, "So what would you do if somebody raped one of your relatives and got away with it? It was the only thing I could do to make him pay for what his family did to my great grandma. . . and what he did to me. I really cared about his nephew, Jason.

If it weren't for the Drummond family, my great grandmother wouldn't have killed herself and I would have a future life with Jason. When he turned his nephew against me, that was all I could take. He was the first guy I genuinely liked."

Smith played along, sympathetically, to keep her talking.

"Don't you think you went a bit overboard throwing away your future over something that allegedly happened more than a century ago?"

Frustrated, her eyes moistened. "You could never understand," she said. "I went through it when my momma's boyfriend raped me and got away with it."

Smith offered a sympathetic frown. "I understand Miss Norton, but you can't take the law into your own hands."

She turned her head away, trying to ignore the logic of his statement, yet, Smith had gotten the message to her that she had no leverage in the interrogation.

With the room momentarily silent, she folded her arms and leaned back in her chair. "So, now that I've gave y'all all this information, I hope you ain't gonna renege on your promise to go light on me."

We did not promise you anything," Smith growled. "Even if we put in a good word, it will be up to your attorney . . . not us, to request some type of plea deal for your information. But since you have been candid and transparent throughout this interview, we won't stand in Mister Combs' way. That's the best I can offer you."

Olivess rolled her eyes and turned her head away, making it clear she was not saying anything else.

The interrogation ended a half hour later as Olivess scribed her account of various encounters with Phillip Drummond and Bennie DeSalvo while at the Devil Island Clubhouse.

Cutter pushed away a feeling of pity, reckoning every police officer holding a suspect had to endure a hard luck story. Olivess Norton's plight seemed to him as desperate as Penelope's. The difference was he had not fallen in love with Olivess Norton.

Chapter 33

The Warehouse Complex

The same day Olivess Norton was being interrogated, Penelope Lane was about to undergo an interrogation of her own, only much more coercive in nature. Her interrogation would be conducted by Bennie DeSalvo's lieutenants and could result in her torture and death if she didn't disclose the information they wanted.

She was being held in the center back warehouse of a nine-building complex on the outskirts of Bullet. The warehouse was windowless, cold, wreaked of odors from open containers and rat feces. The lack of ventilation over the past two years resulted in mold and fallen asbestos particles. It was near pitch black inside, damp, and deathly silent. For three days, she laid in the corner with her hands and feet bound and duct tape fitted tightly over her mouth.

She had intermittent medical treatment to keep her alive . . . not the best care, but by a medical school dropout who joined DeSalvo's organization. He had enough medical training to execute life-saving activities for injured gangsters or those with gunshot wounds.

She slept uncomfortably on her side when her eye muscles gave out and she passed out in a syncope state only to wake up vomiting from nausea caused by anxiety and dehydration. Nobody, including the mob doctor, bothered to thoroughly clean the vomit away, which made her nausea constant.

DeSalvo's bodyguards brought her canteens of water and barely microwaved frozen dinner on metal trays. The first day of her captivity she refused to eat in protest. But on the second day, it did not take long before her hunger and dry mouth overcame her will to resist.

Bennie DeSalvo's hideout was located to the far left of the complex, which allowed for a rapid escape out a back door if raided. The heavily wooded trail and ravine covered in damp leaves and pine needles made it hard for tracker dogs to pick up a scent.

At six thirty that evening, two of his trusted Lieutenants came to DeSalvo's location and escorted him to the building where Penelope was located. As he walked in, she shuddered with fright. It was the first streak of light she had seen in three days except for mealtime. Her eyes blinked rapidly as she tried to adjust to the change in light. The first to come in front of her was DeSalvo. He was a frightening, intimidating figure, a large head with a crew cut and a tattoo of a switchblade along the right side of his neck. He wore a thick gold chain around his neck. He grinned with delight to see what he interpreted as an effective wearing down process. Her eyes were puffy and swollen from crying for hours. Her skin was ashen, and her wrist was bruised and red from flexing her limbs for circulation.

When DeSalvo approached her with a scowl on his face, she nearly hyperventilated with fear.

He stood over her and asked with his Sicilian accent, "So, what are we gonna do with you? Are you ready to talk or do we need to give you a little more painful encouragement?" He turned and glanced at one of his lieutenants who held a police night stick and a fileting knife with a long, thin blade. She shook uncontrollably as he twirled it in his hand.

Her voice broke as she replied, "I told you I don't know anything about any land contracts.

DeSalvo clenched his teeth and smiled, "Now we both know you are lying. Phillip told you everything. He kept the surveys and plans for the development, and I want to know where he kept them."

Penelope trembled. "I don't know anything, I swear," she repeated, wearily.

"And I supposed you didn't tell anything to the cops while you were in that hospital."

"I couldn't talk to anyone. I was in no condition," she lied.

DeSalvo took a deep breath, looked at his two lieutenants with doubt and then stared back at her. "I will leave you here with my two friends and maybe they can help you remember."

He turned and walked out the door.

Penelope screamed as you peered up at the two smirky grins and asked, "What are you gonna do to me?"

As DeSalvo out the warehouse, the two lieutenants approached her slowly.

Penelope proceeded to scream in terror as she winced in pain, not sure if she was about to be tortured or raped. She begged silently for Blake to somehow come to her rescue, although she realized the chances of that happening were remote. And even if he did, she lamented he might not get there in time to save her life.

Chapter 34

It was the day after Olivess Norton's first interrogation that Cutter returned to BPD headquarters and was informed that, based on Olivess Norton's deposition, the district magistrate had issued a narcotic warrant for the arrest of Bennie DeSalvo. That left one question lingering in Cutter's mind. Was Bennie DeSalvo currently in Bullet or had he returned to Miami with the hostage?

Cutter's excitement with the news of the search authorization was doused when he glanced at the date on his desk calendar. He realized it had been seventy-two hours since Penelope's kidnapping.

His optimism dimmed further as he observed members of the BPD recovery task force assembled in the main conference room to lay the groundwork for a dragging operation of several tributaries in the local areas. Based on past discoveries, there were areas deemed conducive for disposing of a body.

Alex McBain walked into Cutter's office with a look of chagrin.

"You don't look like you're bringing tidings of joy," Cutter deciphered.

"Boy, is that an understatement, mate." McBain replied. He then parked himself in a chair, exhaled a deep breath and said, "We just got word that Ryker received a secure message from Washington that the bureau is dispatching a couple of agents down here to take the lead in taking down DeSalvo."

"They wouldn't make a commitment like that without having something more concrete than the evidence we shared," Cutter concluded.

"I can tell you what has been talked about around the water cooler at BPD but it's not very much. Everything significant is being treated as classified and not releasable except to those with a need-to-know. . . and I guess that does not include us."

"Tell me what does include us," Cutter prodded anxiously.

McBain grabbed bottled water from the mini-fridge and pulled a chair next to Cutter's desk and sat. "Apparently, agents from the bureau have been down here for weeks conducting covert surveillance right under our nose."

"At what location?" Cutter asked.

"Shankytown."

"Shankytown? What is out there?"

McBain briefed, "There is a group of abandoned warehouses just south of the interstate. It used to be a Wal-Mart distribution center that closed years ago. Through months of surveillance, they have determined it's a haven for local drug dealers and now they have evidence DeSalvo's organization' set up a throughput operation for high-grade cocaine and other narcotics, along with black market weapons. They cannot say for sure, but something happened two days ago that is reminiscent of a DeSalvo security measure."

"Go on," Cutter urged.

"One of the agent units followed a convoy of vehicles heading towards the warehouse complex but it was dry-cleaned," McBain continued, referring to a counter-surveillance tactic commonly used by mobsters to lose a tail. "The good news is they managed to get the license numbers on several of the vehicles. One of them was a Florida plate registered to a Miami crime boss named Ransom Oliver."

Cutter leapt from his chair. "I thought he was put away. I was personally involved in his takedown for drug and racketeering in Miami."

"You've fallen victim to federal bureaucracy, mate," McBain informed him. The conviction was overturned on appeal due to questionable evidence gathering."

Cutter's face narrowed as he stood and slowly moved over to the window.

"Bullshit! That bust was solid."

"Hold on, partner," McBain warned, noticing Cutter look of eagerness. "If you are thinking about digging into that case, you'll have Internal Affairs crawling up your ass faster than you can shit. Word is the bureau doesn't want any investigation or even surveillance of Bennie DeSalvo until they can prove a direct link to Ransom Oliver."

Cutter paced about the room then turned to McBain, "I gotta in on this. I know it was either DeSalvo or Oliver who ordered the hit on me which killed Jenni."

"The bureau doesn't care about your personal baggage, Blake," McBain remarked. "And they care even less about a hostage who they consider a fugitive. Because of the hospital bombing, you won't get authorization to even sniff this case."

Cutter continued pacing silently, then sat. "Then we need to know everything they are doing, everything they know about Oliver and DeSalvo. We need a contact who knows what moves are being made in Washington and Miami; where they're taking a crap, everything. We need someone from outside BPD we can trust. Even Carruthers cannot know about this."

McBain tightened his jaw and moved closer to Cutter. Whispering, he told him, "I have a contact in Miami who can keep us knowledgeable with what is going on at the bureau. He is in the e-mail network with bureau investigators, and I believe I can trust him. His name is Lee Kim. He is an instructor at Quantico but does consultant work for the Miami field office. He's worked in vice and investigation divisions and has actionable intelligence on the DeSalvo cartel."

"So, what makes you so sure he'll cooperate with us?" Cutter questioned him. "It sounds to me like he'd be sticking his neck out. Why would he do that?"

"Remember my ex-wife?" McBain asked.

"Yes, I remember Lulu. What does Lee Kim have to do with your ex-wife?"

"He's, her brother. Despite the divorce, we're still on good terms."

Chapter 35

Lee Kim was a Korean-born detective with more than ten years of field duty with the bureau. He was tall, handsome, and thinly built with a full head of jet-black hair that belied his age. He spent countless days training on special warfare tactics at Little Creek, Virginia with the Navy's **SEAL** Team 2. So, he was extremely physically fit and highly intelligent and had been a great asset to the bureau, particularly in planning police tactical raids and assaults.

McBain accompanied Kim to Cutter's office for an introduction and conversation about an insertion strategy at DeSalvo's hideout.

"Blake, this is my ex-brother-in-law, Agent Lee Kim," McBain introduced him as they arrived.

Cutter garnered a confused look.

"I know what you're wondering Blake," McBain noted then explained. "That's it's strange that I'd be collaborating with my sister's ex-husband."

"I-I'm not saying…."

McBain interrupted. "Well, after they divorced, he saved my sister's life… donated his kidney. It is a long story we don't have time to go into."

"You've said enough!" Cutter declared as he shook hands with Kim. Cutter then pulled McBain aside side and asked him to step out into the hallway for a moment.

"Excuse us!" Cutter said to Kim.

"No problem," Kim responded graciously.

When they reached the hallway, Cutter spoke softly to McBain saying, "I know Kim is willing to help us. That is not what I am concerned about. Did you smell his breath? It reeks of alcohol."

McBain responded, "Don't worry about him, Blake. He's been handing out with Seals, but I guarantee you, he won't disappoint us."

Cutter and McBain re-entered the room and McBain immediately moved over to Kim and asked, You're good, Kim?"

By the expression on McBain's face, he knew McBain was referring to his alcohol intake.

"I'm fine," Kim reassured him. "Yeah, I partied a bit last night with the guys, but I'm good."

McBain waved his left hand back and forth towards Cutter to asked him to halt any interrogation or concern about the matter."

"Welcome to Bullet," Cutter offered with a guarded smile. "I admire you for what Alex just told me, but if I said I've heard enough to trust you, I'd be lying."

"I don't expect you to," he replied sincerely. "My personal life doesn't affect my work or my commitment to help take down these bad guys. I'm here to help in any way I can."

"Fair enough!" Cutter relented. "Let's hear what you got."

Kim pulled a Bullet City map out of his black travel bag, unfolded it, and laid it out over Cutter's desk. "I will share with you what I know. The bureau has had wire taps on both Oliver's and DeSalvo's communication for a long time. We know they've been meeting frequently in places we believe to be safe houses. As you can imagine, we've been waiting a long time to uncover something big about these two. One of our taps picked up a conversation between the two about the movement of drugs and weapons out of Miami. We didn't have a clue about Bullet, Georgia being the destination until recently. We'll still have a tough time establishing a money trail for drug purchases. They are transacting in cryptocurrency and funneling funds through shell corporations. Money flows have been untraceable to this point. So, they are easily moving their profits from drug and weapons smuggling through various money laundering resources. It will be difficult to slow down their expansion. Bullet is just the start."

"Can we gain any intelligence from their internet activities?" McBain asked.

"Not a chance there either," Kim informed them. "Our IT team could not pick up anything. My guess is they are using IP spoofing to mask the IP addresses. We have evidence that they are also using secure VPN to encrypt and decrypt their e-mail communication. So right now, we have nothing that will stand up in court."

"All this doesn't surprise me," Cutter admitted. "DeSalvo's good at concealing his operation. My question is...why would they pick a place like Bullet as a major distribution hub and transit point of sale?" Cutter inquired. "It's well off the beaten path," Cutter further noted.

"Actually, that's what makes it appealing," Kim explained. "It's a hub for inland narcotics and weapons distribution. There's easy access to I-95 and they don't have to deal with customs agents and the border patrol like the ports of entry into Miami from the Caribbean. We've gotten indications they're using an unknown rogue shipping company to launder their containers through the Bullet port container yard. We haven't been able to identify the exact shipping company because there's over a hundred that utilized that port. We're confident it won't be long before we notice something. We have round-the-clock surveillance."

Cutter and McBain both raised their eyebrows and nodded in acknowledgement of Kim's information.

Kim then pointed to a spot on the map about ten miles west of the Bullet city limits. "Here's where we think DeSalvo has set up shop. It's a cluster of abandoned warehouses just off Tobacco Road…ideal because it's outside the city and far enough away from the port as to not draw attention. It is a strategic gem—isolated, well concealed, yet still close to the interstate. There is a long, narrow, and heavily wooded dirt road that stretches about three miles from the interstate to the complex and the complex is surrounded in the back by rolling hills, mostly with thick woods of mature, evergreen trees. It's an excellent location to place snipers. We've been able to conduct drone surveillance, but it is nearly impossible to get close in without being observed from the air or ground. I would recommend approaching with a small team on foot through the woods. Regardless, a raid will not be easy to pull off, especially if the mission includes hostage extraction. That may reduce options on how the bureau wants to manage it."

Cutter asked, "So you're suggesting the bureau will bypass local jurisdiction and go after DeSalvo with its own assets?"

"I'm not sure that's the case," Kim clarified. "They prefer an interagency operation but since both DeSalvo and Oliver have been high on FBI interest, they will want to lead the planning effort. The bureau doesn't believe the county has the manpower or armament necessary to successfully execute a drug and weapons warrant and they don't want to miss this opportunity to bag at least one of the DeSalvo hierarchy. But we will have to be prepared. DeSalvo always travels with a legion of heavily armed henchmen."

"So, what type of response do they think we'll encounter if we conduct a raid?" Cutter asked with a sudden look of concern.

"We suspect they not only have AR-15s but an assortment of military-grade weapons to include high-powered assault rifles fitted with telescopic scopes, military M4 Carbines, shoulder-fired rockets such as RPGs, grenade launchers and flame throwers. We also know DeSalvo deals in weapons on the black market and through international smuggling. One weapon we know he's acquired is the Heckler and Koch XM8 light assault weapons which were popular with German units during the 1990s to 2000s but were replaced by newer technology. Many were smuggled through the black market to terrorist groups and third world countries." Kim stated. "Don't think they're obsolete. XM8s are still highly effective."

Cutter asked, "And you think those weapons made it through smuggling into the Caribbean shipping routes."

"Precisely," Kim confirmed. "Contrary to popular belief, weapons are easier to smuggle through international waters via container ships than drugs. Then, there's no way to prevent them from getting through the ports and into inland routes. They can use biker gangs, semi drivers, distribution trucks, even small racks transported in the trunks of unsuspecting motorists on normal interstate and state roads. Once they're in country, it's pretty much a lost cause."

"There's the rub," Cutter noted in agreement. "We've don't have enough agents or state and local law enforcement to monitor the endless number of smuggling nodes and routes."

McBain clenched his teeth, then asked, "So, if we can't stop them on the road, what do we know about their warehousing operation?

Kim briefed, "We believed they've placed scouts and snipers as far out as the main road. If we tried a direct assault, they'd pick us off like ducks in a shooting gallery."

CHAPTER 36

Cutter walked around the room cupping his chin in thought and then turned to Kim and declared, "There's still something I don't understand. Why did a Sicilian born mobster like Bennie DeSalvo decide to immigrate to the U.S. to align himself with notorious American mobsters like Ransom Oliver and Anthony Milano?"

Kim briefed, "Here's what I've gathered about the Sicilian cartels while I worked at Interpol. They are very well established and very monopolizing. They don't let other small groups gain power unless they have family ties, which DeSalvo has no Sicilian family lineage. I read his dossier and studied criminal career for several years. DeSalvo started out as a street thug with a high IQ and graduated to become a Sicilian drug dealer. Since, he had a natural acumen for business, he defected to Holland, married a Dutch national in Amsterdam, went to business school for two years and got the European equivalent of an associate degree in business and finance. We traced the woman he married and learned she disappeared without a trace while she was working at a factory there in Amsterdam. There was an investigation by Dutch authorities, but nothing tied him to her disappearance, so the case went cold and was eventually closed. At that point, we learned DeSalvo traveled to Ecuador, recruited a group of paramilitary defectors, and brought them to Sicily to try and take over one of the biggest cartel's turfs. But after several public shootouts, DeSalvo realized his small group would never break into the business of the Sicilian crime families without losing a lot of men, some he's developed personal relationships with. It was a ruthless business in Sicily where rival mob groups are hated worse than police. We don't know exactly how he was brought into the Oliver and Milano crime conglomerate, but we figured his expertise in business, finance and international trade gave them more intelligence collection ability on smuggling operations than one would get through any domestic associations."

"Understood," Cutter acknowledged. "Then why would a Sicilian intermediate boss hire a bunch of Cuban nationals rather than bringing his own people over from Sicily?"

Kim smiled, "It's a simple formula, Blake," Kim revealed to him. "In the brief time since you left, syndicate operations in Miami and the Gold Coast have established an evolving business model that rivals any Fortune 500 company. Due to the competition from street gangs, independent drug smuggling markets and other sources of mysterious world competition, they are beginning to welcome international diversity and outsourcing for cheap labor... in this case, the outsourcing is for murder-for-hire contracts, political assassinations and kidnapping, human trafficking transportation and distribution. It's not just about drug and weapons smuggling. That's small potatoes these days. The other factor is that Sicilian blue-collar criminals would demand the type of funding and perks they enjoyed in Sicily where there's not much differentiation between legitimate commerce and the underground economy. There's just not a lot of investigative prowess like we have in the western world. Miami cartels would be hard pressed to keep Sicilian or Italian born staff satisfied and loyal, which would expose and threaten the organizations. However, with Cuban and Latin American mercenaries, there's wide open sources of cheap and enthusiastic labor that is used to drug running and committing criminal activity for pennies. It's a sure bet business model."

Cutter then understood the logic of DeSalvo's operation in Miami and he was ready to move on with more discussion of actionable intelligence. "So, what's the trigger for the bureau to move in?" Cutter asked.

Kim continued, "They're looking for something concrete to indicate drug or weapons smuggling activity. They need that evidence before they can establish probable cause to obtain a narcotics search warrant and mount a subsequent assault. The magistrate in this county isn't very accommodating. That means they need more surveillance on the target vehicles. It wouldn't be for at least forty-eight hours. Even if they get the leads now, it'll take at least that long to process federal warrants."

"It's gotta happen within twenty-four hours!" Cutter exclaimed bitterly. "Anything beyond that and our hostage might be dead."

Kim glanced at McBain and then replied, "I understand your concern, Agent Cutter. I hate to state the obvious, but we've gotten no confirmation that she's held there or still alive. You go launching something independently that interferes with a federal sting and, as we say in my homeland, you'll be in deep kimchi."

Cutter argued belligerently, "I'm not gonna let a hostage get killed at the expense of taking down DeSalvo or Oliver."

McBain and Kim exchanged a look of deep concern. Cutter was letting his personal feelings interfere with his objectivity and reality once again.

Kim warned, "You'd better produce some logical reason you think she's being held and is still alive. That's your only chance to get support on this one. Once the feds in Washington get all the intelligence on what's going on down here, you'll have Washington agents coming down here out the ying-yang."

Frustrated with the progress of the meeting, Cutter decided to excuse himself from the room as Kim continued discussing pertinent details with McBain. After a couple of minutes outside the door, he walked back in and said, "I appreciate you coming up here, Agent Kim, but you wasted a trip if you think I'm going to stand by and do nothing while we wait on bureaucracy to play out."

"Then what's your move?" Kim asked.

"I'm going to see Ryker." Cutter declared, then turned and walked back towards the door. "We need complete interagency coordination to bring every asset we can bear on this situation. This is a potential game changer in this county."

As he reached the door, McBain shouted, "Hey, partner! Your chances of getting Ryker to let you blow into this operation are slim to none."

Cutter didn't respond and stormed through the bullpen, refusing to be swayed by McBain and Kim's warnings and negative prospects.

Chapter 37

A few minutes later, Cutter rushed into Ryker's office, without knocking, then briefed him on what he had learned—careful not to reveal his source. "Chief, we can't wait for the bureau to take over this investigation. If they wait any longer, the hostage will be dead."

Raising his eyes from a case folder on his desk, Ryker barked, "Here's a news flash, Agent Cutter. Statistics would suggest that she's already dead if they've got her. Once the boys from Washington take over, it's their call what happens after that."

"You know that's bureaucratic bullshit, chief!" Cutter shouted. "We have a sworn duty to investigate and rescue a kidnapped person."

Pulling rank, Ryker sprung from his chair like a jackrabbit, dropped his pencil and bifocals on the desk and said, "You're getting too personally involved with this case, Agent Cutter. Your focus is supposed to be on closing the Norton case." After a short pause, Ryker said, "I've heard enough. You need some down time. You need another short vacation."

"A vacation?" Cutter questioned, rhetorically.

"Yes, and this time, alone." Ryker poked.

Cutter was furious at what he perceived as a cheap shot, feeling like he wanted to take a pair of pliers and twist Ryker's head apart from his neck. He took a deep breath and composed himself, changing his tone as he spoke apologetically, pleading, "Didn't mean to go off the handle, Chief, but I need just one shot to get this woman out. . . one shot before the bureau comes in here and screws it up."

Cupping his chin pensively, Ryker paused, sighed heavily then replied, "Alright Cutter, you better be right about this. You know you're risking the reputation of the entire department. What are you asking me to do?"

"All I'm asking is a chance to get her out before the bureau sends some hot shots out there to shoot up the place." Elaborating on the obvious, he added, "My gut feeling is she's out there. If they took that kind of risk to bomb a hospital and kill and injure people to kidnap her, then it means she knows a lot that the bureau can use to nail these guys. I don't think we should blow this chance. She's a tough woman and she'll resist long enough for us to get there in time to get her out."

Despite long-standing animosity between the two, Ryker trusted Cutter's judgment. Ryker again sighed heavily, then relented. "Alright, Cutter, I'll give you forty-eight hours to come up with something solid about the hostage's whereabouts," he offered. "But be advised of one thing."

"What's that, Chief?"

"I'm not going on record as authorizing anything, but you can't take anybody down without my approval. As the old saying goes, I will disavow all knowledge if this goes to shit, and you will not get any of our SBI resources to support it."

"Best of both worlds," Cutter snipped.

Ryker stared at him without words and waited.

"Alright, we'll do it that way," Cutter relented. "You got my word that I won't tie this to the bureau in any way. At that moment, Cutter winced from the lingering pain as the discomfort of his arm being in a sling flared.

Ryker, noticing Cutter's temporary loss of focus, decided to give him a moment to overcome it. He walked over the door to ensure it was closed tight and then moved back to his desk and turned the volume up on his radio. Squatting back into the chair behind his desk, Ryker informed him, "There's another reason why the county and BPD are forced to delay any rescue operation."

Cutter perked up, witnessing a rare look of openness on Ryker's face. "Take a look at this e-mail I received from Mayor Daniel." Ryker ordered him as he logged on to his computer and pulled up his e-mail.

As Cutter moved over to scan the on-screen e-mail, Ryker continued, "There's someone undermining our intelligence on this case—a mole in the department. BPD believes that one of their officers tipped the DeSalvo organization about Ms. Lane's hospital stay, which resulted in a kidnapping, bombing and innocent casualties. I'd like you to know who they think it is."

Chapter 38

As Cutter remained silent, Ryker allowed Cutter to stare at the computer screen for a moment. Ryker then grumbled, "Looks like this cop thinks it's worth losing his career to help mobsters kidnap a woman who is a confessed murderer."

Cutter reacted, growling "Son-of-a-bitch, Logan Metropolit! Why am I not surprised it's him? I have never trusted him from the first time we met. If there's was any cop that I figured would be on the take, it would be Metropolit."

"How do you figure?" Ryker asked with feigned curiosity.

"I've known about Metropolit's gambling debts for years?"

"So why didn't you take that information about him to Internal Affairs?" Ryker asked.

Cutter grinned facetiously. He realized that Ryker was asking out of frustration. "C'mon boss. You know we don't disclose information about police officers' personal issues without a justifiable reason to do so."

"Even if they've been turned?" Ryker asked.

"Even against a guy like Metropolit." Cutter said. "I loathe him but up until now, he was one of us."

Ryker walked to the window and stared out. It was the obvious sunken feeling of disappointment to learn that a police officer goes rogue, particularly one who was trusted enough to work with federal agents.

"So, how'd we get him?" Cutter asked.

Ryker explained, "One of BPD's undercover vice squad members has observed him driving in his personal vehicle toward the complex of warehouses four times in the past two weeks. Since that area had not been the site of any recent investigations, they got suspicious and tailed him. Then we triangulated several calls from his cell phone which pinged to the area code for South Miami."

"It sounds circumstantial," Cutter questioned. "Just because DeSalvo is from Miami does not prove he was calling him or anyone in the organization. You know that Chief," Cutter pointed out.

"Correct," Ryker agreed.

"So, what was the hook for Metropolit to be drawn in by the mob?"

"As you mentioned, it was his gambling debts. Our sources knew more about Metropolit's problems than you did. He owes a bundle to local bookies who are connected to the mafia in Miami. He's been on the IA's watch list for a while, but they chose to keep it close hold, hoping for an eventual good outcome."

"That doesn't prove guilt," Cutter countered.

"But it was enough for internal affairs to start an investigation and trace his telephone communication."

Cutter shrugged heavily. "I don't think much of Metropolit as a police officer, but the department could be headed for a lawsuit if they're wrong. I heard he has some family high up in the political structure."

"Well, as long as it's not Senator Dayton, nobody will really give a damn."

"So, when were you going to let me in on this?" Cutter asked as his forehead stretched.

Ryker responded, "I thought it was too risky for you to know before now. The bureau put a gag order in place until Internal Affairs and the DA's office produces enough to prosecute. My guess is you would have gone ape shit and blown it. Now that you do know, you will have to be discreet. We don't want to lose the chance of nailing a rogue cop because of the intertwining effect of these investigations."

"I understand," Cutter relented, "So what's next?"

"We are giving this time to simmer before we turn up the heat. Until then, stay out of the way. He may be the key to breaking this case open."

A wide grin surfaced on Cutter's face. He hadn't felt such euphoria since losing his virginity at age sixteen. "Just promise me this, Chief."

"Promise you what?" Ryker asked suspiciously annoyed.

"Let me in on it when we nail him. A rogue police officer on the force is worse than the antichrist in the Basilica."

Tossing the case file aside, Ryker replied sarcastically, "That's eloquently put. I'll make sure you're added to the guest list when we're ready to shake him down."

Before Cutter walked out of Ryker's office, he remarked vehemently, "If he's not interested in your deal, I have a better one for him."

"What that, Cutter?" Ryker asked.

Clenching his fist, Cutter replied, "An appointment with me in a back alley."

Chapter 39

Cutter didn't have to wait long before getting the opportunity to confront Logan Metropolit about his betrayal. He received a call from Internal Affairs three days later, inviting him to the BPD conference room at noon that day when Metropolit would be summoned there by BPD Chief Carruthers. To avoid the possibility of Metropolit being a no-show and fleeing, Carruthers informed Metropolit that he was being summoned to a special coordination meeting to discuss the evidence that had been obtained in the DeSalvo investigation.

At ten minutes before noon, a host of BPD law enforcement officers, led by Carruthers, converged on BPD's windowless main conference room, eager to witness Agent Metropolit's expression when he entered the room. The group included Carruthers, Cutter, Ryker, and Deputy County Sheriff Donald Holloway.

After everyone was assembled, a hush fell over the room. It was a surreal sense of regret over witnessing a promising, young police officer foregoing the silent glory of police work for the fortunes of corruption and temptation. The assembled group jockeyed for the best position near the door, poised for that dubious moment when Metropolit stepped in.

Chapter 40

At 12:05 p.m., Metropolit walked through the door into a room of unwelcome stares. He quickly realized he was not there for a narcotic's investigative coordination meeting as told. The stares followed him as he sauntered over to the edge of the oblong conference table. His forehead stretched with curiosity.

"What's going on, Chief?" he asked with a nervous tick.

In a blunt tone, Carruthers announced, "Detective Metropolit, you're being placed under arrest pending an investigation for a host of felonies to include corruption, conspiracy, accessory to multiple counts of murder and domestic terrorism in the bombing of a public facility."

"What the hell are you talking about?" he asked with a feigned look of shock as a uniformed police officer walked over and placed him in a set of handcuffs.

"Cut the crap, Metropolit!" Cutter shouted moving towards him in a threatening manner. "How much did DeSalvo pay you to sell-out your department?"

Ryker stepped between them. "You get personal and you're out of here, Cutter," Ryker shouted at Cutter.

Cutter backed up and Ryker scoffed then took a deep breath to ease his own tension.

Carruthers proceeded to fire off the counts from the lengthy charge sheet as the uniformed officer guided his prisoner to a chair. Metropolit refused to sit as his face turned red.

Carruthers passed the charge sheet to Deputy Holloway who placed it in a manila folder.

Metropolit, groping for words, stuttered, "Wait a minute, Chief. You think we could speak privately about this. I am entitled to legal counsel before you can charge me with anything."

Carruthers interrupted him, "Cut the crap, Metropolit! SID's been tailing you for weeks. We know what's going on out at Tobacco Road and we know you're involved. We also know your motive. Do I need to elaborate any further?"

Metropolit swallowed a lump in his throat. His hands trembled. "What's the crowd here for, to humiliate and embarrass me?" he asked.

"Just say it's our little payback for you selling out the department," Ryker replied.

"Now sit!" Carruthers ordered. "We've got something to discuss with you."

Metropolit eased into a chair. Then, Carruthers approached him and spoke again. "Look Metropolit, I've asked the key law enforcement leadership here this morning to listen in on something that may prove beneficial for everybody. If you're indicted and prosecuted for police corruption and potentially accessory to kidnapping. If Penelope Lane turns up dead, you may be looking at accessory to manslaughter along with a host of other charges."

Metropolit sighed morosely with a look of resignation.

Carruthers continued, "Now that we've got your attention, we have a proposition for you. We need a way to turn the tables on DeSalvo and get inside his organization. You may be the person to help us get it done."

"What do you want me to do?" he asked, knowing he had to concede and agree to save his skin.

Carruthers pointed toward the door, signaling Holloway and several others to exit the room as their role of intimidation was complete. Cutter and Ryker flanked Carruthers as they moved close to Metropolit, cognizant that even a police officer when cornered like a rat could do something unpredictable.

Ryker then spoke directly to Metropolit, "We know that DeSalvo's setting up a drug and weapons smuggling operation on Tobacco Road. We need you to infiltrate their facility and install some listening devices, paving the way for us to obtain some viable evidence. I can fully guarantee we will have enough to prosecute you if you don't cooperate. However, you cooperate, and it leads to major arrests and drug busts, there may be a bit of leniency for you somewhere down the line. I'm not making any promises no matter what the outcome. There's just a chance we could do something for you if you help us bust DeSalvo."

Metropolit felt his insides recoil into a knot. "No way," he protested. "You're asking me to commit suicide by double-crossing DeSalvo. Nobody double-crosses a man like him and lives to talk about it. Besides, there's no way you're gonna ever take him down. He's set up a fortress out there. They've got security checkpoints echeloned from the main road to the complex. You'd never be able to infiltrate that place no matter how many agents you send out there. They can see vehicles coming a mile away from the hills," he added exaggerating. "And that's only if you get past their henchmen stationed at different points along the route."

Stating the obvious, Ryker interjected, "That's now your problem, Metropolit. If you mess up and fail to succeed with this operation, you could forget about a retirement but start planning to spend the next few years in prison."

"Be careful Ryker," Carruthers warned. "Let's not predict the judicial process." Carruthers shifted the questioning to his knowledge of their capabilities. "Maybe you can clue us in on what we'd be facing if we decide to conduct an assault," Carruthers prodded.

Metropolit sighed heavily, thought for a moment, and then said, "I can't help you, there. I don't know that much about it."

Ryker lunged across the table and looked Metropolit square in the eyes. "Take him and book him," he ordered the uniformed guards. "We'll make a call to the DA's office and request a murder one indictment."

Metropolit raised his hands. "Alright-alright. I'll tell you what I do know."

Cutter took a deep breath, preparing himself for whatever Metropolit was about to divulge, even if it meant learning that Penelope had been harmed or was dead.

Metropolit began, "It's a very heavily fortified site. On the grounds is a stash house with a large cache of high-caliber firearms, munitions, drugs, and pallets of cash bundles that were laundered through Miami. If you're going to assault the compound, you'll have to do it with total surprise and at night. They're well equipped with mines, grenades, assault weapons, snub-nose semis . . . the whole nine yards."

"What about manpower? How many bad guys do they have?" Carruthers asked Metropolit.

"My guess is at least twenty. Most of them are foreign immigrants from Columbia and Venezuela, some defectors from the FARC and a few from Cuba and Honduras. His most trusted lieutenants and henchmen are from Sicily, his home-grown group. DeSalvo's known to hire men with guerrilla and rebel warfare experience. They won't be easy to take down. He pays them well, so they'll risk their lives for their money."

There was a prolonged silence from Cutter and Carruthers, like something had sucked the air out of the room.

"What do you think we'll need to do to take them down?" Carruthers asked Ryker.

Ryker thought for a moment and then replied bluntly, "At the minimum, we'll need a BPD tactical team augmented by SBI and ATF agents armed to the teeth. A nighttime assault is our only chance. If we're to launch, we'll need more intelligence on how their defenses are arrayed and the type of armament they're utilizing at those security checkpoints. We have to do this without it becoming a blood bath . . . and we can't come out on the short end."

Carruthers directed, "This needs to be a cooperative effort between SBI and BPD. I'd like to get this done before the Feds in Washington take over."

Ryker nodded and gave a wry grin. "We can get it done, but we'll need some time to plan it out."

Cutter intervened, looked over at Metropolit and asked him in a frantic tone, "What about the hostage? Are they holding her there?"

"Last time I was out there was two days ago," Metropolit replied. "She was there and alive."

Cutter broke a subtle grin of relief. Noting his interest, Metropolit continued, "I can't tell you what their intentions are with her. I can't assure you they haven't killed her since the last time I was out there."

Carruthers interjected, "What we'll need is for you to go back in there and assess whether or not a rescue operation is feasible." He stared over at Metropolit prodding the obvious.

Metropolit leaned back in his chair. "If I go in there, I'll need backup."

Carruthers turned to Ryker for a moment to gain a visual consensus. Ryker nodded and responded, "We'll have to move in quickly."

"Fair enough," Carruthers said as Cutter nodded in agreement. "I'll leave you to work that out with SWAT and the HRT and get back to me with a plan. How long would it take?"

"Give me a few hours to discuss it with the team chiefs," Ryker requested. "Due to the number of weapons and munitions they're stockpiling, we'll likely need ATF support also."

Metropolit nodded to prevent anyone in the room from suggesting Carruthers reconsider the deal. Metropolit added, "As long as I'm wired and have communication, we may be able to pull it off. But if all goes to shit, then I'll need your help getting out. They find out I've double-crossed them or if I even get made by anyone in there, I'm a dead man." Metropolit was attempting to show resolve, but with the less than confident tone of his voice, it was obviously false bravado.

Carruthers turned to Metropolit and said, "We'll work on it, but no promises. We still need to clear this through Mayor Daniels.

Cutter whispered to Ryker, "You can bet she's not going on record saying she authorized this mission. Remember, if it goes to hell in a handbasket, I assure you, it'll be an unsanctioned raid."

Carruthers spoke to Metropolit, "You'll be strapped with an electronic monitoring device so don't even think about trying to escape."

"Understood," Metropolit responded quickly, realizing that Carruthers' main concern was covering his ass.

Carruthers turned to Ryker, "Okay, Harry. You've got the lead on this. This operation must be on a need-to-know basis. If this leaks to your bureau or worse the press, we'll have to shut it down." Ryker and Cutter nodded in agreement. Carruthers then gestured for a uniformed officer to escort Metropolit to a holding cell.

Chapter 41

The next morning, Carruthers, Ryker, Cutter, and Deputy Sheriff Holloway were summoned to Mayor Daniels' office to discuss the planning for the operation that would be named *Juggernaut*. After they arrived and congregated in front of her desk, Ryker stepped forward and opened the conversation. "Mayor, we've selected a viable plan to launch Operation Juggernaut. What's left to work out is the composition of the assault and entry teams," he added, suggesting to Daniels and Carruthers that the onus was now on her staff to coordinate any involvement by other outside agencies.

"I know what you're looking for, my endorsement of this raid, but it's a tacit endorsement only and completely off the record," Mayor Daniels responded.

It was the good news that Cutter and Ryker were hoping for. Ryker continued, "We need to conduct the operation with a high degree of surprise and deception. So, we'll need some BPD assets to be on-call if we need them."

Carruthers said, "Alright. I need to get my leaders from vice and special tactics read in on the plan early."

"Not a problem," Ryker confirmed.

Then, Daniels' press secretary Nikki Grant walked into the room and came over and whispered into Daniels' ear as Daniels nodded. Mayor Daniels then spoke to the group, saying, "Those hounds at the news bureau can be useful for a change. I'd like to hold a press conference tomorrow to hint to the press about a future operation against drug infiltrators in the county. We need that type of advanced information for the public in case something major goes down before we can react. I want to give them the perception that something's planned but not immediate. Also, let provide a false suspected location. This needs to be the biggest information deception operation since D-day."

Chapter 42

Later that day, the Deputy Chief of the Vice Squad, Lieutenant James Campbell was summoned to Mayor Daniels' main conference room for a meeting with the same group from that morning. He was accompanied by two of his most experienced vice squad members. Campbell was a tall, lanky man with a salt and pepper-beard, thick bushy eyebrows, and a distinctive beaked nose. He was looking for involvement in an operation like Juggernaut to add credibility to a department that had rarely seen significant action in the county in the past two years. Glynn County was considered one of the driest counties in the state until the recent rumors circulated about narcotics criminal activity.

After a rotation of handshake and small talk, Daniels took a seat in the front row and gestured Campbell and the rest of the group to take their seats.

Immediately thereafter, Campbell stood and said, "For this operation to be successful, we'll have to do more than the mayor's press conference to rattle DeSalvo's nerves and lead them to potential mistakes."

Mayor Daniels eyebrows raised. "Okay, let's hear your suggestion, Campbell."

"Ma'am, I suggest we conduct a second press conference shortly after yours in which the SBI Chief and BPD Chief of Police jointly announce that we're sending agents down to Miami to conduct covert surveillance of Bennie DeSalvo's business establishments. We could ask the local newspapers to publish the story in tomorrow's edition. We'd then have Metropolit go out to the compound carrying a copy of the newspaper article. That way, while he's on the inside gathering information on their set-up, he can also gauge DeSalvo's reaction to the publication of the story."

Mayor Daniels interjected, "That sounds like a potentially good plan. Let's work on it."

"I can handle the communication with the Miami field office," Ryker added. "I have a good rapport with the SAC down there, and Police Chief Manual Sanchez is a good friend of mine. We were in the academy together. That's how Agent Cutter got here. I'm sure Manuel and I can work together on when to have the press release the story."

Despite her reservations about Ryker on certain issues, Mayor Daniels felt comfortable the plan could be executed successfully under his leadership.

"Sounds feasible except for one thing," Ryker posed. "Big fish don't usually swallow small bait."

"Meaning?" asked Campbell.

"Meaning, the plan doesn't sound foolproof." Ryker explained.

"What more do you suggest?" Campbell asked with a twitch of frustration.

Ryker added, "We should get someone from the bureau in Miami to follow up with a sound bite criticizing the operation, suggesting it would be a waste of law enforcement resources. We need a retired police officer to come to the station and do a live interview…someone who knows police tactics, someone that locals know, trust and respect. It should be someone who will sound legitimate on the air that the local radio jocks would allow to do a fake interview."

"A cooperative radio station may be hard to find in South Florida," Campbell stated. "We no longer have a good reputation with the local community like we used to."

Ryker cupped his chin in thought, then announced, "I know who we can use. I know a guy who retired about three years ago named Jose Rodriguez. He retired from vice and now operates a soup kitchen on the east side of Miami. He also started a youth basketball league. The local radio stations already know him and would fully cooperate."

After muttering a few words to Carruthers, who offered back a noncommittal shrug, Daniels announced, "It's worth a try. Find a radio station manager that will collaborate with us on this, and we'll put the entire plan into motion."

As the meeting concluded, Campbell and his team departed for BPD to contact the two radio stations in the area. Simultaneously, Ryker and Cutter left to head back to BPD. That left Daniels and Carruthers to consult further on the plan for the media statements.

A half-hour later, Daniels phoned her press secretary to notify all the local broadcast and print media outlets that she would be holding a press conference to announce an interagency surveillance operation to be conducted in Miami.

At nine that evening, Cutter left BPD headquarters for his apartment, satisfied with the initial planning for the operation. He felt anxious, knowing that six days had already passed since the kidnapping. Despite the cleverness of the plan, Cutter surmised the time needed to coordinate, rehearse, and execute it would further narrow the possibility that Penelope would still be alive once they initiated the rescue operation. He also knew agents from the bureau would be arriving in the county within the next few days to take over the case. When it happened, the focus would turn from a hostage rescue to executing an arrest warrant for a federal suspect and his cohorts. But that would all change if they could pull this plan together and execute it.

Chapter 43

The next afternoon at one, the makeshift special task force consisting of a hostage negotiator, members of BPD SWAT, and several SBI agents assembled in the BPD conference room for an initial briefing on Operation Juggernaut. Ryker ordered the masking of all classified information to just those with a need to know in case Detective Logan Metropolit wasn't the only compromised officer in the department.

At that same time, Metropolit was taken from his basement holding cell in BPD headquarters and escorted in handcuffs by Deputy Holloway and an unidentified SBI agent to an alley directly behind BPD headquarters. A BPD detective dressed in street clothes, wearing a black baseball cap and sunglasses was sitting alone in an unmarked sedan on the left side of the alley near the entrance. As the trio stepped through the back door of the headquarters, the detective started the engine and drove slowly towards the three. Once stopped, he got out, gave the car keys to Holloway and entered the building. The deputy unlocked and removed the handcuffs from Metropolit's wrists.

Holloway addressed him, "Okay, you've got four hours to get out there, check things out, plant the listening devices and get back here. We will rendezvous back here at five this evening. Park the car in the parking garage three blocks down Main Street. Make sure you're not followed when you walk back into this alley. If you're not in this alley at straight up five, any plea deal is off the table, and I will assure you we'll get the DA and prosecutors to throw the book at you. Don't even think about trying to escape. All airports and seaports have been notified and given a composite photo of you and we have patrols on roads and highways leading out of town."

Metropolit stared down to the tightly fitted hidden ankle monitors, took a deep sigh and replied, "Don't worry. I won't screw this up."

Holloway thrust the set of keys into Metropolit's right hand harshly and snarled acrimoniously, making it clear he wasn't in favor of this activity but was following orders.

Metropolit nodded once, got in the car, started the engine, turned left at the end of the alley, and drove off.

At six thirty that evening, BPD was devoid of all the administrative staff and law enforcement officers. Earlier, the dispatch clerk had notified the cleaning crew supervisor that their services would not be needed that evening. The stage was set for several clandestine meetings and phone calls in preparation for Operation Juggernaut.

Chapter 44

At seven p.m. Metropolit arrived back at Bullet and ditched the vehicle in the parking garage as instructed. Metropolit then walked to the back alley where Holloway was waiting. When he arrived, Holloway placed Metropolit back into handcuffs and marched into the building.

Cutter and McBain linked up with Ryker and Holloway at Carruthers' office. Shortly after Cutter and McBain sat and briefed the group on the status of preparations, Ryker called the detention department from the administrative assistant's desk and ordered Metropolit to be escorted to his office to meet Cutter and McBain. The group converged at Ryker's office minutes later.

"Let's not waste time," Ryker opened the meeting, prompting the group to be seated. He turned to Metropolit and ordered, "Let's hear what you learned."

Metropolit briefed, "I did as I was told. I placed listening devices in three warehouses occupied by members of DeSalvo's crew. Then I met with DeSalvo to show him a copy of the newspaper article. But I didn't leave it with him, so hopefully he wouldn't think of making calls to the stations."

"That was smart," Carruthers commented with a wry smile. "What was his reaction?"

Metropolit replied, "He was angry and concerned, of course."

"Did he question you about why you brought him the newspaper article and how you happened to stumble upon it?" Holloway asked.

"I told him it was just a coincidence," Metropolit replied. "I pick up the paper every morning."

"And he bought that . . . without any suspicion?" Holloway further questioned.

"Yes, he did, far as I could tell. He didn't ask me any questions about it."

Holloway looked unconvinced. He was always the suspicious type. It came with the territory from years of experience working in homicide and vice. "So, what happened then?"

Metropolit continued, "I remained in the room for several minutes while he called several of his top henchmen in to discuss it. He forgot I was still there."

"That doesn't sound like DeSalvo to be that sloppy," Holloway questioned as Ryker, Cutter and Carruthers all garnered a look of doubt. Holloway had seen many unsuspected individuals become main suspects in criminal cases. He tended to believe just the opposite of what he first heard on just about everything.

Being as it was after-hours, Carruthers didn't want to arouse any unwanted curiosity of their cars of the attendees being in the parking garage, so he hurried the meeting along. "Okay, we will table that issue for now. Tell us what else you learned from that trip."

"They are setting up warehouses to take deliveries of weapons and drug packages, but I didn't talk to anyone about it so as not to arouse suspicion. I saw forklifts moving large crates and pallets around, like it was a shipping and receiving operation."

Holloway interjected, "Given the fact that they are operating out of state, I think we can send an undercover team out there to function as customs inspectors and check building licenses and permits. All we need is to have someone cite one violation and we have probable cause to go in. We could also take photos of the data plates and barcodes on those forklifts and other surrounding equipment so we can trace the acquisitions."

"Do you think it's really necessary to take that type of gamble by sending in customs inspectors?" Cutter questioned.

"We have to, at this point," Carruthers replied. "We don't have probable cause for a search warrant or a raid. If we raid and make arrest and then don't find illegal drugs or weapons, he gets off again, like he's done in Miami. As you know, he has the best attorney that money can buy. Everything we do has to be fool proof."

Cutter and McBain nodded in agreement. Ryker offered a resigned expression.

"What's the status of the hostage?" Cutter asked.

"I saw her. She was still alive," Metropolit answered.

"What's her condition?" Cutter asked.

"She was conscious, but was writhing in pain," Metropolit admitted. "I only saw her for a moment when I walked with DeSalvo and his crew through one of the warehouses in the back where she is being held. Why they are holding her there, I don't know. No discussion of her came up while I was there."

Cutter felt his heart sink in his chest. "Give me her exact location."

Metropolit thought for a moment then continued, "She's inside the smallest of the warehouses. It is on the backside west end of the complex. I couldn't tell how many overhead freight doors there are, but there's a front entrance with another building about twenty feet in front. You would have to secure the front buildings before entry due to their proximity. I noticed her mouth and wrist and ankles were bound with duct tape. You would have to work your way through the complex with minimal noise to get to her without being detected. Getting out with an immobile hostage could be problematic."

Shifting back to tactics, Ryker asked, "What's their defensive posture?"

"They have about five to seven men patrolling in and around the complex. There are approximately ten more stationed as lookouts at checkpoints along the entrance road. They are milling about, trying to look inconspicuous. They keep their weapons concealed inside their jackets or in their vehicles, but you can bet they are heavily armed. Even if a team negotiated past the first checkpoint, we would have only a few minutes to find her and get out. They do radio checks with their posts about every thirty minutes. Once detected, you will be engaged within seconds and then all hell will break loose."

"Got a clue where DeSalvo would be during an assault?" Ryker asked.

"It's impossible to guess," Metropolit shook his head regretfully. "I have no idea where he is sleeping. I didn't see any bunks or sleeping bags or anything of that nature at any of the locations I passed through. But I certainly doubt he is sleeping at the front. I cannot even confirm he sleeps there at all."

Ryker said, "That's why we need to wait 24 hours for time to pick up intelligence from those listening devices. We've got transcripts of him in conversation from our voice recognition software. Because of his heavy Sicilian accent, our techs would easily recognize his voice."

Carruthers asked Metropolit, "Anything else you'd like to share with us."

Metropolit responded, "Yeah, one other thing. Once the engagement begins, they could move him through any of six warehouses to protect him. They may also have an escape route behind the complex through a heavily wooded ravine that would make it difficult to pursue them without ATVs."

Ryker turned to Carruthers, asking, "So can we have more time to gather intelligence about the layout of the area before we launch?"

Carruthers replied, "As long as it doesn't jeopardize the success of the operation. We have no idea if DeSalvo's bringing more manpower into the complex. So, we need to take more time to evaluate different firefight scenarios." Carruthers had touched on a new fear in Cutter with those last statements.

Cutter rushed to interject, "I wouldn't much more time before launching, sir. It's already been over ninety-six hours. If there is any chance of rescuing the hostage, we must do it now."

After a deep sigh, Ryker seemed ready to accept reality. Cutter felt distressed with any thought of changing the operation from a rescue mission to a full-scale assault operation. Despite his personal agenda, Cutter knew Carruthers would not endanger an entire task force to rescue a dirty police officer or a fugitive turned hostage.

Viewing the pessimistic expressions, Ryker declared, "We have two choices. We can launch in a minimal risk posture with a withdrawal option or simply wait for the boys from the bureau to get down here with more firepower and with federal authority to launch without a local warrant. Ryker then looked at Cutter with a cynical grin and said, "I prefer we do the latter."

Among the group of highly charged police officers, Ryker sensed a lack of support for his preferred option. In their minds, an underworld figure threatening the sanctity of their community was local law enforcement's business. But Ryker secretly had his own agenda. He figured if he could get DeSalvo indicted by the feds on both kidnapping and racketeering charges, DeSalvo would turn state's evidence against the real Mafia kingpin, Ransom Oliver. Nabbing Oliver, the mastermind of the most diverse criminal organization on the East Coast, would undoubtedly be the SBI's equivalent of 'capturing the holy grail.'

Chapter 45

The following day at four, Carruthers contacted Ryker to notify him that Mayor Daniels, in consultation with the FBI field office in Atlanta, had decided to give SBI 'carte blanche' authority to conduct the raid. Based on that decision, a more intense phase of preparations began.

Prior to the next morning's daily brief, Carruthers received a call from the senior police trainer at South Ridge, informing him the task force had completed the necessary rehearsals and was ready to execute the operation.

After hanging up, Carruthers then informed Mayor Daniels of the situation. Afterward, Daniels leaned back in her executive chair and appeared lost in thought. She was surprisingly apprehensive about the plan. Though she had been the first to endorse the operation in the previous meeting, she suddenly was getting cold feet. She was about to authorize a high-risk combination raid/hostage rescue operation without the benefit of interagency cooperation or thorough intelligence. It was a type of makeshift, ad hoc operation with a history of ending in a blood bath. She took a deep breath, picked up the phone receiver and called the FBI bureau HQ in Washington.

Later the next evening, Ryker called Cutter into his office. Cutter observed the grim look on Ryker's face. He sensed it was bad news, but hoped it had nothing to do with the fate of Penelope Lane.

"I just got off the phone with Carruthers who spoke with Mayor Daniels. She's decided to delay Operation Juggernaut for forty-eight hours to hand it off to the bureau."

Cutter's jaw dropped. "What's the deal, Chief? I thought we were all set to launch."

"She's decided the operation is too risky for local agents."

"So why the forty-eight hours wait period?"

"That's how long it'll take Agent Ronaldo Kelly and his tactical team to get down here from Washington."

Cutter felt his hair on his neck standing on end. "Son of a bitch! That damn Kelly's a renegade. Things will get screwed up in a heartbeat if he's involved. The last three federal raids he's been involved in resulted in hostage casualties."

Cutter outlined his fears of Agent Kelly's involvement to Ryker. "Ronaldo Kelly is the son of Roscoe Kelly, house representative from the 13th District in Georgia. His paternal ties in politics are the only reason Ronaldo Kelly was not suspended from duty after the third botched raid in Miami which resulted in the death of two hostages. Internal Affairs closed the investigation without as much as a reprimand for Kelly. It is well known that Roscoe Kelly's intervention into the IA investigation was key to Kelly's continuing service with the bureau. Nepotism decisions at its best."

"I hear what you're saying Cutter but it's out of my hands," Ryker replied.

Cutter had no choice but to acknowledge the obvious. "So, if they're sending Kelly down here, that's means the bureau is planning on conducting an all-out assault."

"You've got to face the facts in front of you, Cutter," Ryker urged him. "You're the only cop who thinks Ms. Penelope Lane is worth risking the failure of this operation for."

"I'm telling you, Boss, Kelly's not the right guy for this," Cuter pleaded. "I collaborated with him on several shakedowns in Miami. He's looking to move up in the bureau, just like his father who'll do anything to get the attorney general's job. Every time Kelly's involved, we not only lose hostages, but we lose officers also. He's only in it to make a big collar. Right now, he's just overhead for the bureau . . . a line item in the budget. But if he deems himself instrumental in a DeSalvo takedown, he'll broadcast it throughout the bureau and Washington at large."

Ryker cupped his chin, then rebutted, "That's circumstantial presumptions and you know it, Cutter. Kelly was never admonished or deemed complicit in any of those tragedies. As I said, it's Mayor Daniels' call."

Cutter felt a cold chill down his spine. He needed to make every effort to impress, so he suggested, "Since we've got forty-eight hours before Kelly shows up, I could use that time to get in and rescue her," he suggested.

Ryker moaned in disagreement, then asked, "How are you going to manage that without any assets, Cutter? You're beginning to sound irrational, and you know that's not a good thing in your situation."

FORBIDDEN RESCUE

Cutter was sick and tired of SBI leadership holding the circumstances of his rehabilitative assignment over his head.

"Just hear me out," Cutter pleaded. "Let me take Metropolit and a small team in. I'll sign the custody sheet for him. Give us one shot to get her out. If there's a chance she's there, then it's our duty to rescue her, Chief. You know that."

Ryker furrowed his brow in thought. He asked, "How the hell are you going to assemble a team for an operation that nobody has authorized?"

"I'll manage that," Cutter replied confidently. "If I don't get any agents or BPD officers to volunteer, then it's a dead issue." Cutter hesitated, moved a step closer to Ryker, stared at him, then continued, "You owe me one, boss."

Ryker hesitated before responding in frustration, "You had to be the one cop that saved my ass." Ryker said. "I'd rather reciprocate by taking a bullet in my chest than go along with this," Ryker countered. He stared at Cutter examining him for any hint of insincerity. "Let me speak with Carruthers before we discuss this any further. SWAT belongs to him. It's his ass that'll be on the line also."

"He won't screw this up," Cutter assured him. "You know the guys at SWAT. They're a resolute and resourceful group."

Gesturing him out the door, Ryker stated, "Nothing's going down unless I get full support from Carruthers. I'll call you with an answer."

While waiting for Ryker's call, Cutter drove to South Ridge to brief members of the task force. It took only ten minutes of appealing to their sense of duty and loyalty before two thirds of the team members agreed unanimously on participation in the unsanctioned operation, believing Cutter's idea that all would be forgiven if they were able to rescue Penelope Lane and take a major crime group out of commission. The two-thirds consisted of several of Cutter's close friends and three others he'd gone through the academy with. They were qualified as snipers and expert shooters. The other third objected to participating but agreed to deny any knowledge of the operation if questioned by IA in the future. An unmentioned question was would they have the same position if questioned under a lie detector or under oath at an official hearing or inquiry.

After the meeting with the task force, Cutter got in his car and sped back to BPD headquarters. On the way, he accessed his voice mail where Ryker had left him a message. After clicking off the cell phone, he revved the car engine and sped the rest of the way through town. Once he parked, he scurried to Ryker's office.

"Carruthers gave the thumbs down."

Cutter reacted, "That's bullshit!"

Ryker interrupted, "Wait a minute. I didn't say your plan is being scrapped. Carruthers won't authorize anything official. That just means you use Metropolit, and you don't sign for him. You figure out how to make Metropolit escape but then you must sell it that you rounded him back up. You don't leave an audit trail and you don't connect this to BPD or SBI in any way. You take him out of detention on your own accord."

Cutter noticed an intriguing look in Ryker's eyes, a look revealing he unofficially supported him.

"I'll take care of it, boss," Cutter acknowledged.

At that point, Cutter knew the rest of their conversation would be completely off the record.

Ryker moved towards the door to leave the office, then abruptly turned and said, "Luckily for you, Carruthers shared a secret with me. It's the reason he's stayed in police work all these years."

"What's the reason?" Cutter asked.

"Twenty years ago, Carruthers had a teenage daughter who was kidnapped and murdered. He understands where you're at," Ryker informed him.

Cutter smiled and said, "Thanks, Chief. I'll make this happen.

Ryker retorted, "Don't thank me yet. This gets screwed up and you'll wish you never met me."

With those words, Cutter exited from the room without another word before Ryker had a chance to change his mind.

Chapter 46

That evening, Cutter's unsanctioned raid that could cost him his career would go into motion. With McBain riding along, Cutter departed in his Charger. He drove along Highway 10 until he turned onto an unimproved service road that ran about a mile until it reached an abandoned, wooden farmhouse.

Little did DeSalvo know the farmhouse, located a mile from the warehouse complex, was a previous training post for the BPD Swat team and other special tactics units before the new complex at South Ridge was constructed. Cutter, going on the advice of two friends in SWAT, decided to use the farmhouse as a command post and staging area to launch the clandestine incursion. The heavily wooded terrain surrounding the farmhouse hadn't been trafficked for three years, but it was still familiar to BPD and SBI law enforcement. Located on a ridgeline with an elevation of at least fifty feet higher than the warehouse complex, it would provide assured communications with an assault team up to the point of engagement.

FORBIDDEN RESCUE

Thirty minutes after Cutter and McBain gained access to the house using bolt cutters to break a padlock on the front door, a black Suburban pulled up, carrying five SWAT team members. The group was part of BPD's elite tactical unit and were trained and experienced in hostage extraction. They arrived appropriately outfitted for a ground assault wearing black Kevlar helmets with face shields to protect against fragmentation, tactical waterproof pants, metal reinforced elbow and knee pads, ballistic body armor vests and six-inch tactical military combat boots. They were equipped with the full array of assault armament, including military M4 rifles, optics and scopes, smoke and gas grenade launchers, lethal and non-lethal ammunition, and pyrotechnics along with truncheons, mag lights and hand-held thermal binoculars for improved night vision.

The tactical team leader, a muscular, middle-aged, balding man named Ray Orton, yelled out, "Alright team, gear up and do your safety checks."

The team responded, wasting no time in completing their routine pre-operational checks. Due to the need for secrecy, they would forgo their normal procedure of tuning their two-way radios to the tactical frequency of departmental police-issue scanners, which was a risky endeavor. This means they'd be conducting an operation without any means of calling for tactical reinforcement. Finally, they loaded magazines into their personal automatic weapons, checked spare mags, and were ready to go.

The evening weather was particularly suitable for a tactical operation—cool, light rain with a misty fog and a slight westerly breeze. The climate complimented the dense trees and provided an upgrade in cover and concealment needed for an approach against a heavily defended location. The only downside was the forecast for late evening thunderstorms in the area, which could cause potential interruptions of low-band frequency transmission and hamper communications between the tactical team and the command post if the weather became severe over the next few hours.

CHAPTER 47

At nine fifteen that evening, Cutter parked his Charger in a nearby wood line and concealed it with a camouflage patterned car cover. He then hopped into the lead vehicle of the convoy, a black Chevy Suburban. A uniformed officer from BPD got out of the front seat of the last vehicle in the convoy. He opened the passenger side back door and reached inside. A handcuffed and blind-folded Logan Metropolit was pulled from the car. The two walked past several staring, suspicious SWAT members sitting in their police vehicle until they reached Cutter's vehicle.

One tac team member, the youngest of the crew, yelled out, "Hey sell-out cop. Don't screw this up."

The accompanying officer shouted back, "Shut up, Jackson!"

When they reached the non-descript vehicle, Cutter reached behind him and opened the back-passenger door.

The officer unlocked the handcuffs and removed them from Metropolit's arm and said, "Get in before somebody shoots you."

Metropolit took a deep breath then stooped and silently got in the car. Cutter immediately stared at him and said, "Alright. You know what to do. You blow our cover, give us up or screw up this operation in any way, intentionally or unintentionally, you'll never see the light of day out of a prison again. Cutter knew that wasn't a possibility for any crime less than first-degree murder or government treason, but he made his point as Metropolit looked attentive and acknowledged the words with a head nod.

Just as Cutter was about to give the order for the convoy to move out, he spotted a black Range Rover followed closely by an unmarked police interceptor SUV pulling up to stop at the side of his vehicle. Cutter immediately got on the radio and announced, "Alright, all, hold up until further notice." He surmised it wasn't BPD or SBI vehicles, so he rolled down the window of the Suburban, stuck his neck out and stared at the Range Rover with a look of intense curiosity. He didn't exit his vehicle because he assumed it was a minor issue.

Upon hearing Cutter's radio command, McBain, riding in the second vehicle, turned on the vehicle's flashers which was a pre-determined signal for the convoy to halt their departure. The vehicles behind him repeated the procedure in succession.

Suddenly, a tall, robust black male emerges from the vehicle dressed in black fatigues. He walked to the driver's side of Cutter's vehicle with a purpose and swagger rarely seen in the BPD. Three other men got out of the vehicle and stood there waiting.

Cutter rolled down his window and instantly snarled and said, "Well, well, if it isn't Ronaldo Kelly, here to screw up another mission."

Kelly sighed softly, and replied, "Ease up, Blake. The past is the past."

CHAPTER 48

FBI agent Ronaldo Kelly was a menacing figure with rippling biceps and bulging thighs. He stood six feet, six inches tall on a 270-pound frame. With a third-degree black belt, he was the prototype agent for this type of assault mission. was appropriately outfitted for this type of tactical police operation. Underneath the standard Navy-blue windbreaker emblazoned with the yellow FBI logo, he wore a black commando shirt covering a tightly fitted flak vest, camouflage waterproof cargo trousers with his detective shield clipped to his belt. On his shaved head sat a stiff-brimmed black baseball cap that completed the tactical attire with military-style combat boots. The gleaming detective shield never set well with Cutter who rarely displayed his on any police tactical operation, cognizant that even the slightest moonlight could reflect off a shield and expose the location of an advancing assault team. But Kelly was a showboat, who wanted everybody to know he was with the bureau. The only problem was, Cutter had not invited him along because he didn't want Kelly there.

Cutter leapt out of the truck and slammed the door.

Denied a handshake, Ronaldo Kelly said, "You should be happy to see me. You can't this gang down with just local assets."

"That's a false statement if I ever heard one, Cutter countered bluntly.

With a sigh and feigned smile, Kelly shook his head and said, "Looks like you haven't gotten over what happened in Miami. How long do I keep getting the cold shoulder over that?"

Kelly was referring to the last interagency counter-drug operation in Miami that both Kelly and Cutter participated in when two hostages were killed in a firefight against DeSalvo's hired guns during a botched raid.

"What the hell are you doing here, Kelly?" Cutter complained. "Nobody notified me you were coming out here. Feds from Washington weren't supposed to show up for two days." But Cutter wasn't done. "During the last interagency drug bust we lost two hostages because of your inept leadership."

Kelly bristled, "You need to talk to your boss."

"I should've been notified you were in the area of operation," Cutter complained.

"C'mon, Blake. You know about security. We don't announce every move we make. You really need to talk to your boss."

Cutter was suddenly incensed, realizing Ryker had double-crossed him, after promising he'd have 24 hours to execute his clandestine operation.

"So, since you're here, what do you know?"

Kelly briefed, "Ryker filled me in on what was going down. He told me you are on your own on this one, but you might need us to execute the arrest since there are federal warrants involved."

"I guess you're here to take over and get a bunch of innocent people killed as usual." Cutter snipped.

"Settle down, Blake," Kelly urged with a deep sigh. "I've already assured Ryker I won't interfere in this operation. The bureau doesn't know I'm here yet. I told them I was taking a couple of days of vacation time before coming down. Ryker called me directly. He just wanted me to get here early to gather some facts about the operation. I'm not going in with you."

Cutter accepted his explanation but was too filled with bitter memories from Miami to acknowledge it verbally. "I don't care why you're here. Just stay out of our way!"

"I'm not the guy you have to worry about." Kelly informed him.

"What the hell are you talking about?" Cutter asked.

"There's an agent heading down here from headquarters named Giamatti," Kelly explained. "He's bucking for a promotion by scoring a big federal arrest. He's got a reputation for shooting first and asking questions later. He'll be the real problem if he gets here in time."

"How's that any different from you?" Cutter snapped. Kelly knew he had to soften Cutter up for his own sake.

"Look, Blake. You're justified in hating me for having you sidelined in Miami," he said. "We gotta put this behind us. You were out of control with grief and obsession with rescuing hostages. I didn't intend for you to be taken off the case."

Kelly's response was to a bank robbery in Miami that Kelly and Cutter had worked together shortly after Jenni's tragic death. Though the operation resulted in three of the four assailants being apprehended, it also resulted in the loss of two police officers and three bank employees. Cutter blamed Kelly for losing control and taking unnecessary risks during the assault on the bank. Yet, Kelly escaped any accountability for the tragedies because he was leading a federal task force, and the raid was in Miami PD's jurisdiction. Thus, the federal detachment returned to Washington with their targeted mobster in custody and the local Miami task force was left to clean up the mess of civilian casualties. They spent the next six months doing damage control with the local community and associated lending establishments.

Cutter received commendations and recognition for several minor drug busts thereafter before the grief of his loss finally caught up with him as he became sloppy and distracted in several cases. It became apparent to Chief of Police Sanchez that Cutter was haunted by the deaths and was letting his obsession with protecting civilians override the negotiating procedures. He was subsequently transferred to SBI, which in fact, proved to be a promotion for his long-term good record in Miami.

"We've wasted enough time," Cutter pronounced, observing lighting in the distant sky. "If you're joining us, then you're riding in the tail vehicle of the convoy."

"Fair enough," Kelly responded with a wry grin, realizing it had taken a lot for Cutter to relieve himself of the anger towards him. Cutter realized he needed to leverage the potential usage of a great tactical asset Kelly and his bureau team added. It was a temporary truce . . . but one as fragile as the armistice between the two Koreas.

With tensions easing a bit, Cutter walked the line and introduced Kelly to members of the tactical team. He then pulled out a map and gave Kelly a rundown on the operation. Kelly looked at Cutter with an inquisitive, doubtful expression.

"You got a problem?" Cutter asked.

"It's your show, but it sounds like a suicide mission. You're sure I can't offer some advice?"

Cutter flashed a crooked grin. "Last time I took your advice, I ended up losing my job, remember? If I need your advice, I'll call you."

At that point, Kelly didn't insist but said, "Alright Blake. But I got your back this time. Just let me prove it to you."

Doubting, Cutter replied, "Hope that doesn't mean a bullet in my back."

Kelly shrugged it off and patted Cutter on the shoulder. He knew Cutter had a soft spot for a great tactical police officer, no matter what baggage came along with it.

Cutter knew it was futile anyway to even attempt to keep Kelly out of the fray. He directed Kelly to leave his vehicle in place and pointed him toward an unmarked sedan stationed at the rear of the convoy which Kelly reluctantly entered.

Cutter then walked down the line of vehicles and shouted in a pep talk fashion, "Alright, saddle up, team. Let's get started. We got some bad guys to take down!" He then shuffled back to the lead vehicle and hopped in. He then ordered the convoy drivers to kill their flashers and get the task force in motion.

Chapter 49

At ten p.m. sharp, the convoy departed the assembly point, with Cutter and Metropolit riding in the lead vehicle, followed closely by the tactical van transporting five heavily armed SWAT team members, a late arriving SRT van with five members of the county's Special Reaction Team and an interceptor utility SUV transporting a hostage negotiator. Drivers of the remaining police cruisers for the task force including the unmarked sedan with Ronaldo Kelly were instructed to wait five minutes before departing, remain in radio contact with the lead group and stay at least three to four hundred yards behind.

Once they'd cleared the assembly area, Cutter reached over and untied and removed the blindfold from over Metropolit's eyes. "Guess what!" he said to Metropolit. "You're driving. Take over."

Cutter got on the radio and ordered the other drivers to halt temporarily so that Metropolit could take the wheel.

FORBIDDEN RESCUE

The convoy restarted and moved along at a steady pace of forty miles per hour on the deserted highway, which allowed Cutter's mind to drift and think about the time he spent with Penelope in the Cayman Islands. Having those thoughts reminded him of how much she meant to him, even in her absence. It worried him that he could potentially let his personal feelings affect a tactical decision if confronted face-to face with Penelope being held at gunpoint with one of the SWAT team snipers having her and a captor in the crosshairs of his weapon. He felt a twinge of terror with the thought that a sniper's errant bullet could cost her life. Still reeling from the loss of Jenni, he couldn't afford to lose her too, neither emotionally nor tactically.

Once the convoy pulled off the highway and onto the access road, Cutter ordered Metropolit to pull the vehicle to the shoulder of the road and halt. Cutter got on the radio and directed the other vehicles to pull to the side of the road behind him. He then ordered Metropolit to drive far enough forward to where all five vehicles were able to pull to the shoulder and stop. Then they made their final radio check of communications before proceeding to possible contact. After confirmation that all vehicles were in radio contact, Cutter ordered Metropolit to proceed forward with parking lights only.

A minute later, the flat surface road gave way to a steep incline of one hundred yards until they crested the top of a hill. Metropolit advised Cutter they should stop for a minute to observe the terrain.

Metropolit killed the engine and Cutter got out and trained his binoculars directly in front of him. In the distance and by the moonlight's illumination, he counted the rooftops of the various buildings at the complex. It was eerie and reminded him of prison buildings. All that was missing were searchlights from guard towers.

The convoy was now less than a half mile from the entrance to the complex. Cutter got back in the vehicle and ducked behind the first-row seats. He ordered Metropolit to resume their approach. The remaining vehicles followed but at greater intervals apart to break up the signature of a convoy approaching.

As they reached the bottom of the hill, the road curved to the right. Suddenly, Metropolit screeched to a stop as he observed a black Lincoln Navigator with dark tinted windows and a nondescript white panel van parked near the fuel pumps at an abandoned service station. Standing next to the vehicles were two stocky-built men dressed in black baseball caps, tinted sunglasses, nylon windbreakers over camouflaged-pattern fatigues and brown hiker's boots.

"Two vehicles and two men up ahead," Metropolit informed Cutter abruptly. "This must be our official welcoming party."

Cutter cautiously rose, grabbed a pair of binoculars, and visually scanned the area from east to west. Across the road from the service station were the markers for two underground fuel storage tanks adjacent next to what looked to be an inactive electrical power substation. Cutter traversed the area and spotted an active electrical substation two hundred meters to the north which he assumed the mafia group had tapped into to use as a power source for the powerless warehouse complex. Cutter then focused back on the two men. Though the two appeared unarmed, Cutter assumed they had weapons stashed inside their vehicles and undoubtedly pistols under their windbreakers.

"We don't want to alert or surprise them with any suspicious vehicle movement," Cutter said. "Just keep going but drive slow."

As Metropolit proceeded slowly forward, he said, "I know those guys. It's

DeSalvo's forward security team. They are expert shooters, his best men. This is going to be interesting."

"I think we're about to have a little meet-and-greet party," Cutter said to Metropolit said as he kept the binoculars trained on the two men pacing back and forth.

Chapter 50

Metropolit eased the vehicle forward slowly. As they came within about a hundred yards of the checkpoint, the humming motor caught the attention of one of the watchmen. He signaled his partner over to the vehicles to grab the 12-gauge pump-action shotguns located in each vehicle.

Cutter dropped down behind the seats, keeping his head submerged below the window.

Metropolit sucked in a deep breath and continued driving forward. He had passed the first checkpoint for DeSalvo's operation several times before, while driving his personal vehicle, a Pontiac GTO. This time however, Metropolit was driving a vehicle unfamiliar to DeSalvo's watchmen. As their vehicle came within fifty yards of the station, one of the men pointed the barrel of his shotgun at their vehicle.

"What's going on?" Cutter whispered without rising.

"They're signaling for us to pull over," Metropolit told him as his voice quivered.

"Alright, let's see what happens," Cutter declared as he reached for his Glock handgun while shifting his body to a position where he could spring up and fire.

As Metropolit stopped the vehicle, the taller of the two guards walked forward towards them while the others stayed perched at the hood of their vehicle. When he reached the driver's side window, Metropolit lowered it and the taller guard asked in a deep voice, "Where are you going?" He stared at Metropolit with the type of steely grey eyes that looked lifeless and earned him his nickname, Deadeye.

"What's up, Deadeye. I've got an appointment to see Mister DeSalvo," Metropolit answered nervously. Noticing the quivering tone in Metropolit's voice, Cutter pointed his Glock's barrel at back of the driver's seat, so if Metropolit ratted them out, a round would go directly through the seat into his back.

Deadeye furrowed his brow and then said, "Nobody told us about you coming out here tonight." Deadeye had acquired the nickname early in his career as a mobster because he was a psychopath, known to kill with no conscious and no feelings. He did his job methodically and mechanically. If he were told to kill one of his own men who was suspected of betraying him or the organization, he would do so without hesitation and not blink an eye. For that reason alone, DeSalvo trusted him as the chief of his forward security team.

"DeSalvo asked me to meet with him." Metropolit responded wearily. His mental fatigue with the events of the past weeks coupled with his nervousness about the outcome began to show in his expression. Deadeye read the look instantly.

"Mister DeSalvo went to bed early," the man shot back. "Nobody's going to see him tonight."

With feigned frustration, Metropolit answered, "I'm just doing what he told me to do...and that is meet him tonight."

"*Oh shit*!" Cutter mumbled under his breath.

Deadeye said, "Something don't seem right here."

Metropolit shrugged his shoulders, devoid of another reply.

"Don't move," Deadeye ordered as he pointed the shotgun barrel directly at Metropolit's head. He reached into his jacket pocket and pulled out his radio. Deadeye then moved away from the vehicle and walked back to the other guards, who went by the nickname Oso. With an expression of deep suspicion, he bent down to Oso's right ear and spoke. Oso instantly clenched his jaws and balled his fist. Then, Deadeye and Oso shook their heads in unison, in obvious agreement with the action they would take. They turned and walked towards the Suburban, but they made a grave mistake in the process. Both shotguns pointed to the ground. Neither raised their weapons. Cutter was surprised at their carelessness, but it didn't matter. He wasn't about taking the chance they'd been made and would be shot without a fight.

Cutter eased over to the passenger's side back door, flung it open and leaped out. He landed upright, rose, and aimed his Glock at the two approaching henchmen.

"Don't move! Drop the guns!" he shouted. After a moment of hesitation, Deadeye looked at Oso.

"Don't even try it! Lay the shotguns on the ground," Cutter warned, maintaining his police bearing by not uttering '*assholes*' which was on the tip of his tongue. As they dropped the shotguns onto the ground, Deadeye cleverly activated the voice transmitter on the radio.

A voice burped on the radio, "Is everything all right out there?"

"Shut that thing off and back up from the van!" Cutter yelled. As the two inched backwards, Cutter noticed the shorter man Oso reaching inside his windbreaker pocket.

"Don't try it, asshole!" Metropolit shouted at him.

Cutter nearly signaled a gesture of thanks to Metropolit, appreciating his attention to the men's movement. The moment of appreciation was dissolved as he realized he wasn't partnered with Alex McBain—but with a mob informant who was playing along to save his own skin and could turn on him at any moment.

Suddenly, Deadeye moved his right hand toward his jacket. Cutter reacted by firing a round into his shoulder. He fell to the ground screaming. Then, Oso pulled a handgun to engage Metropolit. Cutter reacted instinctively, firing a round into the man's right arm as Metropolit fired also. Reluctant to surrender, Oso snatched the pistol with his left hand, prompting Cutter to deposit a fatal round into his chest.

Cutter pointed the gun at the wounded Deadeye and yelled, "Get up and start walking!"

Metropolit and Cutter grabbed the shotguns and radios and then dragged the dead guard to the back of the station, where he rolled them onto a patch of tall weeds.

Suddenly Deadeye began to rise from the ground. To separate them, Cutter then marched the wounded Deadeye into the station's male bathroom. There, they were greeted with a caustic stench of urine, the sight of dried excrement around the toilet bowl and gay solicitations scribbled in pen on the bathroom stalls. An iron water pipe extended from the ceiling to the concrete floor. Cutter handcuffed Deadeye's wrists behind him to the bar. Deadeye grunted in pain as he felt like his injured shoulder was being pulled from his body.

Metropolit rushed inside to check on Cutter. "Are you gonna gag him?" he asked.

"No, we better leave him where he can breathe," Cutter replied. "There's very little airflow in here and we need to make sure he stays alive until we can get a unit out here to take him in."

Suddenly, Deadeye roared out at Metropolit, "You fuckin' turncoat police officer!" Globs of saliva spewed onto Cutter's face as his nostrils flared with rage. "We're gonna kill both you fuckin' pigs."

"You're pushing it, asswipe," Cutter warned. The man followed with a callous glare then spat out a chorus of Sicilian words.

Cutter lacked patience with annoying rhetoric and responded by telling Metropolit, "I have changed my mind. Gag this bastard before I kill him right here."

Metropolit gave an affirming nod and rushed back to their vehicle where he retrieved a roll of duct tape. He scurried back to the bathroom and handed it to Cutter, who knotted a piece of rope, stuffed it into the back of the man's mouth and sealed it with a strip of duct tape.

Cutter left the bathroom ahead of Metropolit with his finger resting against the trigger of his Glock. He had successfully resisted the temptation of planting a bullet into Deadeye's skull, while remembering he was saving his remaining rounds for the man, he felt was responsible for his wife's death. That man was Bennie DeSalvo.

Chapter 51

Having lost the element of surprise, Cutter and Metropolit sprinted back to the vehicle with Metropolit driving and Cutter hopping back into the back seat. Cutter's thinking was if their vehicle caught fire from the front, he had a better chance of survival if he remained in the back seat, especially if Metropolit was hit.

"We've been made. Let us get the hell out of here," Cutter shouted, as Metropolit started the engine, took one glance back at the gas station bathroom door to ensure the handcuffed henchmen hadn't escaped, then floored the gas pedal.

Expecting to encounter another security point along the way, Cutter radioed the rest of the assault team and requested the drivers of the second and third series to proceed forward and catch up with them and then back off to about fifty yards behind; far enough as to not create a large convoy signature but close enough to respond if they needed reinforcements in a firefight prior to reaching the complex.

Ronaldo Kelly overheard the radio call, grabbed the microphone from the driver and tried to respond to Cutter to offer his assistance, which would mean he would have to join them in their vehicle at a stop point along the route. Cutter overheard the voice of his law enforcement nemesis and replied, "No way, Kelly. You are not in on this." He then broke contact.

Less than a quarter mile from the complex, Cutter and Metropolit encountered their second obstacle, two new henchmen perched on the side of a hilltop a few yards off the right side of the road, both pointing shotguns in the direction of their vehicle. Metropolit immediately pressed the brake and their vehicle screeched to a stop. Before they could exit the vehicle, two slugs spanked off the vehicle's hood and two more sliced through the driver's side window frame, circumventing the ballistic panel and narrowly missed Metropolit's right shoulder by inches. A shard of glass ripped a piece of Metropolit's leather jacket. He winced from a burning feeling in his left arm.

Maintaining his composure, Cutter ordered Metropolit to peel off the road and into the wood line. They both leaped out the vehicle, dropped to the ground on opposite sides and assumed firing positions. Taking fire from Cutter's right side, they laid down a volley of suppressive fire in the henchmen's direction, which managed to hold off the snipers long enough for two BPD SWAT vehicles from the second series to pull up beside them.

A group of seven shooters sprang out the door of the nearest warehouse, ran through the unmanned gate, and dispersed into the trees. A barrage of heavy gunfire ensued between DeSalvo's shooters and the SWAT unit, prompting Cutter and Metropolit to hop back into their vehicle, maneuver past the strafing rounds and advance at breakneck speed toward the complex.

As they approached the first warehouse, five more thugs flashed into view. They opened on them with AR-15 and sub-machine gun fire.

"Oh, shit!" Metropolit growled as he screeched the vehicle to a halt, while a salvo of rounds exploded a few yards in front of the vehicle.

"Gun it!" Cutter barked. "If we don't haul ass now, we're dead." Cutter then radioed the second group, barking, "SWAT team, we're approaching the target area. We've gone hot, need backup here, now!"

CHAPTER 52

Metropolit floored the gas pedal, and they sped forward. Suddenly, two grenades exploded at the rear of the vehicle embedding shrapnel in the back panel. The follow-on team wasn't so lucky. DeSalvo's snipers engaged the SWAT vehicle with a volley of high explosive rounds from RPGs and AK-47s, nearly disintegrating their vehicle while killing the driver and three Officers.

Metropolit glanced up at his rear-view mirror and noticed the burning vehicle, prompting him to continue speeding forward. A few seconds later, they reached an unmanned gate and barreled through it with the reckless abandon of a suicide bomber.

As they halted near the first warehouse, Cutter grabbed the radio and ordered, *"Alpha 2, this is Alpha 1. We're inside the perimeter. We need backup now!"*

A voice on the radio responded, *"Copy that. We'll be there in two mikes!"*

Aware that the remainder of the task force was behind them by at least two minutes, they veered their vehicle to a spot behind a metal storage building and remained in place.

Then suddenly, Metropolit jumped out of the vehicle and dashed towards the front door.

"Logan, what the fuck are you doing?" Cutter shouted. Within five seconds, Metropolit was out of voice range and totally exposed. *"First he's a sell-out traitor, now he's trying to be a goddamn hero!"*

Before Metropolit could reach the door, a barrage of bullets scattered dust at his feet. He dropped to the ground and low crawled behind a huge concrete planter full of dirt. Through a dusty cloud, Metropolit reached a planter and gestured back to Cutter with his right hand to stay put.

By then, the steady gunfire had alerted DeSalvo's bodyguards who were located inside the middle of the second row of warehouses.

Cutter called again over the radio and learned the remainder of the task force was pinned down by heavy gunfire from several snipers located at the top of adjacent buildings. So, he leaped out of the vehicle and hauled ass towards Metropolit's location. He and Metropolit were now in a delicate situation. With the other vehicles still a minute away and beyond visual contact, they were forced to defend themselves against over twenty of DeSalvo's elite soldiers.

Bullets landed around their position, chipping the planter. Metropolit stayed behind it as Cutter lunged away behind a tree. Despite the sting of several fragments into his face, Metropolit fearlessly maintained his position. Through the noise, he picked up the sound of voices and pounding footsteps from inside the first warehouse. He took a second to brush away the concrete chips from his collar before he'd sprint to a safer position.

As the next round landed inches from his right shoe, Metropolit rose, then sprinted toward the front left side of the warehouse and dove to a corner of the structure.

Cutter sprinted forward and assumed a position behind a landscape wall approximately twenty yards to Metropolit's rear.

There was a brief silence as they evaluated the situation. Hearing blasts in the distance, they realized that retreating to their vehicle was no longer an option. They were now caught in no man's land.

Metropolit acknowledged Cutter's intent by bolting over to the door. He shouted one time, *"Federal agents! We have a search warrant!"* He then kicked it open, and belly rolled into a firing position. Cutter quickly followed. As they paused to observe an empty room, heightened anxiety set in. They asked themselves internally, *"Are we walking into a trap?"* There was again a momentary pause as both silently prayed for reinforcements. With sweat pouring down his forehead, Cutter surmised DeSalvo's men had retreated to sniper positions deeper inside the complex. They stared at each other, realizing they had maneuvered their way into a kill zone.

Chapter 53

At the onset of the raid, Bennie DeSalvo, was asleep next to a naked twenty-something prostitute, in a small room located in a warehouse near the back of the complex. DeSalvo, a Sicilian with dark complexion and silver, slicked back hair had dark wrinkles and several distinctive facial scars which made him appear past his forty-five years of age. He was awakened by the noise of his henchmen clamoring and the clacking of weapons racks being unlocked. Suddenly his main consigliore, Salvadore Bora, barged into the room yelling in his raspy Sicilian voice, *"Signo' DeSalvo, s'arruspigghiassi. Ci stanno acchippanu. I sbirri ci sunnu.* (Wake up! Wake up! Mr... DeSalvo, dammit! We are being raided!)."

DeSalvo, bleary-eyed, dull of mind, and fatigued from hours of meaningless copulation, blew nostril snot onto the floor, and shoved the prostitute's arms from around his shoulders. He leapt to his feet and ordered Bora to alert his other henchmen to assume arms. As Bora tore out of the room, the bare butt, pencil thin, black-haired prostitute sprinted towards a nearby toilet room clutching her bundled clothes in hand.

DeSalvo hurriedly threw clothes on. He reached under his pillow and grabbed a Ruger .357 Magnum semi-automatic pistol and shoved it inside his pants.

A personal bodyguard flashed into the room. DeSalvo shouted at him, *"Igghiati l'aimmi! Pigghiati l'aimmi ea picciotta e puitatimilla* (Bring the girl to me!) The bodyguard rushed out the door to execute DeSalvo's order.

DeSalvo reached into a nearby footlocker and grabbed two more semi-automatic pistols, which he stuffed in the back side of his pants. He barged into the hallway to wait for the delivery of his hostage.

The continued exchange of gunfire outside the warehouse alerted Cutter and Metropolit that the SWAT team members were pinned down behind them. Metropolit overheard footsteps approaching the front door. Spinning around, he caught a split-second view of one of DeSalvo's men through the side window. Metropolit fired. With one pinpointed shot, the gunman dropped out of sight. He shouted over to Cutter, "I think I got one."

"Where's Penelope?" Cutter asked.

"She should be in one of the back warehouses," Metropolit answered, barking over the gunfire. "Do we need to clear these front buildings?"

"Not without the rest of the team. There's too many of them for us to fight through. Our back-up must be pinned down, but if we stop moving, we will die here. Let's go after the middle warehouse in the back."

Metropolit replied, softening his tone during the brief pause in gunfire. "We'll have to clear rooms one-by-one. They know we're coming. I doubt we'll get through without contact." He was hoping with those words, Cutter would dismiss the thought of rescuing her.

"That leaves no choice," Cutter commented, then ordered, "Alright, let's move forward . . . but keep you head on a swivel!"

As Metropolit uttered a silent scoff, they rose and rushed to the first room. Metropolit cracked the door open to a large empty room with door entrances on each corner.

Metropolit whispered 'Clear' first, then Cutter repeated.

Moving forward, they aimed their weapons at the second door straight ahead, realizing the further they proceeded through the building, the more likely they would be to encounter DeSalvo's henchmen at point blank range. Someone was sure to die. Who it would be depended on who got the jump on the other first as the door opened. Realizing they could be walking into a kill zone, Cutter eased the door open, then tossed in a flashbang and smoke grenade. As smoke filled the room, Metropolit instinctively darted into the right. They shared a brief sigh of relief as, through the smoke, they saw no one.

"Clear!" Metropolit shouted. "They must've moved her to a backside warehouse."

The door ahead of them led to a long, vacant corridor, which was rapidly becoming smoke filled from the flashbang.

They eased through the narrow corridor which had no side doors. When they reached the end, Cutter pushed opened the back door. He peaked outside, looked in both directions, saw no one and heard no gunfire. It was a chilling silence.

Directly in front of them and twenty-five yards away loomed the middle warehouse where Metropolit had seen Penelope. They darted across the open space and repeated their entry procedure from the first warehouse, with Metropolit kicking the door open.

As Cutter darted in, he froze. A grey-haired man was holding a gun with his arm around the neck of a palled and markedly terrified Penelope Lane. Cutter stood face-to-face with the man he believed masterminded the execution attempt on him that killed his wife, Jenni.

With the pistol barrel pressed against her right cheek, Penelope peered into Cutter's eyes with a fearful look of relief. Her hair was a disheveled mess. Her mascara smeared across her face down to her chin, which had several cut marks. She thought to herself in fear, *can he save me? Would he do something desperate and get me killed?*

Instantly, Cutter's thoughts moved. *Could she break loose enough to create the space I need to shoot DeSalvo?*

CHAPTER 54

Cutter aimed his sidearm at DeSalvo's chest.

"I can't believe it," DeSalvo chuckled. "It's Detective Blake Cutter. What a small world!"

"It's Special Agent Blake Cutter," Cutter corrected him while dismissing any thought of familiarity. *I don't have a fucking relationship with you because I've tried to bust your ass so many times.* Cutter's thoughts flashed through his mind. *You're just a fucking syndicate criminal I'm either going to arrest or kill today.* "Drop your weapon and let her go," he shouted at DeSalvo.

DeSalvo snickered, "Well, congratulations on your promotion, Agent Cutter . . . like that's going to make any difference here today,"

"Cut the crap, DeSalvo. It's over!" Cutter shouted. "Let the woman go!"

DeSalvo's brow furrowed, "What's over? Agent Cutter" he asked with a smirk. "I see only two of you." DeSalvo turned his head to look at Metropolit.

"Well, we have a traitor in our midst. Whose side are you on today, Logan Metropolit. I guess we'll find out,"

Cutter hoped Metropolit hadn't changed sides. "Drop the gun, DeSalvo," Cutter ordered. "Let the woman go or I'll waste you right here."

"As you Americans say, you and what Army?" he replied, laughing maniacally. "You amuse me, Agent Blake Cutter."

"Well, Logan. I see you're having trouble understanding where your loyalties lie," DeSalvo said, with a smirk. "I guess that's unfortunate."

"I had no choice," Metropolit replied.

"Shut up!" Cutter shouted at Metropolit. Cutter's jaw tightened with anger at his decision to provide DeSalvo with an explanation, knowing any sign of regret expressed by Metropolit would leave him and Metropolit vulnerable. "Let the woman go and we'll talk about a way out of this," Cutter urged, stalling for time as his palms sweated.

"There's nothing to talk about, Cutter. I'm calling the shots, not you," DeSalvo rattled back tightening his grip on Penelope's hair. They all overheard footsteps approaching from the adjacent room.

Penelope shrieked in pain.

DeSalvo grinned in amusement and loosened his grip on her momentarily.

Another of DeSalvo's men, a stocky-built man with a face chiseled with knife scars and a mop of dirty brown hair stepped into view from a side hallway. He put Cutter's head directly in the crosshairs of his Glock.

Metropolit responded, shifting his sidearm toward the man with a nervous twitch, barely putting enough pressure on the trigger to prevent a discharge.

Cutter and Metropolit froze, suddenly entangled in a standoff, with DeSalvo holding Penelope as his trump card.

With a cheesy grin, DeSalvo boasted, "As you should infer gentlemen, you'll soon be outnumbered. I'll be gracious and allow you to say goodbye before something regretful happens. But Penelope stays with me."

"No way, DeSalvo," Cutter contested. "Nothing's happening until you let the woman go."

Suddenly and boldly, she screamed, "Shoot him, Blake!

DeSalvo cupped his crusty right palm over her mouth.

She emitted a muffled shriek.

DeSalvo murmured to her, "Shut up, you bitch, or I'll kill you right now."

"What do you want with her?" Cutter shouted at him.

"Once she turns over the laptop and the money I want, then you can have her," he answered calmly. "If she doesn't, you'll get her in pieces."

"What are you talking about a laptop?" Cutter asked.

Stroking her hair with his gun, DeSalvo explained the more obvious, "The money she's got stashed in a Cayman Islands bank account. But soon it's going to be *my* money, as soon as she does a transfer, right sweetheart?" he asked her before kissing her cheek. The feel of his crusty lips against her skin made her cringe. "Do you know what else I want, Agent Cutter?'

"Let me guess. You want a plane at the airport, right?" Cutter guessed aloud.

"Negative. That's already taken care of for me," DeSalvo added, cockily. "What I want is for you to not interfere with the future."

"Whatever that means, it ain't gonna happen," Cutter barked.

Cutter looked at Penelope inquisitively, noting the remorse on her face. His hands shook slightly as he realized he was dealing with a motivation stronger than he anticipated. *It had to be about money,* he muttered under his breath.

For the next few seconds, no one budged. Metropolit and the shooter stayed locked on each other while DeSalvo relaxed his hand from Penelope's head to give Cutter a moment to digest his intent.

At that moment, two BPD SWAT officers, who'd fought their way through the barrage of gunfire, flashed into the room with guns drawn.

Cutter reacted by shouting, "Hold your fire!"

Short on patience, DeSalvo decided to press the issue. "I've had enough of this, gentlemen. We're getting out of here now. Tell you to back off or I'll kill her right here and now." He again pressed the gun barrel against Penelope's temple and gestured to the other shooter with his other hand to lead them out of the building.

Behind DeSalvo, loud footsteps were heard approaching.

DeSalvo was unaware that his trump card was contemplating a move of her own. As they crept forward past Cutter and Metropolit, she waited patiently for a momentary loss of pressure on her temple. Suddenly, she pulled her right arm away from him, but DeSalvo grabbed hold of her wrist. She felt the piercing agony of his fingernails against her shoulder.

"Don't try that again, bitch," he shouted, spitting mucous on her in a state of rage.

"Shoot him!" she screamed at Cutter.

"Shut up!" DeSalvo shouted in her right ear, clawing her shoulder.

"Do what he says, Penelope," Cutter advised her.

DeSalvo was joined by three more of his henchmen. With a grin, DeSalvo nodded to his henchmen and his bodyguard to proceed toward the door with Penelope in his clutches.

Cutter and Metropolit followed closely behind them, poised for the first opportunity to engage them. DeSalvo, Penelope and the loyal bodyguard disappeared out the back door with the two police officers close behind in pursuit.

CHAPTER 55

Suddenly, Ronaldo Kelly and a SWAT officer named Dave Henderson rushed into the undeveloped area between the buildings. The last henchman in the area fired two rounds at them but missed. Kelly and Henderson leaped behind the corner of the building to take cover. Then, as the arrogant henchman remained in the open firing at them, Kelly discharged two rounds into the henchman's chest. The henchman fell to the ground. Kelly and Henderson thought he was dead.

As they charged forward, the henchmen rolled over and fired two rounds, one round into Henderson's leg and the other into his chest. Kelly responded by firing back, shooting the henchman twice and mortally wounding him. Kelly then grabbed the radio from the wounded agent and called the tactical command post, shouting, *"Officer down inside the complex, middle warehouse on the back side. We need additional units deployed to this location. Expect heavy gunfire and resistance!*" He then noticed Henderson was bleeding profusely. At that moment, several rounds hit the building above Kelly's head. Kelly couldn't tell whether the rounds were coming from law enforcement or if they had been spotted and were being approached by a shooter or shooters from an unknown direction.

Kelly noticed the blood soaking Henderson's pants leg. He grabbed a bandana out of his back pocket and made a tourniquet above the leg wound. "I gotta get you to a safe place before you get shot again. You need medical attention. I'm gonna move you so hang in there, so stay with me."

Henderson, writhing in pain, acknowledged Kelly's words but a head nod. Henderson was pale and his torso began twitching due to the onset of shock.

Kelly grabbed Henderson under his arms and began a fireman's drag away from the front of the building to a position on the opposite end of the middle warehouse.

"Are you doing, okay?" he asked Henderson.

Barely conscious, Henderson responded with a wry smile, "Yeah, I'll be alright. Continue with the mission." It was the kind of smile emitted by gunshot victims right before they died.

"Stay with me," Kelly repeated, panting from the adrenaline rush. "We're gonna get you out of here."

Kelly then inserted a new magazine in his Glock and headed toward the front door. Suddenly he stopped. A trail of blood ran from the spot where Henderson was shot to the side of the warehouse where he'd left him. Realizing he needed to do whatever he could to reduce the chance the wounded SWAT member would be discovered before help arrived, he took a moment to kick dirt over the blood trail to conceal it from view. He could only hope the injured agent wouldn't do anything to draw attention to himself, such as moaning or trying to crawl away from the location.

Kelly ran to the door and rushed into the open room, raising his eyebrows as he realized he was in the middle of a standoff.

DeSalvo, still clutching Penelope's arm, slowly retreated toward the center of the room. As Kelly raised his Glock to aim it at DeSalvo, his attention was diverted by another shooter, wielding a small handgun. Before the henchman could fire, Kelly discharged the first two rounds from his new magazine into the henchman's chest. Cutter finished him off with a third round.

"Give it up, DeSalvo," Cutter shouted forcefully. "There's nowhere to go!" His heartbeat increased from a mix of intensity and adrenaline.

DeSalvo chuckled in defiance.

Penelope, sensing DeSalvo had eased the pistol away from her temple, elbowed him hard to his side. As DeSalvo reflexively lowered his weapon to grab his side, Cutter fired a single round, hitting DeSalvo in the left arm. Before Cutter could fire again, DeSalvo's bodyguard fired back. A single bullet grazed Cutter's right arm. Cutter's eyes rolled back as blood trickled from the flesh wound. Despite taking the round, he managed to stay on his feet.

The bodyguard aimed to fire at Cutter again, but Metropolit got the jump on him and fired two rounds into the man's chest. He dropped to the floor instantly.

Scowling in anger, DeSalvo attempted to fire back, but his gun jammed. Kelly fired a round that ricocheted off DeSalvo's gun. DeSalvo flinched as the pistol snapped out of his hand and fell beyond his reach.

Penelope seized the moment and attempted to escape his grip. For her courage, she was rewarded with a slap to the left side of her face which knocked her to the floor. DeSalvo clutched her pants pocket with one hand and dragged her toward him. At that moment, Salvadore Bora bolted through the door brandishing a sawed-off shotgun.

"*Unni li fati avvicinari* (Take them out)!" DeSalvo yelled at Bora.

Before Bora could aim, both Swat officers shot him, and he fell to the floor.

As DeSalvo eyes froze momentarily, Penelope broke free from his clutches and limped across the floor. DeSalvo fumbled a 9mm from his waistband. The separation between Penelope and DeSalvo provided Cutter enough clearance to shoot him at direct range. A single bullet plunged into DeSalvo's chest. He fell onto Penelope's lap.

Cutter rushed over and pulled Penelope from under DeSalvo. Then, he shoved the mafia leader's body aside like a bag of rotten potatoes.

Suddenly, DeSalvo opened his eyes, grunting.

Cutter calmly walked up to DeSalvo noticing he was wincing with pain but conscious and appeared coherent. Cutter reached into his pocket and pulled out a set of handcuffs. "You're under arrest!" he announced to DeSalvo. DeSalvo stared at him and then at his dead bodyguards. He glared in disbelief.

Kelly approached DeSalvo. DeSalvo noticed him, grunted, and suddenly reached his right hand towards his back where he had a switchblade holder attached to the back of his belt. The switchblade clicked open as he swung his arm from behind his back. It was the move Kelly wanted. In a zombie-like state, Kelly emptied the magazine of his 9mm pistol into DeSalvo's skull. The barrage entered his temple and hollowed out the back of his skull.

Cutter reacted in a state of rage, pushing Kelly backwards.

"What the fuck did you just do! He was no longer a threat. We wanted him alive!" Cutter growled, realizing that the most relevant lead to the murder of his late wife had just expired.

"He was reaching for a gun," Kelly calmly replied.

"The hell he was!" Cutter screamed. He looked down at DeSalvo. "It was a switchblade, Kelly."

"Doesn't matter," Kelly replied bluntly. "A lethal weapon, none the same."

"What was he gonna do with a switchblade while he's on the floor?" Cutter asked, angrily. "You just killed my best chance at tracking down my wife's murderer, you son-of-a-bitch!" Cutter reared back to throw a punch at Kelly but his injured arm from previous gunshots were too painful to get into that posture."

"This was my collar, Kelly!" Cutter scowled. "You weren't supposed to be involved."

"Wrong answer, my friend," Kelly argued, getting into Cutter's face. "We've been after this bastard longer than you've been out of diapers. Go back to small time bust, Blake. My bosses sent me down here to take him out of commission and that's just what I did. So, he's ours, now."

Cutter grabbed Kelly by the throat and wrestled him to the ground, realizing his magnanimous forgiveness of Ronaldo Kelly was premature.

McBain and two other officers rushed in, grabbed Cutter, and pushed him away. "Knock it off, Blake! Yelled McBain. "Leave it up to Internal Affairs to sort this out."

Cutter, now hyperventilating with rage, made another attempt to lunge at Kelly, but McBain stepped in and pushed him away. "Go outside and cool off, mate." McBain ordered him in an official tone, desperate to placate Cutter's anger and prevent an ugly incident.

Cutter, with a deep, frustrated expression, brushed the floor dust off his shirt and walked away. He took a deep breath, composed himself and moved over to Penelope, who still lay on the floor.

Trembling and whimpering from the trauma, she struggled to her feet and embraced him with all her strength as she winced from numerous painful scratches on her hands and arms. Cutter reciprocated the strong embrace as he felt a sense of relief. He then wrapped his arm around her shoulder, and they walked out of the building, leaving Metropolit, Kelly and the incoming SWAT members to clean up the carcasses.

"Thank you, Blake!" she said wearingly as they reached outside. "You saved my life and I love you for that."

Cutter wasn't sure how to react to those words. He wondered if they were genuine, or if she was sizing him up for a sympathy assessment. Yet, he couldn't deny he felt the same about her, and his state of panic followed by relief made him realize it more than ever.

Minutes later, two EMTs arrived on the scene and both Henderson and Penelope were placed on a gurney and administered an IV in prep for transport to the hospital. As they reached the safe confines of the police perimeter, Blake reached down and embraced her while she was on the gurney. She winced in pain and her knees buckled as he touched her. She hadn't recovered from the injuries and surgery, but it didn't matter to her.

Cutter touched her forehead and said, "I'm sorry all this had gone down."

She retorted, "It' okay, Blake. I don't care about my pain. I just needed a hug. I know what my future holds."

He stared into her sunken eyes and exhaled a sigh of deep relief. The stare was followed by a look of resignation as a deputy sheriff gestured to Cutter, reminding him of his duty to have the love of his life handcuffed while on the gurney. EMTs considered all transporting fugitives a threat no matter the circumstances.

As a uniformed officer escorted her gurney to the EMT vehicle, Cutter stood motionless. Penelope stared back. Both realized their enthusiastic embrace, reminiscent of their weekend in the Caymans, was undoubtedly their last.

As the EMT van with Penelope pulled away, another EMT saw blood dripping off Cutter's fingers and pulled him toward an ambulance to treat the wounds.

Chapter 56

Sporadic gunfire continued around the compound for several hours until the remainder of DeSalvo's henchmen were apprehended or killed by the BPD task force. As additional police units arrived, it was evident Cutter and his makeshift task force had underestimated the tenacity of DeSalvo's army.

The final body count of Operation Juggernaut was sixteen mafia dead and five law enforcement officers injured. DeSalvo's body was the first of the casualties to be transported to the morgue for autopsy. Investigators were anxious to learned if and what type of drugs were in his system at the time of death. It would give them a clue to what drugs the mob was pushing into Bullet since DeSalvo had a reputation for personal endorsement of his products via his own use. When his dealers distributed a new line of synthetic cocaine or heroin or meth, DeSalvo would sample the product himself to ensure it was pure. The task force seized over five tons of various narcotics from the warehouse grounds and several caches of weapons. But with the distribution into Bullet in its infancy at the time of the bust, SBI, ATF and the DEA wanted to get a jump on any new drugs that were infiltrating the country through various syndicates.

Overall, SBI classified the operation as a failed event. Anytime multiple officers were killed or injured in a police tactical operation, SBI would be label it a failed event, regardless of the take or number of high value targets (HVTs) taken down. That determination would allow law enforcement leadership to lobby the bureau HQ for greater training resources and funding.

CHAPTER 57

Two days after the raid, Cutter signed his release papers from a local hospital with his arm in a sling, but he'd suffered no structural damage from the gunshot wound. At nine, under a gloomy morning sky, a nurse escorted him out the entrance and to his vehicle, as a precaution in case he had a setback and showed signs of losing consciousness. He used one arm on the steering wheel to drive home.

After resting a few hours, he left the apartment for a short walk in the fresh, clean air. At a corner drugstore, he bought the morning edition of the Bullet Herald. One of the headlines plastered on the left side of the front page immediately caught his eye.

Questionable Tactics Used in Police Raid. Seven Police Officers Dead – Page 6.

He turned to page 6 to read the article and instantly recognized the name on the credit line. It was Sally Smith, the female reporter he had denied an interview after the hospital bombing. Cutter thought, *revenge sure is a mother fucker.*

With the publication of the story in every local newspaper, the die was officially cast. Within days, the story of the hospital bombing, and police rescue operation made national headlines and was broadcast on CNN. The results took effect immediately. Summer tourist cancellations to Devil Island came in droves. Mayor Daniels resigned the next week, a year before her planned retirement in what was a political fig leaf. Joe Carruthers announced he would not seek reelection beyond his current term as Chief of Police. Harry Ryker's name vanished from the 'short list' of police chief candidates, though he remained in his position as SAC of SBI. As political pundits rose from the ashes, there was no forgiveness in the media for the hospital bombing under police security and the loss of millions of dollars in tourist revenues. A local tabloid, critical that Carruthers did not immediately resign with Daniels, followed several negative articles about suspected police corruption and abuse that in effect became a smear campaign. Since Carruthers was the scapegoat, all officers involved in the unsanctioned raid, to include Cutter and McBain were reprimanded in writing but not suspended. For his assistance in the takedown, Metropolit negotiated a plea deal and received a reduced prison sentence of 15 years.

In hopes to diffuse the maelstrom of controversy surrounding the bombing and assault operation, Joseph Ellington, the popular former Bullet City Manager, was brought out of retirement as an interim mayor to replace Daniels. His first task at damage control was to denounce a local tabloid article claiming the county had become the new seat of organized crime. Known to be recklessly outspoken, Ellington countered the story by releasing a statement to the national press claiming the death of Bennie DeSalvo marked the culmination of drug trafficking in the state.

A political snafu followed a week later at a press dinner. A local reporter misquoted him, stating Ellington believed surviving members of the DeSalvo crime organization would resurface in Miami and join forces with Miami top mafia boss Ransom Oliver, a legendary underworld figure who had eluded federal officers for over a decade while building a drug and weapons smuggling empire. The statement not only made Ellington 'persona non grata' with Florida politicians, but also blocked him with most of Florida's law enforcement community.

Olivess Norton's deposition in the Phillip Drummond case along with her testimony at Penelope Lane's trial effectively linked DeSalvo to the organized crime plot in Bullet. However, it failed to provide enough evidence to connect Ransom Oliver to the Bullet drug and weapons network. Her deposition revealed her plot to poison Phillip Drummond. The medical examiner testified that the toxicology screening revealed a mixture of non-lethal substances. She avoided a murder indictment through an arranged plea bargain between the prosecutor and her attorney, Elijah Combs. Instead, the DA's office filed a charge of manslaughter in the death of Jimmy Delray and reduced the attempted murder charge to aggravated assault in connection with the Phillip Drummond homicide. She was subsequently convicted on that charge but given a light prison sentence of ten years followed by ten years of probation.

As the Norton case closed Blake Cutter was left frustrated that a major organized crime figure like Ransom Oliver could still be connected to the death of his wife and no plan was being discussed for a new operation or surveillance of Oliver's network in Miami.

Chapter 58

It was four months after the raid before the Penelope Lane multiple homicide case came before a grand jury. Her defense team, through coordination between the Terre Haute, Indiana Police Department and Child Protective Services gained unfettered access to information regarding Penelope's background and the case involving the drowning death of her parents.

Agent McBain and Detective Holloway of BPD were sent to Terre Haute, Indiana to interview residents from the area where Penelope was raised to gather information about her childhood. McBain was assigned to investigate Penelope's background. He had been there before when he first learned about her parent's drowning before returning to Bullet to discover Penelope taking Cutter hostage on the roof of her apartment building before her fall.

During several interviews with people who knew her as a child or attended school with her, investigation revealed she'd been bullied mercilessly during her school years and suffered physical and verbal abuse by her parents, Robert and Mable Oden. They were found drowned inside a submerged car in a local lake. A childhood friend of Penelope's who still resided in Terre Haute agreed to travel to Bullet to testify on her behalf during court hearings. She verified Penelope confided in her about abuse and said she witnessed, on several occasions, visible bruises on Penelope's arms and hands, but at Penelope's request, she never revealed the knowledge to anyone.

Due to the brilliant defense by one of the best state-appointed attorneys, he was able to seek a mental disorder defense by portraying Penelope Lane as an abused woman with a history of bipolar disorder and mental and physical abuse without any record of psychological counseling. McBain also learned she was adopted, and she had no knowledge of her biological parents. It left doubt in the jurors' minds regarding premeditation in either of the Drummond couple's deaths. After extensive deliberation, Penelope Lane was found guilty of a lesser charge of third-degree manslaughter in the deaths of Phillip and Dorothy Drummond by reasons of insanity. The court ruled Penelope had no previous intent to commit murder but did have afterthought of hiding the act after the fatal assault. Thus, instead of her being released in a not-guilty verdict, she was remanded to a state psychiatric hospital for a period of twenty years.

The judge further ordered a provision in her sentence that, with good behavior and extensive counseling, her time in the psychiatric hospital could be reduced to eight to ten years.

More disheartening to Cutter was the fact that Penelope's account of conversations between Phillip Drummond and Bennie DeSalvo were ruled inadmissible due to her lack of credibility. Miami mafia leader Ransom Oliver again escaped indictment in connection with either the Blake Cutter assassination attempt or the drug smuggling operation in Bullet, Georgia.

Chapter 59

Five Months After the Raid

On a rainy and foggy morning, Agent Blake Cutter trudged up the front steps of the front entrance to the Bullet County Courthouse. As he reached the top step, he noticed Penelope Lane coming out, dressed in an orange jumpsuit. Her legs were bound by shackles and wrists bruised by the cold steel of handcuffs. Flanking her were two detention officers armed with shotguns. They were escorting her out of the main entrance of the courthouse to a waiting non descript white bus that would transport her to Watkins Psychiatric Hospital.

The officers whisked her and seven other prisoners past the blitzkrieg of approaching local and state news reporters hoping for a word on camera from her or one of the detention officers. They could care less about the other six prisoners.

As she stepped onto the bus, she looked back and sighed morosely. From the window of a middle row seat, she stared out at Cutter. Cutter noticed her shivering with a ruefully bland expression. She looked frail, having lost a noticeable amount of weight during her hostage time and subsequent confinement. It was a reversal of the optimistic and confident expression she'd maintained during her arraignment and trial.

The white sixty-passenger bus pulled away from the courthouse and within ten minutes was beyond the city limits of Bullet. In the bus were the seven women prisoners, two correctional officers named Gavin Turner and Ray MacDonald and a contracted driver. The plan was to drop Penelope and two other psychiatric patients at Watkins after the bus had dropped the others off at state women's corrections facility.

Two hours later, the bus was two miles from the psychiatric hospital where it turned off the main highway onto the blacktop entrance road. The road curved to the right and up a steep incline through rolling hills and thick trees. As the bus crested the top of the hill, the driver slowed for an 18-wheel tractor-trailer stretched across the road, blocking both lanes. The driver coasted to within a hundred feet of the tractor-trailer, stopped and idled the engine.

"What's going on?" MacDonald, the senior of the two corrections officers, asked the driver as he walked up from the front two seats of the bus which were separated from the prisoner seating by an iron gate.

"I don't know," the driver responded, nervously. "This son-of-a-bitch is blocking the road. It must be an accident up ahead," he said, assuming.

"I can see that, Mr... Peters," MacDonald snapped at him, already feeling suspicious and in a heightened state of anxiety. He unbuckled the holster strap of his Glock 9mm service weapon and in a more composed voice, said to the driver. "Pull over to the side and I'll see what the deal is."

MacDonald looked back and nodded at Turner, indicating that he was to stay on the bus to safeguard the prisoners while he got off and checked the scene.

Just as MacDonald stepped off the bus onto the ground, a bullet pierced the driver's side window, striking the driver in the temple. The driver's head dropped onto the steering wheel as blood splattered onto the window and seat as he died instantly.

"What the fuck!" MacDonald yelled. "Secure the prisoners on the floor!" he shouted to Turner.

Turner grabbed a shotgun off the rack, unlocked the gate door, and ordered the prisoners to drop to the floor. Two more rounds pierced through a left side window from a sniper on a hilltop five hundred feet away.

As MacDonald took cover in front of the bus, shooters rushed from the tree line, sprinting towards the rear of the bus while firing volleys of rounds toward the back window of the bus and shattering the glass. Two of the shooters used the covering fire to rush towards the front entrance of the bus. As MacDonald stepped from behind the front of the bus, he was struck in the right side of his chest and right shoulder by two high caliber rounds fired by one of the gunmen. They were obviously sharpshooters, much more skilled than the corrections officers. MacDonald fell to the ground instantly unconscious. Turner reacted by slamming the gate shut without locking it, then rushed towards the front of the bus. The shooters had rehearsed the entire scenario. As Turner reached the steps, one of the shooters fired several rounds through the side window striking Turner in the neck and shoulder.

With the two officers down and the driver dead, the shooters had free access to their target. The first shooters entered the bus, noticed the fallen officer, and expelled an additional round into his back, to finish him off.

The women screamed in terror. The prisoner closest to the back door lunged to pull on the emergency exit handle. It wouldn't budge, so she raised her left leg and kicked at the door to attempt to jar it open. But for security purposes, the door was locked from the outside. At that moment, the lead shooters kicked the iron gate open. He instantly recognized the third prisoner lying on her back on the floor. Penelope Lane was the prisoner they'd been ordered to kidnap. Unemotionally, he shot the other women one by one. Penelope screamed as blood scattered around her. The shooters grabbed her by the arm and yanked her from the floor.

At that moment, Turner miraculously regained consciousness, raised the shotgun and aimed it at the gunmen. Simultaneously, the shooters heard Turner's movement and began to turn. As Turner fired the four aught buckshot, the shooters pulled Penelope in front of him. She received the full load in her chest. As she fell to the floor, she winced and uttered Blake's name.

Blake Cutter's body jerked violently as he woke up, sweating profusely and hyperventilating. His vision blurred momentarily as he pulled himself together and realized the entire episode of the bus encounter was a horrible nightmare. After that episode, he needed a drink. Fortunately, there was a quarter-bottle of distilled Grey Goose vodka in the fridge. He emptied it down his throat, followed by two sleeping pills. Cutter thought of the risk of mixing alcohol with medications. But subconsciously at that moment, he convinced himself that his body could manage it and have the effects he wanted. On a normal night, the swig of vodka would've been enough to knock him out. But, with the nightmare, he figured he needed an extra boost. That wasn't dangerous, he told himself. Of course, a stray dog isn't dangerous . . . until it bites you and you get rabies. Nevertheless, within a few minutes, he succumbed to drowsiness and was ready to place the episode on the back shelf of his mental library.

It was a meaningless bad dream he murmured to himself as he slumped onto the bed and proceeded with a meditation exercise of deep inhales and exhales to slow his heart rate and relax his nerves. But as a book fell off a shelf onto his head and woke him, he surmised it was also a premonition that Penelope was in grave danger and only he could stop her from being killed.

Bennie DeSalvo, a hood on the FBI's Most Wanted list had been taken out. Everything else was an afterthought. Nobody really cared that Penelope Lane was still on the higher command's hit list. She was a double murderer and was about to face justice or karma at the hands of the Mafia . . . neither mattered to anyone but him. Paranoia aside, he knew he had to intervene to save her, and he had to do something soon.

CHAPTER 60

Three days after the dream

Cutter paid a visit to Penelope at the county jail. During their conversation with her through the glass visitation window, she hinted there was more she wanted to reveal about DeSalvo and his dealings with Phillip Drummond . . . information that would make her a target for elimination. When Cutter pressed her for more details, she resisted, stating she was afraid of the consequences of exposing the DeSalvo organization to the police.

The night before her scheduled transfer to Watkins Psychiatric Hospital, she called him. As they spoke on the phone, she mentioned a phone call she received at the jail in the prior week from a stranger who would not identify himself. It was a voice she remembered from Phillip Drummond's meetings with the DeSalvo group at the Devil Island Clubhouse. The person asked her to verify her identity. She had accommodated the request without realizing someone could be tracking her whereabouts.

The caller then abruptly hung up but phoned back later that day. She recognized the voice was the same one as earlier that morning. She immediately hung up and reported the call to the jail guards.

The county sheriff, figuring the man would call again, set up a phone taps on the jail's main inmate phone lines. Guessing right, the person called again the next day. This time, the call was traced to an obscure phone booth near downtown Bullet. BPD dispatched local deputies to descend upon the location. When they arrived, they found the booth unoccupied. They dusted the entire booth for fingerprints but found no trace evidence or witnesses to identify the caller. The caller had been incredibly careful.

Penelope knew who he was and knew she had a much greater reason to fear being in a minimally secure psychiatric hospital than being in the county jail or on the streets.

The next day

The morning of her transfer had finally come. This time it wasn't a nightmare, it was reality. In a déjà vu scenario, Cutter drove to the Bullet County Jail and parked in a spot across the street from the jail's main entrance. He stayed in his car until he saw a grey nondescript nine-passenger van pull up in front.

Moments later, he watched as Penelope and five other women were escorted from the jail to the van by two uniformed officers. In the front passenger seat of the van sat a man wearing a blue blazer and a pair of tan slacks. Cutter figured he was an official from the psychiatric hospital. Instead of the orange jumpsuit she wore in his dream, Penelope wore a blue chambray top and loose-fitting blue jeans and deck sneakers. The other two women were similarly dressed.

As the van pulled away and faded into the distance, Cutter revved his vehicle's engine, made a U-turn into the streets, and drove off in the opposite direction of the van towards BPD headquarters.

With the Drummond couple and the James Delray cases now closed, his temporary assignment at BPD was completed. He was supposed to clean out his desk and return to duty at SBI headquarters.

Five minutes later, his vehicle came to a screeching halt in front of BPD HQ. He hopped out and sprinted into the building. Instead of heading to the third floor, he rode the elevator to the basement. There, he grabbed a tan, trench coat from his loaner locker, put it on and popped the collar up over his neck. He then rode up one floor to the armory. He had been issued a key to the main weapons cabinet since SBI agents had been storing their service revolvers with BPD while on attached duty. He proceeded to use his key to unlock the cabinet. Instead of retrieving his personal weapons, he grabbed several grenades and as many magazines of ammunition as he could fit into the pockets of his overcoat. He locked the cabinet and moved surreptitiously toward the main exit.

As he reached the front door, Alex McBain spotted him. "Where you headed, chap?" he asked.

"I'm heading out to pick up an old friend."

"I didn't know you had any left," Alex joked.

Cutter didn't respond; he just opened the door and started to walk past McBain, holding his coat tightly against him to hide the contents in the pockets.

McBain instantly became suspicious since it was a very warm day. . . too warm to be wearing a trench coat. Wait, Blake!" McBain shouted. "Don't go anywhere. The guys are throwing you a farewell party. It was supposed to be a surprise, but you'll miss it if you leave right now."

Agent Cutter again didn't respond but took a few more steps toward the outside.

"Whoa, partner! Hold up. We brought in your favorite rum cake. Don't ditch us like this! Besides, you need to ditch that coat. You're going to burn up in it."

Breaking a wry smile, Cutter responded bluntly, "Sorry. You enjoy the cake. I'm taking a rain check."

As he took the first step, the armory room cabinet key fell out of his pocket and onto the top step. Cutter reached down, retrieved it, and stuffed it back into his pocket. But not before McBain noticed.

"Whoa, chap. Where are you going with that arms room key? You know taking that key out of the building is against regulations. This isn't SBI HQ."

Cutter ignored him and continued walking down the set of steps.

"What's up with that key, Blake?" McBain repeated strongly.

Cutter turned around and answered solemnly, "I'm going to rescue Penelope before that van gets to the facility. I can't let her get locked up in there, Alex. I can't let anyone hurt her. I need to save her." Cutter's eyes looked in a zombie state.

"Have you flipped out, chap. You can't get away with this. Come back inside with me and we'll talk about it."

Cutter stared at him with silent indifference.

McBain then noticed bulges in both of Cutter's coat pockets. "I can't let you do something stupid, Blake. What are you gonna do? Shoot up a transport van. How do you even know you'll catch up with it?"

Cutter turned and shouted, "Stay out of this, Alex."

Feeling he had no choice, McBain pulled out his Glock and held it by his side. "You know I've got to stop you, Blake. I don't want to you, but I will if I must."

Cutter stopped, turned about, tightened his jaw, and stared at his partner.

McBain raised his voice, "Cut the crap, Blake. Jenni's dead! You can't keep chasing a memory. Let's go into the building, now."

Suddenly drawing attention from uniformed officers walking by, Cutter replied, "I'm not losing her again. Stay out of my way!"

McBain then rushed up to Cutter and grabbed him by his jacket sleeve. "Have you lost your mind, chap? I'm not letting you do this."

Without warning, Cutter shoved McBain to the ground. The shock of his partner's aggression left him momentarily motionless. As Cutter made a move toward his car, McBain leaped to his feet, ran up, and grabbed Cutter by his coat again.

Cutter turned about and pushed him to the ground a second time.

McBain, a man who had become Cutter's most trusted friend, was left with no choice. He rose to his feet, aimed his Glock at Cutter, and shouted, "Stop Blake, or I'll have to shoot you!"

A gasp sounded from the officers who had stopped to watch the altercation.

As Cutter's hand rashly moved inside his coat pocket, McBain fired a round into Cutter's left leg, knocking him to the ground.

Several police officers sprinted to the scene. Bystanders screamed in horror. McBain dropped his Glock to the ground and sat down on the bottom step in disbelief of what had just gone down.

Blake Cutter was placed in handcuffs by one of the onlooking BPD officers. After McBain explained to the officer what had just happened, Cutter was read his rights and asked to remain sitting on the steps as McBain called the dispatcher to report the incident then proceeded to call for an EMT van as blood gushed from Cutter's leg.

Ten minutes later, an EMT van arrived and the police officer and EMT assisted in getting Cutter onto a gurney and into the van. McBain chose not to ride in the EMT or following the van to a nearby hospital but rather phoned SAC Ryker to inform him of the incident. As the EMT van pulled away, McBain despondently walked towards his car for a trip to Ryker's office. He was still in a state of shock of having to shoot his SBI partner.

As he turned and watched the EMT van pull away, followed closely by a BPD police cruiser, McBain fought back emotions and murmured to himself, *Damn you, Blake! Is she worth throwing your career down the drain?*

After completing a debriefing to the Ryker and BPD Chief Carruthers regarding the incident, McBain walked out of the building shaking his head in disbelief. He decided to take the afternoon off to come to terms with what had occurred between him and Cutter.

Chapter 61

Three Months Later

For the first time in twenty-two years, Blake Cutter did not wear a police badge. He was now just another private citizen who had to let licensed law enforcement deal with the criminal underworld. Three months had passed since he'd been shot by his SBI partner, Alex McBain, at the front steps of Bullet Police Department Headquarters as Alex thwarted his attempt to free Penelope Lane from a transport bus heading to Watkins Women's Psychiatric Hospital. To Cutter, the time away from investigative police work felt like an eternity for a disgraced ex-cop who'd lost his own identity and went past the line in pursuit of forbidden love.

The Christmas season was supposed to be a time of joy and celebration. But for Blake Cutter, it was days spent roaming through want ads looking for work. Instead of sipping apple cider with his SBI cohorts or curling up with Jenni Cutter beside a roaring fireplace, he spent his nights drowning himself in shots of vodka and falling asleep in despair and a state of depression.

The morning before Christmas Eve, Cutter was in a particularly somber mood, sitting alone at his apartment, recollecting times when he was a decorated police detective. It was a happy time when Jenni was alive, and their marriage was thriving. But now she was dead, and his thoughts were being shared with another woman whose face popped into his mind more often than Jenni's. She was the woman he'd hoped would someday fill the space in his heart left by the loss of Jenni.

For the next moments, his thoughts shifted between the two loves and the confusion of how he should feel coming into the holiday. He wondered where his devotion laid, and could it include two women. *Am I betraying Jenni by thinking about Penelope?* he thought to himself.

Suddenly, his daydream was interrupted by the vibration of his cell phone. He wasn't in the mood for a conversation, yet the sense of responsibility he upheld while on the force led him to pick up the receiver and answer it in a professional tone.

"Blake, it's Penelope!" she uttered in a frantic voice.

He couldn't believe he was hearing from her after all these months. He had been forbidden from contacting her after being fired by SBI.

He rose from the bed and sat upright. "Yeah. This is quite a surprise," he replied, attempting to hold back his excitement and shock. "I didn't think I'd ever hear from you again. What's going on?"

Tearfully, she replied, "I'm surviving it, Blake. . . as well as I can being locked up in his nut house."

"Hang tough. You'll get through it, "he urged her, consolingly. "One day all of this will be behind you, then you can start your life all over again."

"Blake, I need to see you," she said. "Can you come here and visit me?"

Cutter sensed desperation in her voice. Without the words to comfort her, he asked, "It's been a long time, Penelope. I wish I could see you…but you know I'm under a no contact order. We're not even supposed to be in phone contact."

"I know all this, Blake. But I figured out a way we can do it," she said. "I received a letter with a picture from a cousin in Florida. His name is Larry Smith. I couldn't believe how much the two of you resemble each other."

Stunned by the suggestion, Cutter replied bluntly, "What you're contemplating is crazy, Penelope."

"It's not crazy and I'm not joking Blake. It'll work," she urged. "The only thing you'll need is a fake ID and a Florida license plate on your car. You did say you kept the one you had from Miami."

"I have it somewhere," he replied hesitantly.

She went on, "That's all you need, Blake. I've been transferred to a minimum-security unit. It's more relaxed here, especially during the holidays. I know the woman who sits at the security desk. She just needs to see a license number when you sign it, just something to cover her ass."

Blake studied the proposition for a moment in silence. "Let's say I can get the ID. What makes you so sure we won't get caught? If this blows up in our faces, you'll never get out of there."

"Please Blake," she pleaded. "You've got to trust me on this."

"They might call this cousin's number."

"I doubt they'd reach him. He's single and a trucker. He keeps a mail address in Florida but he's always on the road."

Cutter hesitated before responding. Just hearing the persistence in her voice reminded him how much he missed her, how much he was fascinated by her persistence and persuasiveness. "Well, it's not like I could lose my job," he joked. "What's so important that you'd risk your neck to see me?"

She paused, took a deep breath then said, "I need to talk to you about a man named Anthony Milano, one of Bennie DeSalvo's associates. There are things I couldn't talk about before now."

Cutter was at a loss for words. He wasn't sure how to react to the subject since he was no longer an investigator. He found his voice a moment later and asked, "If you had something to reveal about Milano, why didn't you tell it during your trial? It may have made a difference. Why didn't you tell me?"

With her voice breaking, she replied, "I couldn't tell anyone about this before now, Blake. If I did, I'd be dead. I felt safer getting locked up here in this nut house and keeping quiet. But I have a good reason to talk now."

"Okay, I'm listening."

She hesitated for a moment and then spoke, "I know things that will connect DeSalvo to Milano and Milano to Phillip's drowning. The mob knows I have this information. I can't go into detail over the phone. You must come here before it's too late." She then asked Cutter to wait on the line as she walked down the hall to ensure no one was overhearing their conversation. Moments later, she returned to the phone, and whispered, "Blake, I saw two men come in here the other day."

"What men?"

Trembling and dabbing her tears, she continued in a softer tone, "I was walking down the main hallway when I noticed these two men dressed in business suits at the front security desk. I stepped behind a door so they wouldn't notice me, but I recognized one of them, Blake. It was one of the men I frequently saw in the company of Phillip, DeSalvo and Anthony Milano during their meetings at the Devil Island Clubhouse. I overheard that voice, the same voice that called me while I was in the Bullet jail."

"Are you sure about this?" Cutter questioned her. "There was no mention during your trial about Anthony Milano ever being seen on Devil Island."

"He was there, Blake, I'm positive."

Cutter shifted back, "And these men at the desk, you think they were asking about you?"

"I'm sure they were, Blake." Her voice became shaky as she continued. "Why else would they come here? Blake, honey, they've come to kidnap me or even kill me. You've got to get me out of this place. I wouldn't doubt they've placed listening devices somewhere in here."

It seemed an irrational and hysterical notion to him, but he decided to remain sympathetic to her concern."

"Okay. If you think something like that is going on, then I'll figure something out. But don't tell this to anyone else."

Suddenly hearing footsteps rapidly approaching her, she hung up without saying goodbye.

Blake was suddenly listening to silence. Penelope! Penelope!" he yelled through the phone.

Chapter 62

Two days later at a quarter past noon, Cutter was enduring rather than enjoying the day with a nap on the sofa in his apartment. It had been agonizing not hearing from Penelope for two days after calling more than a dozen times and being told she wasn't available to talk without getting an explanation. He was beside himself and about to lose his mind. Then, his cell phone buzzed, waking him up.

He recognized the number and frantically pushed the green button and yelled, "Penelope. What the hell's going on. I've been calling you for two days and nobody's let me talk to you. I was about to come there and find you."

She hissed then said, "I told the attendants not to give me any messages from you."

"Why the hell would you do that?" he asked as he sat up rigidly.

"Blake, I can't talk to you by phone anymore. I know they're not tapping your phone."

"What do you mean, tapping my phone. What are you talking about?"

"Oliver and Milano's got people who can do anything they want…and they want to get to me, Blake. They've got paid hackers who can triangulate our calls."

"What if they do?" Cutter challenged. "We're not together and you're safe in there. Give me names and I'll ger a friend of mine to hunt them down."

"Hunt down, Blake? You're not a cop anymore." She reminded him. "You can't go after these people."

He stayed silent for a moment not wanting to admit she was right.

She looked around the area near the house phone and lowered her voice to a whisper. "Look, Blake I need to see you. I don't want you to come here. You can put us both in danger."

What are you talking about?" Cutter asked. "What about that idea for me to come there under a false identity?"

"Too dangerous, now, after what just happened." She paused for a moment, moved as close to the window to shield noise as possible. "Milano's got several technicians who had been heavily involved in tapping and monitoring phone calls of several rivals mob leaders in Florida."

"How do you know this?"

"Blake, do I need to remind you? I was with Phillip for three years. He told me everything…pillow talk and at dinners. He trusted me, but he just needed to have someone to confide in . . . and to brag about. I was his trophy girl. I know DeSalvo spied on everybody he was involved with, friend or foe. With him dead, Milano will be doing it now."

Cutter paused and put the phone down to his side in deep thought.

"Are you still there, Blake?" she asked.

"Okay, I'm tracking what you're saying. I won't call again, and I won't try to come there. I don't think they could have my cell number. I wouldn't doubt they could get a listing of all police-issued numbers when I was on the force, but how could they do that now."

"Please, Blake." she pleaded.

He relented, noting she sounded even more emotional. "I'll stop calling if it makes you feel uncomfortable."

She clarified, "It's not your phone I'm worried about Blake. They're monitoring every call that comes to this place. I know for a fact they did it when I was in county."

"So how will I see you?"

"I can sneak out, Blake. I know a way I can sneak out in the middle of the night. On Wednesday, there's no one surveilling the grounds after dark. I found this out from a girl who's been here for ten years. She befriended me as soon as I got here. We eat lunch and dinner together every day and we talk often when we're let out on the grounds. I know she's transparent with the staff in here."

"And you trust her?" Cutter questioned.

"I have to Blake. I had to trust someone. I need to see you and tell you something important. My life is on the line."

"Okay. I can find a location to meet. How are you gonna get out and you'll for sure be spotted out in public in hospital-issued clothing."

"Barbara's a trustee. She gets picked up one day a week by her family. She's supposed to get out in about a year. She can buy me a dress and give it to me. I can wear it underneath my uniform, and I'll make sure no one knows."

"Why would this woman risk her future freedom by helping you. You get caught and she could be remanded there for a longer time."

"I know, Blake. But she's gotten to know everything about my entire life. She had a father who was an undercover police office and was killed by the mob when his cover was blown. That happened when she was seventeen and she nearly went crazy and attempted suicide several times. She was committed to this place three years ago for mental health treatment and she's been here ever since. She wants to do something to have influence by helping me."

"So, you've already told her you're planning this," Cutter asked, curiously.

"No, Blake. I didn't tell her anything about trying to leave here to meet you. I just asked her how I could sneak away if someone got in here and was trying to get to me to harm me."

"Okay, then we'd better move fast," Cutter said. "Here's an idea, as crazy as I am to suggest this. You could meet me about one in the morning, downtown. Could you do it tomorrow night."

"Not tomorrow night, but early Monday morning. I need time for her to go onto the hospital grounds this weekend and map out an escape route. Then I need Sunday to make sure everything around here happens as normal. They don't even do bed checks on Sunday. I can leave out the back, cross the back garden, climb over the fence, and disappear through the woods. I just need to confirm nothing's changed since I last walked out there. She told me there's a taxi stand about two blocks north of this facility behind the woods."

"Okay," he acknowledged. "You've obviously thought this through. Well, there's an alley in the west district between Broad and Hurley Streets. There are a lot of clubs around there and you can blend in with the crowds of people exiting bars, then make your way down the alley. I don't want you around there alone, so you will meet me exactly at one a.m."

"I'll do it, Blake." She said confidently, then hung up abruptly as she noticed ward nurses walking in her direction.

Chapter 63

On Monday morning, shortly after midnight, Blake spoke to Penelope via phone, then left his apartment and drove twenty minutes until he reached the trendy West End district. Her voice echoed in his head the entire drive. The night was cool with only a light mist mixed in with a dense fog hovering in the area.

Even on Sunday nights, the district was abuzz with patrons at lively bars and nightclubs and restaurants that stayed open until two a.m. West End was the last bastion of hope for a declining and deteriorating city. Investors made a last-ditch effort to revitalize Bullet by dumping millions of dollars into the West End while leaving other areas in more need wanting. In the past two years, all West End streets have been repaved, broken cobblestones have been repaired and new ones installed, including Broad Street, the main thoroughfare through the downtown district. Several establishments reopened with major renovations to their interiors and new signage.

FORBIDDEN RESCUE

Hurley Park bordered the West End district on the north side and was named after a legendary 1940s city commissioner Robert Hurley. It had been renovated with new playgrounds, several walkways, an amphitheater, a manufactured lake, and a commitment by BPD to add it to its overnight patrol routes.

Arriving on Broad Street, Cutter slowed his speed on the cobblestone street, then parked his car on Broad Street and killed the engine. He was two blocks from the corner of Broad and Hurley where the long dark alley he'd planned for their meeting was located. He reached in the back seat, grabbed a tan-colored trench coat and a hat, put both on, and then pulled the collar of the trench coat around his neck. He then reached for the overhead visor, retrieved sunglasses, and put them on. Stepping out of the car slowly as not to attract attention, he looked down the street in both directions to ensure he wasn't being observed. Briskly, he crossed to the opposite side of the street from the designated alley until he reached it. He overheard horns and drums vibrating from side-by-side bars with live bands. As doors opened to release smokers, Cutter recognized a Glenn Fry tune that was one of his favorites. He paused for a moment to take it in, but then refocused. Then, he jetted across the street, dodging one oncoming driver and hurried down the alley.

A few steps into the dim space, he stopped and checked his watch. It was twelve fifty-five. He noticed two large dark green dumpsters, which were full and nearly overflowing at the end of the alley. They bordered the backdoors to a pizza joint. Given the lingering smoke coming from the chimney and the overflowing trash from the weekend garbage, the entire alley wreaked of trash stench, decayed meat, and other choking odors, which was to be expected since city dumpster empties didn't occur until Tuesdays.

Cutter felt a twinge of uneasiness being in an unsecure alley for an undisclosed amount of time, but there was no way to contact Penelope to ensure she would show up because patients at the facility were not allowed to have cell phones. He stood behind the dumpster on the left side for twenty minutes.

Chapter 64

At one fifteen, Cutter glanced at his watch to start his mental countdown to the moment he would abandon the location due to concluding she was a no-show. Noise from nearby bars dwindled as the facilities prepared to close. He could see various couples and groups passing by at the entrance to the alley heading home after a night of drink and partying. The last thing he needed to see was a person or a couple wandering down the alley as a shortcut to their car on a nearby block. He was losing faith that she would show. . . like he really had a lot of confidence in this risky and crazy meeting, in the first place. He asked himself several questions, Was *this just a ruse? Did she get caught trying to leave? Am I foolish for getting further involved in her life?*

Then, two minutes later, he suddenly heard the clicking of high stiletto heels through the momentary silence. He peeked from behind the dumpster and noticed a curvy figure approaching wearing a tight-fitting red dress that accentuated her hips enticingly. Her hair was shoulder length and highlights glowed from the corner streetlight. He figured Penelope was wearing a wig or it had grown fast since he'd last seen her being taken away on the prison bus when it was still a black pixie cut. But it had been months since he'd seen her, and it was possible it had grown on its own.

As her face became recognizable, he peeked from behind the dumpster and bellowed, "Over here!"

As she reached him, she wrapped Blake in a strong hug and wouldn't let go. He tried to pull away, trying to balance his emotions with discretion, but she dug her nails into the back of his jacket, clutching him like a vise . . . like a wife would a husband returning from a long military deployment . . . like a farewell hug from someone who wouldn't see him again. She clung to him without saying a word but then suddenly trembled and sobbed.

"Blake, I missed you so much. I'm so scared!"

He hesitated to return the verbal sentiments, but instead grasped her cold hands and lightly pulled her to a position behind the dumpster.

"Boy, it stinks back here," she whispered, reacting to the putrid, rancid odor. At that moment, Cutter realized he'd picked the wrong alley and the wrong spot. He didn't remember those dumpsters being in that alley since the restaurant had just opened six months ago.

"We won't be here long," he reassured her. "I almost gave up on you. Are you okay? You're a little late. Did everything go well with you getting here?"

"I told you I'd make it, Blake. I just had to pick the right time. You should know by now not to doubt me," she teased. "Shouldn't a girl always be fashionably late?"

She got the chuckle out of him because she wanted to relieve her own anxiety.

"You look great," he said. "I wish we could share a dance in one of these clubs. It's a shame to waste a great outfit like this."

"Oh, I plan to keep it, Blake. As Arnold said, we'll be back," she joked.

"Aren't you cold?" he asked, offering to take off his jacket and wrap it around her.

"I'm from Indiana, Blake," she pointed out, resisting the offer. "I'm not like you Southerners who have a fit at the first hint of a nippy night."

He broke a wry smile at her remark.

"Besides, this is all she could find that would make me blend in. It's not like she has access to a lot of clothes."

Cutter acknowledged with another grin. He appreciated her jolly mood. "Listen, we don't have much time. What do you have to tell me?"

Diverting, she said bluntly, "I can't go back there, Blake. Can you take me away from here? Those mob guys are trying to kill me. I know everything about the forgery and there's a lot of laundered money involved. The FBI's getting close. I got a call from an investigator named Agent Ronaldo Kelly."

Cutter spoke under his breath, *that son-of-a-bitch,* Cutter then bit his tongue. "What the hell was he calling you about? He's not a friend and he's not working this case. He's just trying to make a name for himself by getting involved in a situation that's none of his business."

"Well, this Kelly guy told me he would be coming to the hospital this week to talk to me."

"Let's talk about him another time," Cutter demanded, shifting. "Tell me about the calls."

Not focused on his inquiry, she continued, "If the mob finds me in there, they will get to me, Blake." Her voice was breaking as she spoke. "They know I'm there. I saw two men outside my window in the woods two nights ago."

Suddenly she started sobbing but held back tears.

Cutter took a deep breath. "I know this is stressful Penelope, but I need you to keep it together. I can't be seen with you right now. If anyone even finds out we're meeting, I can go to jail. You've got to go back and give me time to figure this out."

She exhaled a deep breath, then replied, "Okay, if that's what you think I should do."

She pulled off her left shoe and a business card and small key dropped out."

"I've never seen anybody put a business card in their shoe," he pointed out.

"Again, Blake. I'm a country girl. I walked on sharp rocks barefooted my entire childhood."

She then handed the business card and key to him. "Blake, this card is from a teller at the Cayman National Bank on Grand Cayman. On the back is a username and password to an offshore account. This key is to a large safe deposit box at that bank. There's ten million dollars in it."

His eyebrows furrowed with curiosity. "Where did you get this key?" he asked.

She continued, "I stole it from Phillip. He's been funneling drug money and laundering it through a person in the Caymans who's been placing money into the box."

Cutter's eyes widened with astonishment. "That doesn't seem possible."

She explained, "We had a contact who we wired money to . . . a man named Robert Beauchamp."

Cutter's jealous memory kicked in as he recalled Beauchamp immediately, "Oh, yea! That's the guy you called Beau. What would make a tour guide get involved in mob money laundering."

"It's not just him, Blake. A guy from Western Union accepted large receipts and passed it to him. Down there, everybody plays and gets a piece of the pie."

Suddenly, he frowned.

She continued, "I took some documents with me when we went there. It's evidence of a guy named Harry Stillwater's involvement in forgeries, fake powers of attorney, the works."

Cutter thought for a moment, then said, "He's the guy being investigated by the Georgia Real Estate Commission."

At that moment, the back door of the restaurant creaked open, and two workers walked out carrying black trash bags.

"Look, we've got to get out of here, but we can't leave together. Can you meet me somewhere else tonight?" Cutter asked her.

"Where?"

Cutter turned his back to the workers and said, "Walk up the alley and turn left at the street. Once you pass the downtown district, you'll see a park. It's only a few blocks. Find a safe place there and sit tight under I get there. I'll be there in about thirty minutes. I've got to hear the whole story tonight. That's the only way I can help you."

They noticed the workers rapidly approaching with the trash bags, close enough to overhear their conversation.

"Okay," she agreed, folding her arms and trembling.

"Go now!" he said to her firmly. "Go! Everything's gonna be okay, I promise."

Their farewell kiss was passionate. Then, he took her hand and led her around the dumpster.

"Promise me, Blake. If anything happens to me tonight, you'll go to the Caymans and get those documents."

Cutter looked perplexed but feigned agreement to ensure she complied with his instructions without further delay.

She scurried out of the alley as he walked to the dumpster on the opposite side from the one the two workers stood smoking and pulled his collar tighter to his neck. He didn't want to be seen walking with her out of the alley, but he also didn't want to be identified by the two restaurant workers. He turned to light a cigarette and stood with his back to them until they dumped the garbage bags into the dumpster and trudged back inside. The door slammed as Cutter looked up the alley and saw Penelope had disappeared. He assumed she was doing as he asked her and would be somewhere in Hurley Park when he got there.

CHAPTER 65

Cutter walked into O'Connor's Irish pub, a joint that had seen too much of him in the past few weeks. It was the place where he'd spent many evenings sitting alone at the bar until midnight listening to local bands performing to mostly empty chairs. It was the place he'd gone too often when he needed to think. Now, he had even more to think about.

As he sat at the bar downing a boilermaker, he pulled out and stared at the fake ID, produced by a contact on the street who owed him a favor. The card displayed the name Larry Smith.

"Another shot," he said as he motioned to the bartender.

"I'm sorry, Mister Cutter, the bar is now closed," the bartender replied. It was customary for bars and pubs in Bullet to shut down at midnight on the eve of a major holiday.

Cutter grabbed his jacket off the next barstool, dropped a two-dollar tip on the counter, and walked to the door. To maintain a degree of anonymity, he'd parked his car a block away at the corner of 4th Street and Wilshire.

In between O'Connor's and the corner was a 24-hour convenient store. It was a place he usually stopped in to pick up his companions for the night, a twelve-pack of beer. Only this night, he'd opted to grab only one can, needing to be alert and sober for the trip to Watkins the next morning.

As Cutter neared the front entrance of O'Connor's, his cell phone rang. The caller was Alex McBain.

"Blake, we've got to talk. Where are you?"

"Somewhere you're not," Cutter snapped back.

"C'mon, Blake. It's time we talked about what happened. It's been months."

"There's nothing to talk about," Cutter resisted, impatiently aware of his meeting with Penelope in the park in less than ten minutes.

"Just give me a chance to discuss it, ole chap," McBain pleaded. "Your friendship means a lot to me."

"You picked a fine way to show it," Blake reminded him. "I guess that's the way you Brits show your friendship . . .," Cutter poked. ". . .shooting your partner." At that moment, Cutter was seeing things one-sided.

McBain fell silent, deeply hurt by the remark. If there was one police officer on the force who thrived on loyalty, it was McBain. "That's not fair Blake and you know it. I was doing my job. You had to be stopped. You were way over the edge."

"It doesn't matter. It's over," Blake replied sighing with resignation.

"It's not over," McBain refuted strongly. "Let's just take some time and talk this out and you change your attitude towards me."

Cutter let the phone receiver hang near his lips for a few seconds.

"What's it gonna be, Blake?" McBain asked. "It's Christmas Eve."

Cutter broke a sneaky smile silently.

"Let's grab a couple of beers somewhere and get together," McBain suggested. "If you feel the same way afterwards, then we can forget about it and part ways. We've had a lot of good times, bloke."

Cutter hesitated again and sighed. Beyond the hurt, he missed Alex's friendship as much as he missed Penelope. "You're not exactly the Christmas Eve date I had in mind."

"I'm the best you're gonna get tonight," Alex pointed out, sensing the silent smile. "Even hookers take Christmas Eve off in this sleepy town. How about I link up with you? What's your location?"

"How far are you away from O'Connor's Pub on Broad Street?" Blake asked relenting.

"My car's parked at the corner of Wilshire near the front of Jay's Quick Stop," McBain replied." I'm on a stakeout with BPD. We've been investigating a string of liquor store robberies and based on some chatter we noticed, we think Jay's Quick Stop could be the bandit's next target." You can join me in the car."

"Give me about a half hour or so," Cuter requested.

"Take your time, chap," McBain said. "I won't be going anywhere and will be right here unless something goes down."

"Roger that," Cutter replied. Cutter laughed bleakly with appreciation and then hung up. He walked from the alley and turned right in the direction of Hurley Park. It was an eerie night, foggy and chillier than normal for Georgia. The path along the sidewalk was pitch black with every bulb in the streetlights either broken or burned out.

As he passed another liquor store about two blocks from the park, Cutter overheard a loud blast from inside, followed by a shrill scream. His eyes flashed towards the window as he accelerated his pace towards the front entrance of the store. Then, he heard another blast. But there was no scream. He knew it was a gunshot, something big. He assumed the second pop had finished off the intent of the first. A chill rushed down his spine. He sensed death in the air. The BPD had guessed right about an impending robbery in the area, but they had picked the establishment.

When he reached the entrance, he stopped and peered through the glass door toward the front counter. His eyes dropped to the floor. A woman lay behind the counter in a pool of blood. Cutter rose and saw a tall gangly man wearing a white T-shirt and faded blue jeans. He was clutching a 3D printed single shotgun in his left hand. A black skull cap covered his face except for the cutout nose and eye areas.

The shooter shuffled back a few steps to a point where a tall store shelf concealed him. The barrel of his shotgun remained in view, pointed at the terror-blanched face of a gray-haired Hispanic male. Cutter assumed he was the store manager. There was one thing he didn't have to assume. He was witnessing an armed robbery that had turned into an aggravated assault with a deadly weapon.

His thoughts shifted to Penelope, waiting for him in a nearby park in a not-so-secure part of town. He suddenly had to make a difficult choice; the safety of a psychiatric hospital escapee, who was alone in a park in danger of being mugged or a couple of liquor store employees who were obviously in imminent danger. His police instincts took over, though he failed to consider he was no longer a police officer and had no arrest or apprehension authority.

He was a private citizen with a privately registered Colt Python revolver he'd purchased at a local pawn shop for self-protection.

With his line-of-sight obscured by several store shelves, Cutter wondered if there was an accomplice somewhere in the immediate area. Three scenarios raced through his mind. *The robber could have caught the female store worker activating the behind-the-counter police alarm and shot her. Either the main shooter or an accomplice's gun accidentally discharged, striking her. The robber shot the woman indiscriminately, at point blank range. The third scenario.*

The scenario didn't matter. It was now his choice whether to intervene and attempt to prevent a horrific massacre. Unlike the past twenty-two years, his authority was merely that of a citizen trying to preserve human life. He no longer carried a police officer sidearm with which to execute that authority.

As he glared through the glass door, he saw another man pop into view on a surveillance mirror on the opposite side of the store. As he suspected, there was a second shooter, an African American who was in his early 20s. The man was dressed in similar clothes but was slightly taller. He also wore a black skullcap but hadn't seen any necessity to cover his face.

Cutter concluded he could take out the first shooter but doubted his ability to engage them both. Thus, he backed away from the door and stood behind one of the columns at the front entrance. He looked once again through the window and watched the storeowner move back behind the counter. Cutter assumed he'd been ordered to empty the cash register.

At that moment, Cutter could've just called 911. But he figured if he prevented an armed robbery single-handedly, it might score points towards his reinstatement to a law enforcement position somewhere, if not with BPD or SBI. So, he remained stationary momentarily in thought. He felt his heart throbbing, fearing the shooter would mow down the store owner as soon as he handed over the cash from the register. Cutter was beset with anxiety, realizing he was not only void of any arresting authority but also outnumbered. Despite the precariousness of his intervening, he decided to act. It had been a while since he'd allowed the good judgement of restraint to overshadow an instinct to act. It wouldn't be this time either.

Chapter 66

As Cutter darted over to a position behind the side wall, an unmarked police cruiser sped down the street approaching the store. Cutter, knowing the unit was responding to someone's call about the incident, Cutter was forced to abandon his heroic plan. He ran to the street waving until the car halted in the road. McBain leaped out of the driver's side, caught sight of Cuter and approached him at the corner. Cutter waved McBain towards him. McBain never forgot Cutter's propensity to find himself caught up in an unexpected, sticky situation.

"Blake, we got a call from the dispatcher about an armed robbery. What the bloody hell are you doing here?" McBain whispered as he knelt next to him.

"I'll explain later, but there are at least two armed gunmen inside," he told McBain. As Cuter reached for his weapon, he continued, "There's a female gunshot victim on the floor laying behind the counter. I can go cover the back if you're ready to go in."

McBain grabbed Cutter's arm. "Wait a minute! Appreciate the info, mate, but you're not a cop anymore," he reminded him. "You better back off and let me handle this. I can't authorize you to assist in this situation." At that moment, McBain glanced down the street and noticed a blue Camaro with a Florida license a hundred feet away. He recognized the license plate number.

"This might sound crazy but look at that Dade-County plate number. I recognize it . . . and I know you do too."

"Son of a bitch!" Cutter said. "That's the car those two hoods drove who participated in a string of drug crimes in Miami that we were never able to nail. They were Ransom Oliver's boys. I believe their names were Spector McShane and Rico Calderon."

"I bet you a hot pistol, this robbery is connected to a cash cow for interstate drug running," McBain noted. "That'll make it a federal collar if I can take it down."

"Too big a coincidence," Cutter agreed. "Are you gonna call BPD for back-up."

McBain replied, "There's no time for that. I've gotta make a move."

"How the hell you gonna do that?" Cutter asked in an aggressive tone. "You can't charge in there alone. You need my help."

McBain paused momentarily to absorb the reality of Cutter's words. "Have you been shooting lately, mate?" McBain then asked.

"I've been on the range once or twice since you shot me," Cutter snipped. "C'mon, you know I can hold my own. You can't go alone against two or more shooters."

Overlooking the former comment, McBain remarked, "That means you're probably rusty," McBain muttered, brushing off the wisecrack.

"I can still shoot well enough to save your ass," Cutter hissed.

Before responding, McBain took a deep breath and paused pensively as he scanned the area. He realized if they charged the door to confront the shooters, they would need someone to cover their movement. He feared an innocent bystander could pop into the line of fire and get caught in the crossfire. He suddenly felt he had no choice but to utilize Cutter as the chance of another unit arriving in time was problematic.

Just as McBain was about to speak, another gun blast came from inside the store.

"Oh shit, we may be too late," McBain whispered as he leapt to his feet. He could only assume the other employee had been shot. "Get ready to back me up."

McBain crept forward two steps and dropped to a crouch, to acquire a clear line of sight at the first man exiting.

"Be careful, partner," Cutter advised McBain. "I'll cover you."

McBain broke a smile without turning as he aimed his gun at the door and crept forward. Before he could collapse the smile, the first shooter dashed into view.

"STOP WHERE YOU ARE!" McBain shouted, traversing his weapon between the door and the gunman. He was expecting the second shooter to rush out momentarily or perhaps even engage him through the glass.

As he stood in a firing position, the shooter, with his pupils bulging out, pulled a pistol from his pants.

"DROP THE GUN AND GET ON THE GROUND, NOW!" McBain spouted. The shooter cautiously knelt and laid the pistol on the concrete sidewalk.

But then, in a surprise move, he popped to his feet, appearing to ready himself to make a run for it.

"I SAID, ON THE GROUND!" McBain barked a second time. The man dropped to his knees, then lay prone.

It was now obvious to both Cutter and McBain that the other shooter must've caught wind of the situation and halted somewhere inside.

McBain approached the crook as he recited the Miranda rights. He pulled the crook's right arm back and put him in handcuffs. McBain then smarted off, "Now try to run, chap."

From Cutter's position near the corner, he looked at the side door. By the dead silence, he assumed the side exit had not been engaged. McBain and Cutter had no choice but to assume the second shooter was still inside the store with no intention of being disarmed peacefully.

In a twist of fate, Blake Cutter now found himself backing up the man who he felt, just three months earlier, had betrayed his trust and friendship.

Chapter 67

McBain resisted the temptation to revisit their past partnership in police cases. He ordered Cutter to remain next to McBain's vehicle while he approached the front of the store. He advised Cutter to only assist him if requested. It would be the only circumstances that a civilian would be allowed to assist a police officer, a situation where there's an imminent threat of death or severe injury to a police officer or a civilian bystander.

Seconds later, McBain reached to open the entrance door of the store. But by then, the suspected second shooter, who exited out the back door, had flashed around the left side of the store where his getaway car parked a short distance away. McBain spotted him and yelled, "Stop where you are!" McBain tripped and stumbled over a raised section of broken sidewalk and was off balance. At that moment, the shooter raised his weapon in a split second and wildly fired one round hitting McBain's left leg. McBain fell to the ground and his Glock fell out of his hand and tumbled a few feet away.

The shooters started to run away but looked back and noticed McBain dragging himself on the ground towards the weapon. The shooter thought he might have been identified and seized the sudden opportunity to eliminate the witness.

With disdainful arrogance, the shooter approached McBain to finish him off. He moved to within three feet of McBain, trained his .45 caliber Smith and Wesson on McBain's forehead and paused for a brief second to savor the moment. McBain looked up at him, emotions split between sudden terror with the thought his life was about to end and desperate hope that some Godly intervention would occur.

Suddenly, there was a loud bang. The right side of the gunman's skull burst open with spewing blood as a single bullet pierced his temple. In a split second, his face contorted to paralyzed shock before he plummeted to the ground. He was dead on impact. The fatal bullet came from the personal weapon belonging to ex-cop and former SBI partner Blake Cutter.

Cutter ran up and quickly leaned down to the injured McBain. "Are you alright, partner?" he asked. Cutter quickly tore the right sleeve of his own shirt and wrapped it around McBain's wound. "I'll get you an ambulance."

McBain muttered in pain, "I'm alright. Just call dispatch for back-up. There may be another shooter somewhere in the area."

Chapter 68

Meanwhile, Penelope sat at the edge of a bench in a secluded part of the park waiting for Blake to arrive. It had been over an hour since she'd arrived there, and due to a recent spike in assaults in Bullet, she feared for her safety. She didn't have a phone to call him, so she was faced with a decision. Should she wait longer and risk some group of rogue teenagers harassing or even assaulting her? Or should she forego the meeting for her own security. With her martial arts training, she felt confident she could defend herself against one assailant but not a group of thugs.

She thought, *where the hell is he? Is he standing me up? Is he waiting for the police to arrive so he could escort them to the park and arrest me?* She realized her OCD, which always crept in when she was nervous, was orchestrating the thoughts. But with her freedom at stake, she couldn't risk it was. She bolted away from the scene before being recognized. What she didn't know was that Cutter was attending to his injured former partner and had decided to wait until the police and ambulance arrived.

When the first responder team arrive, McBain informed them of the shooting and gave them a verbal statement. Fortunately, for Cutter, the first police unit to arrive were two patrol officers who knew him and didn't question his role in the incident. When the EMT van arrived, it took the emergency technicians less than five minutes to IV McBain and then took him away from the scene for transport to the nearest hospital.

Minutes later, Cutter jogged up to the entrance to Hurley Park. He looked around and then proceeded directly to the playground and recreation area where he'd told her to wait. Once he arrived at that location, he peered around the area, but she was nowhere to be found. He spent the next twenty minutes circling the main pedestrian areas of the park until he was convinced, she had left. *But where did she go?* His feelings were mixed between anxiety and concern that he couldn't locate her. He assumed she headed back to Watkins because he was late.

Cutter returned to the convenient store in time to speak to the BPD onsite officer in charge who was busy conducting a preliminary investigation. He informed Cutter he'd received a radio call from the EMTs that McBain had been transported to BRMC, the same hospital where the bombing and the kidnapping of Penelope had occurred. Despite his concern and curiosity about Penelope's whereabouts, his first obligation was to check on the recovery of his former partner. He decided to drive to BRMC.

At three a.m., while Cutter patiently sat in the waiting room, the wounded McBain was transported from the Surgical Ward where a team of surgeons and nurses removed the bullet from his leg and provided the necessary post-op care. He was then transitioned through the recovery room to an inpatient bed for overnight observation.

At three thirty, Cutter was notified by the attending surgeon that everything had gone smoothly with McBain's surgery, and he would be released the next day at noon provided there were no setbacks or infections from the surgery. He gave Cutter permission to visit him but for no more than ten minutes.

After stopping briefly at a vending machine to grab a cup of coffee, Cutter walked into McBain's room and found his former partner woozy but conscious and alert. He was heavily bandaged around the wounded area of his left leg. Cutter saw the thick wrap through the hospital nightgown as McBain lay on top of the bed sheets with an IV in his left arm and a breathing tube in his nose. His face appeared bloodless, but his expression was upbeat and welcoming to Cutter's arrival.

"You'll do anything for a day off!" Cutter commented jovially as he approached the head of the bed and squeezed Alex's left arm above the IV.

"Careful mate!" McBain barked as he winced in pain from the sensation. "Why don't you just kick me in the leg and call it a day?"

"Sorry, Alex!" Cutter bantered back. "How are you, partner?"

"I'm alive," McBain responded appreciatively. "I guess I should thank you for saving my life."

"That's what ex-partners are for," Cutter added.

"You're still my favorite partner and I owe you a big one," McBain noted.

Cutter broke a grin but then walked back to the room door and shut it. He returned to McBain's beside with a somber expression. "Well, I really need one now."

McBain scooted upward in the bed. "Anything I can do for you, mate.""

Cutter paused and sighed, "Well, this one can't involve the SBI. . . only you. Penelope Lane's in danger, and I need your help in a big way."

"But she's confined to the psych hospital," McBain noted.

"I know," Cutter interrupted. "But look, since DeSalvo's dead, she fears she'll be targeted. She's sure DeSalvo's men are coming after her because she knows some things about them. I was supposed to meet her tonight and I think she was going to reveal some information to me, but then this happened to you. She told me earlier she'd received suspicious phone calls at the hospital but can't identify the caller."

"And how can you be sure about this? How do you know she's being honest about this?" McBain asked, grumbling with an inquisitive, doubting look. "You're under an indefinite no-contact order along with your suspension. You screw that up and you'll never get back a job back in law enforcement, much less SBI or MPD."

Cutter paused and scoffed, saying, "Look Alex, I met with her tonight before the convenient store incident. She left the hospital tonight and met with me near there, and we were supposed to meet again."

"McBain sat straighter and furrowed his brow. "You mean, she escaped from the hospital?"

With McBain staring upward, Cutter confirmed his statement. "Let's just say she left, but she intended to sneak back in before daylight."

"I would ask how, but I really don't want to know."

"Good," Cutter acknowledged. "I didn't get to talk to her but for a few minutes. She's got a lot more to tell me about what's happening. I asked her to wait for me at Hurley Park. Then, I ran into you and your robbery buddies.

After the EMTs got to you and I gave my statement, I went to the park, but she was gone. I don't know if she's missing, if she went back to the hospital on her own or what happened to her."

McBain glared at him. "A fine mess, chap. That's sounds like it's the state's problem now, not yours." McBain argued. "How many times do I have to say, you and this woman?"

Cutting to the chase, Cutter gritted his teeth and talked on, "Look Alex. I know this seems crazy, but I feel personally responsible for her safety. Plus, she knows things from her relationship with Phillip Drummond that can help me find out who murdered my wife. This is about justice, Alex. I don't have a lot of time to discuss it. I just need to know you got my back and I can call on you to help me or get information for me discreetly if I need you in the next few weeks. I'm especially interested if you hear any talk around the water cooler about DeSalvo's connection to a big mob boss in Miami named Ransom Oliver."

"You're talking about the reputed leader of the east coast syndicate?" McBain asked rhetorically.

Cutter nodded.

McBain laid back on his pillow and rolled his eyes momentarily. He then raised his head and looked intensely at Cutter. "You better be right about this, mate. I don't know if helping you in this situation is payment for you saving my life."

Cutter knew McBain was being sarcastic and was subtly giving him the green light. Without an affirmation, Cutter said, "Thanks, partner. Don't worry about anything. I won't ask you to jeopardize your career for me . . . just get you a date with Internal Affairs."

"You're about to fuck this up, already."

Cutter leaned down and gave him a fist bump. "You're the best partner a guy could ever have."

As Cutter walked to the door, McBain said, "I'm not really your partner now, if you haven't noticed."

Cutter stopped, turned, and replied, "That's not what you said earlier. I'm holding you to it."

As Cutter exited the door, McBain leaned back, shaking his head in disbelief and deep concern.

Moments later, Cutter exited the BRMC, got in his car, and drove back to the west end of Bullet to Hurley Park. He had to make one last search for Penelope before he'd plan a secret early morning visit to Watkins.

Chapter 69

4 a.m. – Watkins Psychiatric Hospital

Rico parked their white, non-descript panel van in a secluded distant parking lot on the Watkins Psychiatric Hospital grounds. The twenty-year old facility located on 110 acres of state property in Southern Georgia was the only remaining long-term psychiatric institution in the state and housed over one hundred long-term patients and over fifty rehabilitative patients.

Rico and Spector were exiting out the same nondescript white van they'd used in the BRMC hospital bombing. Minutes later, they approached the main security booth a hundred yards from the driveway that led to the circular entrance to the main building. Each wore thin black windbreakers over olive green coveralls, brown work boots, and plain green baseball caps. They wanted to appear as service workers.

They feigned the complacent security guard, who was finishing a 24-hour shift, with a false identity and work assignment, then signed in and proceeded on the dark path between several adjacent annex buildings. A dead roving security guard with two bullet holes in his skull was deposited in an unused dumpster located behind a row of hedges near the entrance road. There were no witnesses to the shooting. No one overheard any noise to them groaning as they dragged the overweight man to the dumpster. As they retraced their steps, Rico collected the shell casing for the semi-automatic pistol that he'd used on the guard.

Next, they needed to convince the night security guard at the entrance desk, who would respond to the bell and come to the locked, security door, to let them into the hospital. They each had only one extra magazine remaining with ten rounds. They wanted to preserve the ammunition for any potential but unexpected shootout within the facility. They had rehearsed the day before when they'd conducted a dry run of the security of the facility. They didn't know if the guard would allow them unaccompanied access to the wards or if they'd have to take another innocent victim's life to complete their mission.

With DeSalvo dead and the Bullet drug and weapons smuggling terminated, Penelope Lane had become expendable. Ransom Oliver, the Miami-based head of the entire East Coast consortium, had ordered her elimination.

After three minutes of waiting outside, the graveyard shift security guard approached the glass door allowing him to view the two visitors prior to granting access to the front reception area of the hospital. What it didn't do was prevent a bullet from being fired through it. The glass, which was installed years prior than when architectural, tempered glass was available on the market, was stronger than normal or annealed glass. But it was not bullet-proof.

A blonde-haired, thinly built man in his late twenties named Tatum Holmes approached the door. He glanced at his watch and noticed the time was four a.m., four hours before he was expected to see the normal hospital staff walk in after utilizing their card key badges to access the hospital.

Attached to the glass door was a two-sided metal compartment where a driver's license or other identification could be passed through to the guard to verify.

"May I help you?" Holmes asked through the glass.

Spector said, "We're here from maintenance. We have an order to check the AC system."

Holmes brow furrowed. He glanced at his watch again. "At this hour? Nobody told me any maintenance crew would be coming this early."

The two men remained silent. Spector shrugged and gave a bland expression. Holmes instantly became nervous and felt suspicious. "You mind passing me your identification?" he asked.

At that point, Rico reached into his jacket, pulled out his Glock pistol and pointed it at Holmes' face.

"What did you ask?" Rico asked, arrogantly.

Holmes panicked and nearly shit in his pants.

"Open the goddamn door!" Spector barked.

"What the hell's going on?" Holmes asked. "We don't have any money in here."

"Open the damn door or he'll shoot you through this glass!" Spector shouted.

Without delay, Holmes nervously reached into his pocket and retrieved a set of keys and used the largest one on the key ring to unlock the door. He wasn't about to reveal to the intruders that a single button was the automatic unlock device.

Both Rico and Spector glanced behind them to ensure they weren't being observed. Then, as they entered, Rico shoved the gun barrel against Holmes' chest and ordered him to lead them to the front desk. "Don't do anything stupid or I'll blow your heart out your back," Rico snarled.

Approaching the front desk, they noted it was unmanned for the night. There was one receptionist on duty, but she spent most of her time hanging out in a nearby office due to not expecting to have any inquiries or visitors at the reception desk during the early morning hours. She certainly didn't have an order for a maintenance team to visit.

"Where is Penelope Lane's room?" Spector asked Holmes.

Holmes eyebrows raised. In a high-pitched tone he replied, "How the hell am I supposed to know? I only work night security."

"I'm gonna kill you right now if you don't tell us where she is?" Rico barked, assuming he was stalling and unaware of hospital protocols. He pointed his gun directly at Holmes' forehead.

Holmes nervously swallowed hard. "Wait! Let me page the front desk receptionist. She can look it up." Holmes had spent many nights working the graveyard shift with Tammy Fontenot, and he knew what number to call to reach her. Keeping his eyes on the gun, he cleared his throat and dialed her cell number. She answered and he asked, "Can you come down here, Tammy?"

"I'm busy, Tatum," she complained. She had nodded off for a catnap on the office sofa when her cell phone buzzed. She had another part time job as a hotel receptionist and had worked the day shift, so she was exhausted and extremely irritable the entire night. "This better be something important or I'm gonna kick your ass for messing with me. I came in here to get some sleep and now you want to screw with my life after midnight?"

"I need you to look up a patient's room number," he said to her in a stronger tone. "We've got a call on the landline from—from . . ."

"From a relative!" Spector helped him out.

"It's an emergency call from a patient's relative," Holmes stammered.

Tammy wanted to ask for the patient's name and just provided the room number on the phone but instinctively felt wary of the request. She realized she needed to be careful not to give a patient's room number to a security guard, allowing him to enter a patient's room and commit a sexual assault on her watch. Selfishly, she feared being fired from a part time job she desperately needed to pay her rent more than concern for patient safety. But she knew Tatum well enough to trust him.

"Goddamn it!" she scowled. "It's four in the frickin' morning! Okay, I'll be right down," she relented with a big yawn.

Chapter 70

Minutes later, a haggard and drowsy Tammy approached the front desk and encountered the two intruders and Holmes. Then, she glared over at the front door and observed that the front security door was open and the red light indicating 'locked' was not activated.

"What's going on, Tatum?" she asked as she stared at the two rough looking men.

Before Holmes could speak, Rico moved the gun from behind his back and pointed it at her face. "You do anything stupid and you'll both die."

Tammy shrieked. "Oh! Please don't shoot me. What do you want with us?"

Spector said, "Listen, lady. You won't get hurt if you take us down to Penelope Lane's room. We just need to speak to her and then we'll be on our way."

"Who are you guys?" she asked. "I'm not allowed to send anyone to patients' rooms without authorization."

Holmes heart nearly jumped out of his skin, and he knew they were one objection away from being shot. He interrupted and pleaded, "Just—just find her room number and do whatever they say, Tammy . . . please." Holmes eyes shifted to where a buzzer was located under the middle of the desk. Then, he stared at the shooter to see if they were looking at his hands. So, he made a slow movement toward the buzzer.

But Spector was quick to notice the shift in Holmes' eyes. He'd been involved in convenience store robberies as a teen. "Don't even think about it." He barked at Holmes as he reached for his jacket, pulled his gun, and pointed it at Tammy's face. "Get over there and look up her room number," he ordered Tammy. "You do anything wrong, and I swear I'll kill both of you."

Shaking violently, her face blanched and tears began to stream down her cheeks. She wanted to comply but was suddenly frozen and traumatized.

"Get over there, NOW!" Spector shouted at her. "Don't make me tell you again!"

There was about twenty yards of separation in both directions between the front reception desk and the first set of patient rooms. Spector felt confident the change in pitch in his voice was not overheard. Nevertheless, he took a moment and walked down each side of the hallway and glared down them to ensure no one opened their room door and looked out.

Spector sprinted back to the front desk, spurting out to Tammy, "Let's go!" as she nervously flipped through the room assignment book and located Penelope Lane's room number.

In the meantime, Spector told Rico, "Anyone come down these hallways, you kill 'em."

As Tammy nervously announced, "Ward B, Room Two Nineteen."

The two-man execution squad felt panic and decided to take another casualty rather than risk being identified or risk being overtaken by the guard as some stage of their mission. Spector pulled from his windbreaker pocket a pistol with a silencer and shot Holmes in the chest.

Holmes gasped, then fell to the floor with a hard thud. Blood immediately began seeping through his shirt. His eyes were locked open as his body began shaking, but he was conscious.

Tammy screamed and nearly fainted on the spot. As she stumbled to her hair and horror, Rico walked over to her, grabbed her by her disheveled hair, and put his wrought iron-like right paw over her mouth. She maturely composed herself sucking in deep hyperventilating breaths.

"Take us to her room," Rico ordered her.

Spector grabbed the legs of the unconscious bleeding security guard and dragged him behind the receptionist desk to a storage room behind it. He then shut the door. He noticed the trail of blood on the floor but decided they didn't have time to attempt to clean it up.

Ward B was in the east wing of the hospital and consisted of a nurse's station, a cafeteria, a visitor's lounge, a laundry room and thirty-two patient rooms. It had been modeled from 3-star hotel chains to try to make patients feel at home and relaxed. It took less than five minutes to walk from the main hospital area, through a long corridor and to the east wing.

It was the longest walk of Tammy's life as the burrito she had devoured an hour earlier elevated into her throat cavity and she vomited. Her legs felt like they were weighed down with chains as she struggled to maintain her balance. Her complexion became blanched. She had a protective nature for the patients in the hospital and her thoughts shifted to fear that one or more of them would emerge in the hallway.

The two shooters followed her to the elevator with Spector keeping the barrel of his pistol over her left shoulder. He was ready to take her hostage if they confronted another security guard.

Rico's eyes became locked on the emergency pull lever. As they entered the elevator, he pushed her over to the opposite side of the lever, so she had no opportunity to grasp it.

"Are there any security or guards on these floors?" Spector asked her strongly.

"No—no!" she answered. "Please don't shoot any of our patients if they wander into the hallway. They are not coherent and would never try to bother us."

As the elevator rose, Spector widened his lips in acknowledgement, but then retorted, "You just shut up and worry about your own damn life."

As they reached the exit floor, Tammy's thoughts shifted from total terror to remorse that she had not taken a bullet by rushing over and pressing the emergency buzzer behind the reception desk. *They do not shoot women. They only wanted to talk to her,* rationalized thoughts raced through her mind. Truthfully, she knew she was dead once they reached Penelope's room. But she had no idea what to do other than comply with their orders.

Chapter 71

When they reached Ward B, the first thing they saw was an unmanned nurse's station. Looking closely, Spector saw a woman with her head down on a desk asleep. An elderly woman with a walker passed in the hallway. If she had been younger and fully in control of her faculties, she would have become the second hostage. But she had been in the psychiatric facility for over fifteen years and had dementia. She was wondering aimlessly and without attention to them, so the shooters passed by her without concern as Tammy resisted the temptation to alert the woman of her plight while simultaneously feeling a sense of relief that the elderly woman wasn't shot.

As they quietly passed the desk without awakening the receptionist, they continued down the hallway. Spector pushed his weapons into Tammy's back and asked complaining, "I thought you said no one else was on these floors?"

"You asked me about guards or security?" she replied stammering.

Recognizing his fault in questioning, Spector simply responded, "Alright, just keep moving."

The tenth door on the right was Room 219. Tammy's heart palpitated as they approached it. She thought of her five-year old son who was being cared for by her sister overnight. *What if he kills me and I don't get to say goodbye to my son?* She thought to herself. Tears streamed down her face, and she envisioned her last moment on earth being her son standing over her grave.

As Rico craned his neck to look down the long hallway, Spector ordered Tammy to knock on the door.

"What are you gonna do to me?" she asked shaking.

"Once she comes to the door, you can get the hell out of here," Spector told her. "If you pull that alarm or tell anyone, I'll be back to see you."

"Please don't kill our patient," Tammy pleaded with him.

"Shut up!" Spector whispered in a soft but strong tone. "Knock on the door!"

Tammy knocked lightly three times but there was no answer. She felt relieved and exhaled another deep sigh.

"Knock again, harder," Spector quickly ordered her.

Tammy did. Once again, there was silence.

Spector nodded to Rico. Rico moved the handle and the door opened slightly.

Spector and Rico entered the room, but very sloppily took their eyes off Tammy. She instinctively seized the moment and darted down the hallway toward an emergency stairway

Rico reacted and stepped into the hallway and pointed his pistol towards her back. Before he could shoot, Spector grabbed his arm.

"Do not worry about her. Let her go," Spector said to him. "No noise. Let us just do for what we came here."

As they darted into the room, they were shocked to find that no one was inside. There was a queen size bed, a dresser mirror and chest, a small table and chair, and a 30-inch flatscreen TV attached to a light green painted wall. But there was no occupant.

"Fuck! Don't tell me that bitch lied to us. Look in the bathroom!" Spector ordered Rico as he scratched his scalp.

Rico flashed into the small bathroom and saw it unoccupied. "She ain't here."

"Fuck!" Spector repeated as he stood momentarily in thought. "Let's get the hell out of here." Then, Spector stopped in his tracks, looked at Rico and said, "Wait a minute. As Rico watched, Spector reached inside the right pocket of his jacket and pulled out two miniature wireless audio listening devices, both fitted with a solid adhesive to stick to a surface. On the sofa, he placed one under the bottom near one of the back legs. He then moved to the coffee table and placed the second device under the middle bottom of the table. "Okay, now we can go," he said to Rico.

Moments later, Spector and Rico exited the ward out the same emergency exit stairway as Tammy. They thought for a moment to head back to the main reception desk to find her and kill her. But they realized if she was smart and courageous enough to risk her life and flee, she was smart enough not to return to where she was taken hostage.

Once they reached the ground floor exit door, they kicked it open, which activated the hospital alarm system. They hastily left the hospital to access the parking lot where they'd parked their vehicle.

Rico and Spector's mission to locate and execute the patient Penelope Lane was unsuccessful that misty early morning . . . but they would be back.

Chapter 72

Penelope Lane was missing.

Minutes after the two mob intruders left the Watkins Psychiatric Hospital, police responded to the scene. It was four thirty a.m. when they approached a visibly shaken Tammy Fontenot. She had frantically made her way back to the front desk-delirious and horrified, but unharmed after she escaped from the mobsters. She was emotionally terrified when the biggest thug murdered one of the staff members in front of her because he didn't cooperate fast enough.

Several uniformed officers, detectives and tactical team members spent the next two hours interviewing her then fanning out and scouring all three wings of the facility including patient rooms, bathrooms, closets, and stairways in hopes of locating the missing patient, Penelope Lane. Tammy couldn't confirm if the missing patent had been kidnapped by the thugs or if she had escaped on her own.

The police patrolled the outer grounds of the hospital, checking unlocked cars, inside the hospital, and behind mature trees and bushes. They searched every potential hiding place in case she'd stayed on the property and tried to return to her room after the danger had passed.

There was one place the police had neglected to look. It was behind the tall hedges at the back of the hospital. That's where she hid until the police had departed the area. Now, the next part of her plan was about to be set into motion. She moved from behind the hedges and proceeded over to behind a storage shed closer to the side door. From that location, she had an unobstructed view of the activity at the back of the hospital entrance. Her plan was to sneak back to her room, pick up her belongings and medications and leave for good. She hated being holed up in a filthy county jail and then remanded to Watkins. But she realized it was a safer place than being locked in a women's prison. Inside prison, there would've been plenty of female mob associates who would've been utilized to carry out Ransom Oliver's order to eliminate her.

At six thirty, two Bullet Police Department detectives arrived on the scene. They were briefed on the situation and immediately escorted by a hospital administrator to Penelope's room. As expected, they confirmed Penelope was missing and made a cursory search of the entire floor and then her room. What they didn't detect were the electronic listening devices under the sofa and the table that Spector had planted there hours earlier.

Spector and Rico had fled the facility but remained hiding out near the entrance road hoping to spot Penelope if she returned.

Cutter arrived at the facility about ten minutes after the two BPD detectives. After parking at the far edge of the front lot, he got out and noticed the flashing beacons in front of the building, A chill ran down his spine as his first thought was Penelope Lane had been killed inside the facility by Oliver's assassins.

Given his current view of several police cruisers out front, he concluded it would be equally unlikely he would be able to sneak into the hospital to try and help her escape from the facility. Aiding or abetting the escape of an incarcerated patient would land him in jail and eliminate any attempt to be reinstated to the police force. He couldn't risk losing the opportunity to hunt down his wife's killer. But he also couldn't risk going into the hospital to look for Penelope until the police departed. So, he slipped back into his car and waited.

Chapter 73

At seven that morning, storms clouds gave way to a burnt orange eastern sun. Blake Cutter rose from his crouched position in his car and noticed a slew of police cars and emergency vehicles departing the hospital grounds with only a few remaining to continue the initial investigation. There were also two news media trucks stationed near the entrance road with their towers extended, waiting to broadcast a follow-up story and see if anything else developed that would be considered newsworthy.

Just as Cutter was deciding to drive and park closer to the entrance, he noticed a nondescript, extended, black van passed through the unmanned front gate and proceeded up to the front of the building.

Exiting the passenger side front door was a grey-haired, hunchbacked man wearing a tan all-weather coat, khakis pants, loafers, and carrying a black leather satchel. Then, a younger pony-tailed white male in his thirties wearing a blue denim shirt and jeans followed. In near unison, they moved to the back of the van, opened the door, and pulled forward a mobile stretcher. The legs expanded before the wheels touched the ground, and the driver pushed it towards the front door alone behind the elderly man. Cutter was too far away to recognize them, but he surmised it was the county coroner and his assistant, arriving to retrieve a deceased person for what had obviously been called in as a suspicious death.

The two men were greeted and escorted into the building as Cutter continued to remain in place in his vehicle.

Ten minutes later, Cutter patience had run its course. He felt it was time now for him to spring into action. He got out and went to the trunk of his car, opened it, and removed a leather hat that had a wide floppy brim he would use to conceal his identity from security cameras as he approached the hospital.

Suddenly, he spotted the coroner and his assistant departing the front entrance with the assistant wheeling a stretcher with a body covered in a white sheet. The coroner assisted the driver in loading the stretcher into the back of the van. They then hopped into the van for a trip to the county morgue. A chill slithered through his spine as he wondered if the person on the stretcher Penelope was indeed. But then, a few minutes later, he got the answer.

Two men approached the front entrance from the left side of the building. They opened the door and casually walked in as the entrance was temporarily unsecured due to the chaos and confusion from the earlier morning police incident.

As the taller of the two men came back to the front door and looked out toward the parking lot, Cutter's eyebrows raised, as did his blood pressure.

It rose to a boiling point. He recognized the man immediately. It was the same man who had assaulted him in Penelope Lane's hospital room. He had the same dreadlocks, and the same robust physique with an oversized upper frame. Cutter only had a two second glance, but it was long enough. There was no mistaking the thug. It was Rico Calderon, accompanied back into the hospital by Spector McShane.

Two emotions rocketed through his soul. The first was fear; a realization of why they were there. The second was rage; a burning desire to satisfy his need for revenge against the man who had assaulted him.

As the man in dreads turned away from the entrance, Cutter stepped out of his car and scurried briskly towards the front entrance. Moments later, he entered the front doors unchallenged and observed activity near the reception desk.

Four uniformed police officers, two detectives and a hospital administrator stood before two news crews clamoring for details regarding the criminal incident and murder which occurred hours before. What Cutter didn't see was the two mob henchmen. They, too, had slipped past the hysteria and were somewhere in the hospital.

Cutter couldn't afford to be noticed or recognized. He eased past the loud chatter with his head cocked while looking off to the side and sauntered down the hallway to the left. He instinctively chose left when faced with a choice. He decided to trust his instincts again.

As he proceeded down the long hallway, several heads extended from rooms to listen and learn what was happening with the frequent footsteps marching past their doors.

Once Spector and Rico turned off the main corridor and entered C-wing they stopped for a moment. Spector grabbed a remote monitor from his pants pocket.

"I'm picking up sound from her room," he said. "Hopefully, she's inside and it's not staff or cops. Let's find this bitch and do her!"

Cutter reached the junction of the C-wing and saw the two men walking down the corridor about twenty yards ahead of him. Cutter followed them. He stayed far enough behind and hugged the wall so they wouldn't detect him. His sidearm was in his right hand near his thigh. Then, he noticed the rapid pace and instinctively knew where they were going. They continued to check the placards located next to doors until they reached the door for which they were searching.

As they knocked on Penelope's door, Cutter slid behind a tall food cart in the hallway, four rooms away from the thugs.

A young woman in a pale blue uniform approached and removed two food trays. Cutter held his firearm behind his back and wished her a Good Morning.

Penelope stood near a couch with a window behind it. She overheard soft voices from the hallway as she opened the window. She would have to return later to retrieve the evidence she wanted Cutter to have.

As Cutter observed, Rico used a credit card to breach the locked door. He conferred with Spector momentarily, then opened it surreptitiously. As the men slowly eased the door open, Penelope crawled out the window to escape. Spector saw her and raised his suppressed 9mm pistol. He fired two rounds at the window opening.

As Penelope fell, the first bullet grazed her left heel. She shrieked in pain as she landed clumsily in a heap on the ground outside.

Cutter overheard the suppressed sounds of both shots and Penelope's scream. He leaped from behind the food cart and ran full-bore towards the door.

Patients poked their heads out to see what caused the sharp noises. But nobody came out of their rooms.

As he reached the open door, he saw Rico following Spector out the window in pursuit of Penelope. Beyond them, she was hobbling away to the center courtyard area. Cutter raced across the room and saw Spector couch, aim, and fire three rounds at her.

Both of Penelope's arms rose over her head as she screamed, stumbled, and fell to the ground with a hard thud.

Cutter had one leg out the window when Penelope was hit.

Chapter 74

Rico ran towards Spector as he stood over the wounded, moaning Penelope. Spector was poised to finish her off.

Just as Spector grinned and aimed his pistol at her head, Rico noticed a security camera on the side of the building with the lens pointed in their direction. He grabbed Spector by the arm and said, "Forget her man. Let's get the hell out of here! We're on camera and those police officers at the entrance will be here quickly after hearing all the shooting you've done."

Spector immediately put the pistol in the back of his belt loop before the two turned to hustle toward their car.

Cutter had his gun in hand, assumed a two-handed shooting stance, and shouted, "Stop where you are!"

Rico turned. Cutter recognized him.

Rico fired a shot which whizzed by Cutter and shattered a window behind him.

Cutter fired two rounds back, one striking Rico in the right shoulder and the other hitting Spector in the chest. Both thugs cried out as blood flowed immediately from their wounds.

Rico cursed as he grabbed the bent over Spector and dragged him along.

"Fucking shit!" Rico shouted as they sprinted toward their van in the parking lot.

Rico clutched his partner with his left arm and righted him when he stumbled and almost fell.

Cutter fired another shot, but he missed as his thoughts had instinctively shifted to Penelope sprawled on the ground lying on her back and sobbing loudly in pain. Her legs were limp from the bullets embedded in her back. Blood trickled and pooled underneath her dress. Her eyes were sunken. She squinted and winced from the excruciating pain.

Cutter knew instantly if she didn't get immediate medical attention, she could die. He ignored the retreating thugs and committed himself to attend to her. As he knelt beside her, Penelope uttered as she swallowed blood, "I'm gonna die, Blake, I feel it. I'm sorry I let you down!"

"Please don't try to talk, just breathe deep," he pleaded. "Help is nearby. We're on the grounds of a hospital." He noticed the pool of blood widening next to her body and clenched his teeth in frustration. His nerves were on edge as his hands shook.

"You're gonna be okay!" he falsely assured her. "Just don't pass out on me, sweetie!" He took her cool hand in his and held it gently.

"Blake, I wanted . . ."

"Sweetie don't try to talk!" he urged her.

She gasped for air as she spit up blood and said, "No, I have to say this. I love you and I wanted so much to be your wife after my sister died!" Globs of blood continue to roll from her mouth.

Cutter eyebrows raised. He stuttered, "Sister . . . what sister? What are you talking about? Stay with me, sweetheart." he followed in a tender but desperate voice. "Don't try to talk anymore."

She swallowed hard then spit up another botch of blood. "Jenni . . ." she uttered in a faint tone. "Jenni . . . Jenni was my sister! Her eyes widened in pain. Her head jerked and shifted to the right as her eyes rolled toward the sky and stared blankly. Her breathing was faint . . . then nonexistent.

Cutter felt her pulse. Her split was gone. Her body had stopped moving. He held back a river of tears. Out of desperation, he started chest compressions. Blood spewed out of her mouth and nose with every compression. There was no breath, not even a bubble of oxygen in the crimson discharge. After the second set, he stopped and stared at her face. There was no sign of life. He checked her pulse again.

Nothing.

He used two fingers to close her open eyelids.

Penelope Lane was not breathing.

Cutter did CPR for another minute hoping to revive the gunshot wounded Penelope Lane's breathing. He had to face the inevitable as he had exhausted himself.

Penelope Lane, the doppelganger of his slain wife Jenni Cutter, was dead.

Chapter 75

Cutter pulled himself together to prevent breaking down. He wiped his bloody hands on the grass as thoughts about his next move flashed through his troubled mind. He couldn't be found by her body. He had to leave the crime scene.

Keeping his hat tilted toward the building where security cameras were mounted, he ran to the back corner of the building and waited. He guessed no more than five or six minutes had elapsed since the barrage of shots were fired. Police and hospital personnel should be appearing at any minute.

Finally, two uniformed police officers rounded the hospital's front corner with two figures in white following them. Seconds later, a plain clothes detective crawled through the window of Penelope's room and onto the grounds.

Cutter had seen enough; Penelope was in good hands. He turned and darted away toward the back woods. He would be seen by patients some of whom could describe the man they'd seen running away. A change of clothes and escape from the parking lot were his next priorities.

Moments later, he climbed over the exterior fence, ducked behind a tree, and glanced back at the converging crowd.

His heart sank as he noticed two paramedics approaching Penelope on a dead run carrying their first aid cases and pulling a stretcher. A small crowd of patients and staff were forming near the side of the building but made an opening for the techs to pass through.

He couldn't watch any more. He safely slinked from the area, circled the grounds, and eventually saw his car. Cutter imagined a large crowd of ward nurses, hospital administrators, and nosy patients gathering onto the outer grounds to watch as the EMS waited for the coroner to return to Watkins for the second time in four hours. The news media trucks were still parked waiting for further developments. He was sure reporters and camera operators were in the crowd.

Cutter sat in his car at the edge of the parking lot. He started the car and slowly drove across the asphalt to the exit. Police sirens blared in the near distance as they responded to the third murder of the morning.

Cutter drove three blocks at the speed limit to a nearby diner where he sat in a corner booth facing away from the entrance door. He ordered a cappuccino and a bagel and frequently glanced at a flat screen TV on the wall behind the main counter. He watched to see if there was any breaking news coverage on the local station about Penelope's murder.

He stayed there until ten, but nothing was broadcast about the incidents at Watkins. He figured it would be on the midday news at the earliest, so he made a mental note to stop somewhere to watch it. He didn't want to be seen going back to his apartment.

While waiting, he finally had time to recall the shocking news Penelope revealed to him right before her death.

Jenni was her sister; she had said just before she died.

Cutter then punched McBain's number on one of his burner phones. He needed someone to talk to; someone he could trust.

Chapter 76

Alex McBain was still in BRMC recovering from his wounds from the convenient store robbery. Given McBain's dedication to duty, Cutter felt confident that Alex's cell phone was at his bedside and activated. Cutter hoped McBain had been taken off the strong pain medication, so he would be coherent enough to take his phone call.

As expected, when Cutter called, McBain answered.

Cutter was tempted to skip the normal pleasantries but didn't want to come off as insensitive. "How are you partner?"

"Lucky to be alive, I guess," McBain replied in a shaky voice. "That perp got the jump on me, so I guess I'm lucky I survived."

"Yes, you are," Cutter said in agreement. "The angels are with you, partner. I'm hedging by bet you'll make a full recovery sooner than expected."

"I've never you as a consoling, cheerleader type, Blake," McBain noted. "I can sense this is a prelude to a favor you need. So go ahead and lay it on me."

"You know me, Alex. As usual, I need your help. There is a big problem."

"Let's hear it," McBain replied cautiously, not sure he wanted to know what Cutter had gotten himself into now.

"Penelope's dead!" Cutter told him bluntly.

"Wa-What?" McBain asked, stammering."

"They got to her."

"They who?" McBain asked.

"Oliver's henchmen . . . the same ones DeSalvo used in the hospital bombing. They shot her at Watkins. But that's not the only shocker. Before she died, she said she was Jenni's sister and knew about something terrible Oliver is planning."

"Why don't you go to SBI HQ to see Ryker and read him in on your involvement in all this?" McBain inquired.

Cutter countered in the raised voice, "Are you kidding, Alex. Haven't you forgot I'm suspended and if I show my face or even call Ryker, he'll have me arrested and prosecuted."

"I think you're wrong here," Alex argued. "Ryker can underwrite your involvement actions. He owes you a few favors and enough time has passed that he might got to bat for you if you've got something concrete that can lead him to Oliver."

Cutter retorted, "The problem is that it's out of Ryker's control. As soon as the Feds would get wind of this, I would be sucked into the wind tunnel of prosecutions. I'm not taking that chance."

McBain paused momentarily to suck in a deep breath. He was confused by how to proceed. "You are right, chap. Where are you now, Blake?" he asked Cutter instinctively, to get an assessment of the situation.

"I'm at a coffee shop, several blocks from Watkins," he admitted without revealing his exact location. His two burner phones were untraceable, but he felt uneasy talking details over unsecured lines. There was no room for gambling.

"I need a favor, Alex."

"Another?"

"Yeah another, and this is big."

"Let me guess," McBain huffed. "You believe this woman wasn't delirious in her death confession and you want me to verify the sibling relationship."

Cutter paused to prep his justification and calm his annoyance with McBain's perceived reluctance. "She was telling me the truth, Alex. People tend to clear their conscious when facing their mortality."

"I get it," McBain agreed.

Cutter continued, "Before this incident, Penelope sneaked out of the facility and met with me downtown. After we talked, she left to go back to the hospital to get something and then she was going to leave for good. She felt they would try and kill her there and they succeeded."

"Why did she meet with you?" McBain sounded alarmed.

"Another story I'll tell you about later," Cutter cut him off. "She was already off the hospital ground and could have escaped. Oliver's henchmen were there waiting for her at the hospital and shot her. I shot and wounded them both, but they escaped when I stayed with Penelope."

"I really need to bring Ryker in on this," McBain declared. "This is gonna be complicated.

"No!" Cutter argued. "I really don't want Ryker or Carruthers knowing about my involvement in this. She has been picked up by the coroner so things will transpire as usual with a homicide death. Will you help me with this, and how soon will you be able to?"

McBain rose to a sitting position on the bed and thought for a moment.

"Look, Blake. I won't be released from this place until tomorrow at the earliest. Ryker's already ordered me to bed rest for a few days. He's gonna have agents coming to my house every day to check on me. I can't go back to Terre Haute until early next week. I'll do this on my own time and my own dime, mate."

"I don't care if it takes until next week because I don't have any other options, but I can reimburse all your expenses," Cutter pointed out. His agreement was simply necessary to get off the phone.

"Serious, chap," McBain retorted. "You barely can pay your own tab at the bar. If I go, I got it covered." McBain enjoyed pulling Cutter's chain a bit during serious conversations. "I'll see if I can slip away tomorrow before their surveillance of me begins. It'll have to be a very short-day trip and find out what I can under the time constraints."

"I appreciate your effort, partner." Cutter said.

"So, what are you gonna do while I'm gone?" McBain asked.

"I've gotta get into her hospital room and find what she lost her life going back for if the police haven't already found it. She didn't have anything with her when I met with her and when she was shot. I have a feeling there may be something in her room that's a clue to why she was killed."

"How are you gonna do that, mate?" McBain asked in a frustrated tone.

"She's just been murdered. The entire hospital, especially her room, will be a crime scene and cordoned off and secured."

Cutter didn't have an answer or a plan. "I'll get back with you soon. You find out if she was Jenni's sister and we may learn why she was murdered." Cutter reiterated. He glanced at his watch and realized they had been talking for several minutes; it was more than enough time to trace a phone call. He said goodbye abruptly and ended the call.

Chapter 77

As Cutter departed the diner, he emptied his pockets of loose change and a ten-dollar bill and dropped it on the table as a tip. It was larger gratuity than he was used to leaving because he wasn't about to use a credit card.

As he reached the diner front door, he glanced back at a flat screen TV on the wall behind the center of the counter. He read the ticker of the morning headlines as a meteorologist was briefing a weather chart, but there was no mention of the incident at Watkins Psychiatric Hospital.

Once he was in his car, he again phoned McBain at the hospital. There was no answer. He figured they had taken him somewhere in the hospital for some final labs and vitals checks before releasing him.

Cutter hung out at his apartment until midday before driving back to Watkins. He'd guessed right. The activity had died down by the time he arrived. There were no police, EMS, or other municipal vehicles remaining in the vicinity of the front entrance. It looked as if things had gotten back to some semblance of normalcy.

He drove onto the hospital grounds to check out the scene, then drove back off and turned left onto the main street. He then made his way to a gas station located about a mile from the hospital. and exited right. Once there, he parked in a space at the far end of the exterior bathrooms and killed the engine.

After waiting a few minutes for passersby to clear the area, he walked back to the trunk of the car. He opened the trunk, reached in, and grabbed a suit bag which he kept in his trunk. He briskly entered the unlocked restroom where he found a vacant stall, opened the suit bag, and donned the black suit, a white dress shirt, and a black necktie. He clipped his unauthorized police badge onto his belt.

Minutes later, he was at Watkins and parked at the farthest parking space from the front entrance under a row of trees lining the curb. As he walked slowly and inconspicuously towards the entrance, he stopped as his cell phone buzzed. He ducked behind a tree and pulled it from his pocket.

"Blake, this is Alex. I checked out an hour ago and I'm back at my apartment. I just booked a flight for tomorrow afternoon, and I have a hotel reservation in downtown Indianapolis for tomorrow night."

"I'm glad you feel up to it," Cutter commented.

"Let's just say, you'll owe me a big one for risking my neck and getting Riley Thompson to agree to cover for me."

"The next time you and Riley play golf, tell Riley I owe him a beer."

"He's not gonna wanna hear from you, chap. Let's just leave it there."

Riley Thompson had been one of the few agents who had been a character witness at Cutter disciplinary hearing. Without Thompson's strong character testimony, Cutter could've been terminated rather than suspended. But it left Thompson on Ryker's watch list, as with every other agent or BPD police officer who'd been involved in Cutter's unauthorized raid and his hearing.

"Okay, chap, so how do I go about verifying Penelope was a long-lost sister of Jenni?" McBain asked.

Glancing around to ensure he was not being observed, Cutter stepped further towards the back fence, not sure of the range or audio capability of video cameras on the grounds. As he reached the back fence, he spoke again. "Take down this address, 1301 Cherrywood Road. It's in the Fall Creek Place Sub-division in the Martindales Lincoln Park district of central Indianapolis. Jenni told me a lot has changed in the neighborhood over the past thirty years. You'll have to nose around and see if there's anyone who remembers her parents. Their names are Ross and Margaret Sullivan. I haven't talked to them since Jenni's funeral in Miami two years ago. I'm not in their good graces since I buried her in Miami instead of near their home in Indy. I'll email the complete information to you later tonight."

McBain scoffed through the phone. "Didn't you think it was a bit insensitive, chap, not burying her near mum and dad?"

Cutter replied, "I followed Jenni's wishes. We talked about our deaths and we each wanted to be buried in Miami. Her parents never accepted it was her wishes. She knew I loved working for MPD and the city of Miami. She wanted to be close enough where I could visit her grave if she died." Cutter choked up with those words. "I never imagined it would become a reality."

"You couldn't explain this to her parents to smooth things over?"

"They were so beset with grief, and they wouldn't even talk to me. I called several times a week after they returned to Indy, but they wouldn't answer or return my calls."

"You should've traveled there to see them, Blake," McBain said firmly.

Cutter felt annoyed and defensive with McBain's badgering. He thought for a moment to hang up on McBain but realized his friend and confidant made the point solely out of concern. He'd always appreciated McBain's candidness, except in these circumstances.

"Can we skip the interrogation, partner?" Cutter requested.

"Okay, chap," McBain eased off. "I still have the case notes from Penelope's parents drowning in Terre Haute. It's only an hour from Indy, down I-70, so I might have time to investigate a connection between the two. But Riley can only cover for me for a weekend."

"Copy," Cutter replied. "Call me tomorrow!" Cutter then hung up.

Moments later, Cutter conducted a dry-run visit at the Watkins Hospital by sauntering along the main hallway unchallenged and blending in with the few remaining hospital employees following-up on the morning's incidents. He made no attempt to approach Penelope's room, but with the lack of suspicion shown to his presence, he felt confident he could return the next day.

Chapter 78

The next morning, Cutter rolled out of bed and donned the same suit and shirt as the day before. He powered down a breakfast burrito and mocha cappuccino and grabbed his DLR digital camera before departing the apartment and driving to the hospital. At nine, he arrived and hurriedly parked in the short-term visitors' lot. Once inside, he approached the front desk and was greeted by a receptionist named Carla Dunlap. He informed Carla he was a BPD detective conducting a follow-up investigation. She didn't question it after he flashed his fake badge.

He requested access to Penelope's room to take crime scene photos. She seemed hesitant and mentioned calling her supervisor for clearance. But Cutter's suave demeanor coupled with her typical early morning workload persuaded her to bypass procedures and comply with the request. After retrieving a universal key from the key box, she escorted Cutter to Penelope's room, which was about a minute's walk to Corridor C. There, she quickly unlocked the door for him.

She seemed in a rush to get back to her desk, so Cutter asked, "Do you mind if I call you when I'm through taking photos? This is going to take a while to record everything here. I'll need to do a thorough recording and I don't want to keep you from your work."

She hesitated, but then remembered she had been assigned inventory duties, which she avoided working on earlier. She didn't want any more interruptions.

She replied, "Okay but call the front desk when you're finished, and I'll come back and lock up. Please don't take anything."

He offered an appreciative smile as she walked away. "Don't worry. I'll leave everything as I see it." Establishing rapport was critical in gaining the lady's confidence and avoiding suspicion.

He waited until she'd turned the corner into the connecting corridor before he stepped in and shut the door behind him. Then he locked it.

He walked to the window and stared out at the courtyard grounds. Crime scene tape was still strapped around the middle of light poles bordering the area where Penelope had been shot and perished. A few feet away lay six numbered evidence markers, indicating they'd recovered spent shell casings or some other evidence. His heart pounded with the renewed shock of her murder. He quickly closed the mini blinds as if it would be enough to close off the mental vision of what had happened.

He stepped away from the window and began canvassing the apartment. After seeing nothing obvious exposed in the living room area, he searched all the furniture with drawers first. Then, he checked beneath and behind the furniture for anything attached and out of place. The mattress was raised to search between it and the foundation. Both pillows were fluffed for hidden objects.

Finally, he moved toward the closet. Miscellaneous items cluttered the floor area. Shoe boxes and cloth bags were searched thoroughly. Clothing on hangers was patted down and pockets were checked individually.

Cutter grew frustrated. Some type of evidence had to be there to draw Penelope back to her rooms unless the police officers or forensics personnel had already recovered something. A shelf above the hangars was packed with extra bedding and a spare pillow. He raised each item to run his hand underneath them. He shook his head dejectedly, then stepped back and stared at each item. There was only one place he hadn't checked thoroughly, but it was such a long shot. He gripped the edge of the closet door to close it. He hesitated. *What the hell*, he thought. *Do it.*

His hand slid inside the pillowcase above the pillow in a last-ditch effort. His fingers touched something solid toward the back. Raising his toes and stretching, he gripped the object and pulled his hand back. A tablet computer came into sight.

Cutter smiled.

He sat, powered up the tablet. It was not password protected. It took only a few seconds for the blue desktop screen to appear displaying the expected icons; Recycle Bin, Microsoft Edge, Acrobat Reader, and McAfee Live Safe. There were only two folders on the desktop; one was titled Miscellaneous. The other was titled Cayman Islands.

Cutter took a quick glance toward the door, then clicked on the Cayman Islands folder and four sub-folders appeared; bank accounts, Bo *he assumed was Robert Beauchamp*, real estate and the bottom one titled Phillip Drummond.

Just as Cutter was about to click the Phillip Drummond folder, the door handle rattled. Then there was a knock at the door.

"Mister Cutter, are you in there?" Carla Dunlop spoke.

Cutter quickly stuffed the tablet under his jacket and moved to the door to unlock it.

As he opened the door, she peeked into the room to see if anything had been tampered with, per the request of the BPD investigators. Then, she looked at Cutter and declared, "You'll have to leave this room now. My supervisor received a call from the police wanting to know if anyone had made inquiries about Miss Lane. She said no and was told to keep this room locked until they released it. I didn't tell her a police officer was already here taking pictures. If you have questions, I can give you the detective's name and phone number and you can talk to him directly."

"That's not necessary, Miss Dunlap. My boss sent me here to take crime scene pictures, and I'm finished." he said, lying while patting the camera strap hanging from his shoulder. "I'm ready to leave."

Cutter held his elbows tightly against the side of his jacket so the tablet wouldn't fall out as he moved past her.

As he waited in the hallway of the C-Wing corridor, Carla locked the door. She then escorted him back to the front entrance. He had to walk briskly to keep pace with her as she was obviously in a hurry. The last thing she wanted was more communication with anyone about the murder incident. She was grappling with her own anxiety as she worked a shift soon after three violent murders occurred.

Moments later, Cutter was back in his car with what he hoped would be a clue into why Penelope was murdered. He pressed the power button on the tablet, but it didn't power up. He surmised the battery was likely dead. He remembered he had a universal power cord back at his apartment. He hoped it would be compatible with the tablet.

He reached into the back seat and stuffed the tablet into his black bag before rapidly driving away from the facility to head back to his apartment. He was more than anxious to see what information would be revealed within its files.

Chapter 79

McBain's plane touched down to heavy rain at Indianapolis International Airport at five p.m. the next day. After deboarding, he made his way to the food court and hung around consuming a beer and pretzel and reading a magazine until the torrential rain subsided. By the time he left the airport, taking a shuttle to the rental car agencies a mile away, the storm had fizzled to a light drizzle. Due to the two-hour delay in arrival in Indi, he decided to forego any investigation of the Penelope Lane case for the rest of the day to rest his weary shoulder.

He picked up the reserved mid-size sedan near six and drove away from the airport. Fortunately, the hotel he'd reserved, Comfort Suites, was located near Interstate Loop 465 and was only a ten-minute drive.

Moments later, he noticed a service station on North Perimeter Road. He stopped in and bought a few necessities for his stay; a half dozen donuts, a few toiletries, breath mints, a bottle of hand sanitizer and an Indianapolis Metropolitan map.

As he drove toward the interstate entrance, he alternated between focusing on the road and glancing down at the unfolded map. He needed to locate the areas of interest that Cutter had mentioned but he also needed to get some rest. So, he decided to let the map sit and not become a distracted driver.

Ten minutes later, he arrived at the parking lot in front of the Comfort Suites hotel, parked, and before exiting, took a yellow highlighter out of his bag and circled Martindales Lincoln Park District on the map. He hoped to get a good night's sleep before he would head to the downtown neighborhood where he planned to locate and visit Jenni Cutter's adopted parents.

The next morning, McBain woke at five, showered and dressed in a pair of nondescript khakis, a plain blue golf polo shirt and a plain black windbreaker. Before leaving the hotel parking lot, he paused momentarily to grab the Indianapolis city map off the seat and perused the route to the Martindales Lincoln Park District. He noted it was just south of downtown.

After a brief stop to grab a morning coffee and a fast-food breakfast, he arrived at Fall Creek Place sub-division in the Martindales Lincoln Park District about twenty minutes later.

Fall Creek Place of Lincoln Park was an inner-city gentrification of approximately 120 housing units. Previously nicknamed "Dodge City" for its high violent-crime rate, the neighborhood fell into disrepair in the 1980s and '90s when entire city blocks were left abandoned. In 2001, the gentrification project was begun by the city and aided by a $4 million HUD grant to stimulate other public and private investment in the redevelopment. Vacant lots and abandoned homes were acquired. New sidewalks, lighting, utilities, and trees were installed, and special financing packages were assembled for homebuyers.

The neighborhood was soon transformed into a model community of Victorian homes, townhouses, duplexes, and modern upscale apartments.

McBain parked at the end of Cherrywood Road and killed the engine. He stared down at an oak lined vista. It was a stark contrast from the old, notorious Lincoln Park, known as a haven of panhandlers and homeless vagrants and urban sprawl located only two blocks to the north. He saw no trash on the sidewalks and no potholes in the asphalt. There were no clouds of pollution from cars and buses stalled in traffic and no drug dealers or gang symbology.

Two elderly ladies across the street knelt while working in flower beds. They each wore large brim straw sun bonnets to protect themselves from the beaming sun. One of the ladies was a Caucasian and appeared to be in her 70s. She was wearing denim shorts and a dark blue top. In the yard next to her an African American geriatric had on light blue pedal pushers and a flowery print top. Neither appeared worried about an errant bullet from a drive-by shooting as they were facing away from the street. The African American lady intrigued him because an internet article about the community stated the Lincoln Park district was historically predominantly Caucasian, Jewish, and Catholic. It made no mention of other racial demographics or groups. It was only in the past two years that several Asian, Hispanic, and African American families purchased homes in the area.

McBain cautiously exited his vehicle and walked towards the Caucasian Jewish lady whose garden was nearest to his vehicle. He sauntered across the well-manicured yard and approached the lady. "Excuse me, ma'am," he spoke in a light tone.

She didn't raise her head or respond. He noticed her hands shaking as she transferred dirt from her potting bag to the flower bed as if suffering from Essential Tremor, Parkinson's disease, Multiple Sclerosis, or several other conditions. He also surmised she could have diminished hearing because she didn't respond to his first calling.

He cautiously stepped closer. "Excuse me, ma'am."

She turned and looked up. Her eyes were dull and cloudy. Her sliver hair was thin. Her smile showed teeth that were yellowing and several missing. Her lips were dry and cracked. Her pale, wrinkly skin resembled dry sailcloth.

She grabbed her cane and slowly rose, wincing as she slowly stood. She placed her left hand in the lower part of her back and wiped her brow. Erect, she revealed a hunchback stature.

"Oh, lord, Jesus." she exclaimed as he placed her empty left hand over her heart. She dusted off her hands. "Can I help you?

"Yes, ma'am," McBain smiled warmly. "I'm Agent Alex McBain of the State Bureau of Investigation."

She grinned mischievously. "Did you take a wrong turn somewhere, sonny? This is Indianapolis." she quipped, proudly.

"No ma'am," he chuckled, politely. "I came here from Georgia on an investigative case."

"Are you a Brit?" she asked, noticing his accent.

"Why yes, ma'am. I am originally from the United Kingdom, but I work for the SBI here in the states now."

Her brow furrowed. "Glory be! Well, I'm Hannah Goldstein and this is my house and my yard."

"I don't mean to impose ma'am," McBain offered.

"It's all right, sonny. What can I do for you?"

McBain started to compliment her on her garden, but decided to cut to the chase, after quickly realizing it might provoke a line of conversation which might last half the morning.

"Ma'am, I'm looking for a couple named Ross and Margaret Sullivan, the parents of a woman whose birth name was Jenni Sullivan."

Mabel's face suddenly blanched and her eyes watered. "Poor Maggie. It nearly broke her heart when her daughter died."

"So, you know about her daughter being murdered."

Hannah wiped her brow, reached down, and folded the top of the potting bag, then walked over to the top step of the porch and sat. McBain followed behind her but stood nearby.

"She never told me her daughter was murdered," she murmured as if to herself.

"So, you know the Sullivans well?" McBain asked her.

"I sure do," she answered proudly and then pointed, stating, "They live there down there in the house with the brown shutters." Her cheeks suddenly drooped. "Maggie has been through so much. Her husband, Ross died last year. I'm sorry. I forget sometimes he's really gone. I've known Maggie for almost forty years. I remember when they put little Jennifer's twin baby sister up for adoption. The losses she's endured. Oh, Lord, have mercy on her soul!"

McBain sucked in a deep breath. He was startled by the revelation but hid it well.

He then asked, "Do you think it would be okay if someone talked to her about Jenni?"

"I don't think she'd mind," Hannah answered. "She's a wonderful, friendly lady. Her eyesight is not what it used to be, but I'm sure she'll be cordial about it."

He then asked, "Is there anything I need to know before I talk to her, like does she have a health condition."

"Oh, she has COPD, but she's a tough ole gal, so I think you should be alright to talk to her," she advised him. "We've talked many times about her daughters and how she loved them."

McBain turned away from her for a moment and stared at Mabel's house in pensive thought. He remembered his mother in England talking about a friend of hers who lost three children in a house fire and never was the same.

She interrupted his stare, by saying, "She's retired so she's usually at home all the time, except for doctors' appointments and such."

He motioned to the neighbor lady in her yard. "I assume your neighbor is a recent addition to the neighborhood."

She followed his view with her own.

"You mean Olive? Yes, she is a great friend and neighbor. She is a widow and has been with us a little over a year. She is truly a dear."

McBain reached out and shook her wrinkly, thin hands. "Thank you for your time, Mrs. Goldstein. I will let you get back to work."

McBain quickly walked across the yard and street and sat in his car. He put his hands on the steering wheel, took a deep breath, and closed his eyes. It was already a humid morning. Then, he straightened and stared down the street at Margaret Sullivan's home, while in deep thought and reflection.

The realization should have been clearly apparent for months but was now evident. Penelope Lane was a perfect likeness to Jenni Cutter because she was her identical twin sister.

Chapter 80

Cutter arrived back at his apartment from Watkins Hospital at noon. He had witnessed the murder of Penelope Lane on the hospital grounds by henchmen of Bennie DeSalvo, the mob hood from which he had rescued the kidnapped Penelope during the police raid in Bullet Georgia.

Now he was left with the task to capture her killers while simultaneously trying to avenge the mistaken bombing death of his late wife Jenni Cutter. He had to accomplish this without being detected by his former boss, Harry Ryker.

Settling in for the afternoon, he immediately found a compatible charging cable and connected it to the tablet and the wall outlet. While waiting on the slow internet connection, he took care of business in the bathroom, then hustled over to his fridge to grab a Miller Lite beer. After discovering an empty fridge, he reached in the cabinet and grabbed a can of tuna fish and minutes later he returned to the bedroom with a tuna sandwich on a dinner plate. By then, the tablet had powered up. So, he punched in McBain's number on his burner. After the fifth ring without an answer, he disconnected before it went to voicemail. Since he was just checking in, he was not desperate to speak with Alex right then.

As the desktop icons populated, he keyed in on a folder titled Miscellaneous. Multi-tasking between sandwich bites and beer, he clicked on the folder and noticed a sub-folder appear with the title Bei'an Mining Company. His brow furrowed and his mouth gaped.

He thought to himself, *what does Penelope or anyone else involved in her death have to do with a mining company?* Unfamiliar with the name, he minimized the folder, clicked on Google Chrome, and typed *Bei'an Mining Company* in the Google search window.

It took a few seconds for page links containing the words to appear. As he clicked on the first link, he discovered Bei'an was a municipality in the west-central Heilongjiang province of Manchuria in the People's Republic of China. A map showed it bordered North Korea and Russia.

His eyes widened as he was totally perplexed. His next thoughts were *this cannot be relevant. Could there be a city or small town in America with the name Bei'an or a family name of Bei'an. Could it be a French word, like the water with the Evian label or Chardonnay wine?*

He scrolled down the rest of the page and saw nothing explaining the name. He then scrolled through the next three pages of internet headings until the word dropped off the listing. Every mention of the word Bei'an referred to the city in Heilongjiang province or a listing of available hotels in the city or just headings depicted in Chinese language, which he didn't bother to try to have translated. There were no other references to the word Bei'an on the web. He felt now felt certain the Bei'an Mining Company referred to the city in Manchuria, unless it was a fake or decoy title, which the thought quickly entered his mind.

His heart was beating rapidly, and he swallowed hard with nervousness as he maximized the folder and hesitated momentarily before clicking on it.

He took a deep breath, consumed the remainder of the beer, and clicked on the link. Several numbered JPEG photos appeared in the window along with document files. They were numbered in order with the word BMC proceeding the number. He assumed BMC was an abbreviation for Bei'an Mining Company. He opened the first photo.

The photo was a grainy JPEG, appearing to be copied from a camera file. It depicted the entrance to a mine shaft which was dug into the side of a mountain, about twenty feet wide and fifteen feet high at its entrance. A set of rail tracks extended into the center of the shaft. As the photo appeared to be taken on a limpid and dreary day, the shaft entrance appeared pitch black.

In college, he had studied Eastern European and Asian history as his minor in International Studies. He remembered reading Japan had invaded the province of Manchuria in 1931 to seize the rich oil and iron ore resources. After World War II, when Manchuria was returned to China, the new communist government invested heavily in mining operations, particularly in the Zhejiang and Heilongjiang provinces of Manchuria. Thus, he was not alarmed to see a photo of mining in that region.

The question that was reiterated in his thoughts was *why would it be on Penelope's computer tablet?*

Since there were no people in the photo, he archived the question in his mind for the moment and clicked on the next photo down the list. In this photo were three men posing in front of a coal pile located many yards left of the entrance to a mine shaft. One of the men appeared to be an Asian in his early forties of medium build with dark thinning hair to his shoulders.

The second man was a man who was in his late fifties or early sixty, who was Asian. But he was wearing a traditional mining robe with no headgear. He had lighter skin than most Asians, so he was indigenous to the region.

The other man was from the western world and a visitor to the mine, based on his attire. He wore overalls, a dark poplin shirt, a hard-shell hat, work shoes, and knee pads, indicating he was taking extra safety precautions local workers often ignored.

In the background of men were two diminutive Asian men dressed in traditional working robes and sandals with conical hats covering their head as they stood on top of a salt pile. The hats cast a shadow from the sun which made it difficult to see their facial features.

As Cutter inched forward to the screen, his eyelids rose. The westerner closely resembled Alex McBain but of a thinner build. Yet, the facial features were too blurry to identify him. His enlargement of the JPEG did not enhance the image enough for positive verification. He then accessed his email, composed a new message, attached the photo, and saved the file as a draft.

Moments later, he retrieved the image from his own computer, downloaded the email attachment and ran it through his downloaded Amped software to enhance the photo. It provided a marginal enhancement which offered better clarity but not to a degree of certainty to know the image was Alex McBain. He had no reason to expect his former partner and current SBI agent would have been in Manchuria at a mining site.

Suddenly, his cell phone buzzed. He recognized the number. It was Alex calling from Indianapolis. Cutter took a deep breath before answering. He decided not to disclose the discovery of the photo files to McBain at that time.

Chapter 81

"Blake, I just had a conversation with an elderly neighbor of Maggie Sullivan who claims she knows Jenni and Penelope were twin sisters," McBain said to Cutter.

"Are you serious?" Cutter replied as his mouth gaped, surprised but not shocked by the revelation.

"Isn't that the news you were expecting?" McBain asked. "Quite frankly, chap, I am surprised you didn't suspect this from the first time you first saw Penelope. The resemblance was too striking to be just a coincidence, so why didn't you ask her about it?"

"I guess I'd gotten too close to Penelope to notice. It wouldn't been here something I'd been likely to ask, anyway." Cutter responded.

"I can understand that, but Jenni was your wife," McBain replied. "It's hard to believe you missed it."

Cutter paused and cupped his chin. He felt a chilling sensation with the revelation he had been in love with twin sisters who were both dead. He decided to the change by asking, "Tell me everything that's going on right now."

McBain briefed, "Well, I drove to the neighborhood and saw this Caucasian woman gardening in her front yard, which was several houses up and across the opposite side of the street from the address you gave me. She identified herself as Hannah Goldstein. I had a conversation with her to see if I could gauge the situation before approaching the Sullivan house."

"Wise move," Cutter interluded.

McBain continued, "Obviously, I got more than I could've imagined by her revealing Penelope was given up for adoption."

Cutter was momentarily speechless.

McBain asked him, "Did Jenni ever mentioned she had a sister given up for adoption?"

Cutter stammered, "N-No, but maybe she did not even know. People sometimes keep those things secret from other siblings forever."

"I guess I can envision a reason for that, McBain interjected.

"Anything else significant she told you?" Cutter prodded.

"She's a long-time friend of Maggie. I'm talking decades. She had known her for so long she remembered the adoption taking place and it was shortly after Miss Lane's birth. She also told me Margaret' husband recently died."

Cutter's eyebrows furrowed. The last time he had spoken with Ross was at the funeral in Miami and although he looked thin, Cutter didn't surmise he was gravely ill. Again, he was momentarily tongue tied. In one conversation, he had learned his dead wife, and his forbidden love interest were sisters. Now, he learned his former father-in-law was dead.

McBain sensed Blake's state of shock but pressed on. "It's a lot for a woman to lose the daughter she raised and a husband. Now she must learn that the daughter she gave away met an early death. I'm glad I spoke to this lady before I went to the house, which is why I am calling you. This is a little too heavy for me, chap! I don't think a stranger like me should be having this conversation with her."

Cutter paused again and took a deep breath. A part of him was terrified of wanting to learn more but he knew he had to face the truth. He also had to face Maggie and give her the news about Penelope.

"Blake…are you okay?" Alex responded to the sudden silence.

"Yeah, yeah," Cutter stammered. "I'm just floored by all this."

"Well, why don't pull yourself off the floor, mate and tell me what I should do now."

"I agree that this isn't our job to lay this on her; the daughter she gave up for adoption killed her parents and now she's dead."

"So, you're gonna try to call her?" McBain asked, suggestively.

"No, I've got to come there," Cutter told him as he went pensive in thought for a moment. "I'll try to hop a flight tomorrow. It's not like I have a day job and need someone to cover for me," he noted.

"Well, I do, but if you want me here with you, you'd better make it tomorrow," McBain advised him. "I'm not on a paid leave."

Cutter sat in the chair, placed the cell on speaker and stared at the tablet screen, shifting his thoughts. "There's something else I need to ask you about…but not right now."

"I hate when you do that to me, mate!"

"Forget I said anything for now. It is nothing important at this very moment." Cutter quickly closed the tablet. "Just stay in town overnight."

McBain acknowledged and hung up, slightly confused but not wanting to pile more on Cutter after the news he had just provided.

Three hours later, McBain was nursing a beer back at the hotel bar when Cutter phoned him and asked to be picked up the next day at Indianapolis International Airport for his two-fifteen p.m. arrival on Southwest Airlines Flight 451.

Chapter 82

A severe storm front along the Mid-eastern US caused Cutter's flight to depart the Atlanta area thirty minutes behind schedule. After a bumpy ride and reroute around the worst of the storm, the plane touched down at Indianapolis International Airport over an hour late.

McBain pushed aside impatient frustration and circled the arrival terminal six times because he refused to pay the one-hour minimum fee to park in a cell phone lot. On the sixth loop, he noticed Cutter exiting the terminal concourse, blew his horn and pulled to the curb.

Cutter tossed both carryon bags in the back seat then entered the car.

"If I had to make one more loop around this terminal, I would've left you here, mate!" McBain greeted.

Cutter buckled up and stared forward, then suddenly remembered the photo of the man resembling McBain at the mining site in China. Cutter didn't return the banter, which surprised McBain.

"Everything okay?" McBain asked. "Not that I was expecting any thanks for saving you an uber fare."

Cutter sighed heavily, partly from exhaustion. Shifting from his true, thoughts, he replied, "Hey, partner, I'm sorry. I didn't get much sleep last night." Shifting, he asked, "Where am I staying?"

"H.I. Express. Got you a room on the same floor as me," McBain informed him.

"Good. I was not ready to smell your stinky feet?" he bantered with a wry grin. What he really meant was he was eager to explore more of the tablet photos in private before confronting his partner about them.

As they entered the interstate for the remaining ten-minute drive to the hotel, there was dead silence until Alex said, "You sure you don't want to go straight to Margaret's home and get this over with? You seem very distracted."

"Nah, just tired," Cutter countered. "I'd rather be well rested when I talk to her. She will cut me like a butcher with a knife . . . with her tongue if I am not careful when I talk to her, because she hates my guts."

"Wow, I didn't get that impression from her friend, Mabel." McBain countered. "She made her sound genuinely nice, even tempered I would suspect.

"She didn't bury Margaret's' daughter twelve hundred miles away," Cutter pointed out. "Remember, with women, especially grieving ones, there are layers, pal."

"Don't be so doom and gloom, mate," McBain critiqued. "Time heals. Lay your charm on her and I'm sure you'll be okay. You'll have a better outlook once you get some rest."

Cutter nodded and leaned back on the passenger side head rest.

When they were three minutes from the hotel, Cutter grabbed his phone out of his pocket and clicked on the email he sent to himself with the JPEG photo. He enlarged it on the phone and was certain it was his partner.

McBain caught a glimpse of Cutter's stare out of the corner of his eye.

"Something wrong, Blake?"

"No!"

A few seconds later, Cutter, asked him, "Have you ever been to China, Alex…say like, Manchuria?"

McBain turned to stare as he released the steering wheel for a moment. Then, Cutter noticed McBain's left eye twitch. To Cutter, it was a sure sign of nervousness.

"What? Where is that question coming from? What are you talking about?" McBain stammered innocently.

Cutter noticed and found it an interesting reaction. McBain had always who offered direct eye contact in conversation. Cutter didn't expect it while he was driving but gestures were just the opposite to an extreme degree.

"Just wondering." Cutter replied deceptively.

McBain broke a grin while he paused in thought. "I don't even know where the hell Manchuria is, other than somewhere in the far east," McBain answered "You have some far east trip planned for us?"

Cutter did not respond.

With obvious nervousness, Cutter surmised McBain was lying or at the minimum avoiding further discussion of the topic. *But why? Why would he lie about not knowing where Manchuria is located? Why would he be in a photo at a mining site on Penelope's computer and then deny ever being there?*

Then, his friendship and devotion to his former partner led him to question himself. *Is this person just a look-a-like? Everybody has a double somewhere,* he tried to assure himself. But after another moment of deep thought, Cutter couldn't convince himself that the man in the photo was a doppelganger of Alex. *One doppelganger in his lifetime is enough*, he thought.

Cutter did not want to believe the man who had been his investigative partner, his confidant, the man he had trusted with his life, his police battle buddy, would lie to him on something he hoped was so trivial and insignificant. He decided to remain quiet and stoic for the rest of the ride.

McBain nervous remained quiet, also.

CHAPTER 83

When they arrived at the hotel, McBain accompanied Cutter to the reception desk to get checked into his room. Cutter was assigned a room three doors down from McBain on the second floor.

As they reached the floor, they stopped in front of Cutter's room 237. McBain was growing more concerned with Cutter's hushed and somber mood. He felt like he had been spending the entire afternoon trying to break the ice with a stranger.

"Wow, Blake, you sure are traveling light," referral to Cutter's only luggage, a small cargo bag. "I hope you at least have a change of clothes balled up in that gym bag, so we can go somewhere and have a beer."

"I'm not here on a vacation, Alex," Cutter replied gruffly.

"So, what's all in your Gucci man bag?" Alex asked, poking fun.

"A tablet I recovered from Penelope's room at the hospital," Cutter told him.

"You took it from an active crime scene during a police murder investigation?" McBain asked incredulously. Cutter detected a flutter in his voice.

Cutter stared at him momentarily, in a suspicious way before saying, "The police had been through the room before I went there. They had their chance to get what they wanted. They didn't take this tablet, so I did."

McBain had never seen Cutter stare at him that intently before.

"I'm planning to do some research about mining in Manchuria. You know anything about it?"

They stared at each other for ten seconds.

McBain finally broke a grin but did not respond right away. "I don't know what you're getting at, chap, but obviously, you need to get some rest." McBain followed the statement by immediately walking away towards his room.

Cutter eyed him from the hallway to see if McBain would look back.

He didn't.

Cutter watched until McBain entered his room, shutting his room door with a loud thud.

CHAPTER 84

Cutter and McBain met the next morning at seven to partake of the continental breakfast in the small dining area across from the hotel lobby. As they sat at a table and ate, Cutter was tempted to inquire again about McBain's connection to Manchuria but decided against it. He realized he needed to focus all his energy on talking to Margaret Sullivan about her daughter's death and her knowledge of Jenni's twin sister Penelope.

Before Cutter's arrival, McBain had planned to checkout of the hotel that morning and catch a mid-day flight back to Atlanta. But Cutter's late arrival prevented Cutter's trip to Margaret' home on that same day. So, Cutter asked McBain to delay his departure until Sunday morning, so he could consult with him throughout his visit.

McBain sensed Cutter's anxiety about the meeting with Margaret and its potential to rekindle unresolved grief with the death of his late wife. He decided to ignore his previous concerns about his unauthorized absence and place the needs of his friend and colleague first. He agreed to stay.

"I wonder if you should call her and tell her you're coming rather than catching her by surprise," McBain debated to Cutter.

Cutter argued, "I can't risk her knowing in advance and her leaving the house or refusing to see me. I'm just hoping she's softened after Ross's death . . . or at least changed her focus. I think if I can talk to her at the door, she will eventually let me in."

"They say, time heals old wounds, chap. I hope in your case it holds true."

"It's time to find out," Cutter prompted, gulping down the remainder of his coffee. He wasn't interested in further conversation about the matter.

Thirty minutes later, they arrived at Cherrywood Road and per Cutter's request, McBain found a parking spot along the street a half-block from Margaret' house. Cutter asked McBain to remain in the car, then he slowly walked along the sidewalk towards her residence.

From the curb, he noticed a late model blue Buick LeSabre parked in the driveway and Margaret's garage was open.

Approaching the driveway, he saw the back of an ermine white classic two-door sedan parked in the garage. He recognized it as a '63 Gran Turismo by the Studebaker hawk nameplate across the width of the bottom of the trunk lid. Cutter was a fan of classic cars and was the owner of a vintage Ford Fairlane before it was blown to bits in the Miami bombing. The sight brought a subtle smile to his face. He was tempted to walk inside the garage and take a closer look but resisted.

Cutter walked around the back of the Buick and along the sidewalk to an iron grill covered front door. The door had cherry wood trim which appeared to have been added years ago to match the street name.

Before Cutter rang the doorbell, he noticed the window curtain to the left of the door was open, enabling him to peek inside the main area of the home. Since it was an open floor plan, he could see all the way through to where a person wearing a red apron over a white blouse and a blue skirt shuffling about in the kitchen.

Not wanting her neighbors to perceive him as a peeping tom or potential home intruder, he quickly moved back to the center of door and rang the door chime. He waited for ten seconds after the first rang before ringing the door chime again.

Then, he heard a pleasant voice, "Just a minute. I am coming."

He was familiar with the tone of her voice, a sweet soprano voice that reminded him of Jenni's.

He took a quick peek again through the window and noticed her stripping off her apron and tossing it onto the kitchen island.

She opened the door and his nose picked up a saucy aroma before the door completely opened.

"Hello, Margaret!" Cutter said, faintly.

She gave him a once-over, hesitated, then spoke, "Blake, what are you doing here?"

"It's been a long time, Maggie."

He noticed her eyes were watered and bloodshot and had heavy bags under them. She was a natural blonde but due to stress and aging, it had become a dirty dishwasher blonde. Her hair was partly covered under a red-checkered bandana matching the apron she had discarded. Her normal radiant complexion had become dry and blanched. He noticed that she had lost weight . . . but it was not a healthy weight loss. It was not an athletic weight loss, either. Her hands trembled and her eyebrows had faded to near nothing.

Her face paled and contorted into a frown as he waited for a reply. He assumed the grim expression was a signal she was still incensed over his decision to bury Jenni in Miami. His appearance at her door appeared to have renewed her despair of the loss of her daughter.

"I would like to talk to you, Maggie. I'd like to talk about Jenni and her sister."

The request clearly shocked her. Her eyelids widened and she stood motionless in a trance, as if she had been confronted by something ghastly.

"Is this a bad time?" Cutter asked courteously. "I could come back."

"No. C'mon in," she replied as she reached into her pants pocket and grabbed her keys to unlock the iron gate. "I supposed we do have a lot to talk about."

"I thought this was supposed to be a safe neighborhood now," Cutter commented as she swung the gate open.

She replied, "I'm an old lady living alone so I don't take any chances," she noted as she led him through the living room." The safety and security of a husband being around was long gone.

"Yeah, you're right, Maggie. You cannot be too careful these days. It's getting to be that it's not safe anywhere," he agreed, trying to make icebreaker conversation.

As the gate swung open, it brushed against a set of tubular metal wind chimes hanging from a light fixture over a hedge. It produced a pleasant tinkling, which Cutter advantaged to offer a nicer icebreaking pleasantry.

"This is a nice way to enter a house, the chiming," he complimented. "I like the oriental look of them," noting the ancient dragon designs on them.

"They actually serve a practical purpose," she explained. "They let me know when a storms' brewing."

Cutter started toward a couch to sit, but Maggie ushered him into the kitchen.

She had a good reason for not wanting to sit in the living room. The last time he had sat in her house on the living room sofa was when he and Jenni had a final conversation with her and Ross on Black Friday, the morning before they left to return to Miami. She remembered Jenni and Blake joking playfully and Jenni kissing Blake on the cheek in front of them as she talked about how happy she was being his wife. She wanted to forever savor the memory.

It was the last time she saw her daughter.

Chapter 85

As he entered the kitchen, he offered up the perfect icebreaker.

"Something smells wonderful!

"It is a strawberry rhubarb pie," she replied proudly. "I'm baking for a neighborhood's women's coffee I'm hosting tomorrow, but I could cut it for you if you would like a piece."

"That is really inviting, but no thanks, Maggie. It's too flawless to cut ahead of time. Its looks delicious, though."

She wiped her brow, offered a wry smile, but didn't respond to the compliment and remained emotionally guarded. Blake and Maggie stared at each other as their thoughts were in unison.

He decided to change the topic to try and fully break the vibes of acrimony she was emitting to him.

"I see you own a Studebaker?"

"Yes, it was Ross' car. He bought it from a collector after he retired from his job at the Studebaker plant in South Bend. I was so glad he retired because I was tired of seeing him commute such a long distance every week. He called the purchase his way of contributing to Indiana culture. When he died, I couldn't see myself getting rid of it. He loved it so much he would drive it every Sunday afternoon. I always sat in the backseat. I felt like he was 'driving Miss Daisy. It was the playful thing we did."

Cutter chuckled politely.

She continued, "We had so much fun with that car before he passed. Ross became somewhat of an expert on Studebaker before he died. Many times, I heard him tell me how the company was founded."

"I'm interested to hear," Cutter said, urging her to continue.

"They have an interesting history, Blake. The company was founded before the Civil War, and they began making horse-drawn carriages. With success, the company evolved into selling horseless carriages shortly after the turn of the twentieth century. They built a variety of cars, wagons, and military vehicles. Our Hawk model debuted in 1956 in the middle of the Studebaker's hierarchy, but the cars took on a whole new identity in 1962 when Brook Stevens redesigned the Hawks with a European look and flair clearly inspired by European car makers and exported to countries all over the world."

Cutter watched a glimmer of delight on her face reflecting on her late husband's good times in the car.

She continued, "I haven't been in the car since, other than to wash it occasionally. I just open the garage a couple of days a week so the paint can get some air, start it weekly, and let it run to keep the battery charged."

Having lost his collectable, Cutter thought momentarily about making her an offer for it, but he deferred that conversation for a later date.

"C'mon and sit," she urged, gesturing him to the living room. "My feet are beginning to hurt. 'I've been standing nearly all morning."

As he moved to take a seat, he hesitated momentarily to glance back at her photo wall over and around the living room fireplace mantle. He noticed there were no pictures of Jenni on the wall. There were photos of Maggie and Ross and one of just him wearing his military uniform from his Army career as a chopper pilot. It was a photo of him with his pilot comrades in Mosel, Iraq.

Cutter had hoped to see a picture of them holding the twins, but there was none there. He imagined her going into the bathroom or kitchen momentarily and he would find a photo album lying around he could quickly browse through. It was wishful thinking for a woman who kept her living spaces immaculately clean and free of clutter.

As they sat, he picked a somber comment to make, a result of his nervous energy, "I was sorry to hear about Ross. Are you doing, okay?"

Her eyes watered further as she replied, "As well as I can. What choice do I have?"

"How did Ross die?" Cutter asked.

"He died suddenly three months ago from an aneurism. It was a blood clot in his brain. An autopsy concluded his death was due to a stroke, brought on by the prolonged stress and grief from Jenni's death that exacerbated other underlying health issues. Jenni's death led Ross into a period of depression, heavy drinking discontinuance of exercise and abandonment of his diabetic diet.

Blake sat quietly for a few minutes. Then, shifting respectfully, he asked, "Bars on doors, Maggie?" he asked. "I'm sorry it had to come to that."

She responded, "Ross told me before he died the worst thing someone can say about your neighborhood is that it is safe. The complacency of that message is music to out-of-town criminals' ears." She moved to the stove, turned off the burner under a teapot, and powered the temperature on the burner underneath a boiling pot of noodles. Jenni had said several times Maggie had a tradition of preparing lasagna and butter beans on the weekends, particularly for her anticipated Saturday visits by Hannah.

Then she continued, "Criminals look for open garages, unlocked doors, open windows without blinds, etcetera!"

Cutter nodded and replied, "Wise advice I guess."

Growing weary of the small talk, she prodded, "I know you did not come this far to chat about this neighborhood or classic cars. Why are you here?"

Cutter nodded in agreement. He paused, sighed softly then took a deep breath. He was not about to reveal her forty-year friend Hannah had confirmed the adoption of Jenni's twin.

"I have sorrowful news, Maggie," Cutter lamented. "I know you don't need anymore."

"I am numb to bad news by now. I will listen if you share a cup of tea with me," she urged as she heard the tea kettle whistle.

"Okay, sure," Cutter agreed.

She moved back over to the teapot containing lemon tea. As she poured two cups of tea, Cutter glanced again over at the photo wall. The lack of photos of the twins made him nervous as to how the conversation would go. She brought the teas and a dainty, covered sugar bowl to the table and sat it down while she stared at him, prompting him to respond to her previous question.

"Maggie, I have something to tell you about your other daughter," he said softly. He reached to grab her right hand, but she pulled it back.

"Your other daughter passed away."

She raised an eyebrow and suddenly all the color disappeared from her cheeks. "When did this happen? she stammered.

"A few days ago in Bullet, Georgia."

She immediately looked resigned, but then, oddly, turned away. She hastily grabbed her cup and took a sip of the tea, then slowly lowered it to the table. Her eyes watered as she took a deep breath and closed her eyes. "I'm so sorry, Maggie. I was with her when she died. That's when she told me she had a sister, right before she died."

Maggie said, "We put her up for adoption when she was born. I learned later her new parents were not the most desirable people."

Cutter was too curious and focused to partake of the tea as the steam from the cup quickly dissipated. "I'm sorry you had to separate the twins."

"We were extremely poor. We had no health insurance. Ross was a drug user then and was only working part-time with no steady job prospects. Jennifer came out first and the doctors said she was okay, but when I got ready to deliver Penelope, there were complications and the doctor told us there was a strong chance she would have a birth defect. They thought it might be fetal alcohol syndrome, as I drank when I was pregnant. But it would be years before it would come about. We had no money to take care of one healthy child, much less a child who would have a disability. So, I signed paperwork to put her up for adoption shortly after she was born. I was told by social services they would try to find a couple in-state to adopt her so I could one day have a chance to get to know her. I didn't realize then it was a false promise. That decision has haunted me all these years. I had to choose one child over another. But we were young, afraid, and unprepared for the challenges of raising children."

She trembled and sobbed profusely.

"Don't be so hard on yourself," Cutter said as he reached across the table and caressed her left hand.

This time, she squeezed his palm. It was the first time she had displayed some sense of comfort during his visit.

"How did she die?" Margaret asked.

Cutter inferred by her asking the question she had no knowledge of Penelope's complicated plight. She obviously didn't know of Penelope's murdered parents, her decision to disappear to a double life, her indictments of murder which lead to her near-death accident from a fall off an apartment roof, being committed to a psychiatric hospital, her involvement with a shady real estate investor who was murdered, her being kidnapped, rescued, and then murdered by mafia henchmen after she became a target for execution. Cutter was not about to heighten her grief and sorrow with revealing the sordid details of this mysterious woman who was one of her twin daughters.

Chapter 86

"Penelope was murdered two days ago," Cutter informed her.

Margaret's reaction was as expected of a birth mother, she became hysterical. First, her eyes rolled in her head, and she was about to slip from the couch when Cutter grabbed her arm. She wept inconsolably. Then, she started wheezing with a sudden shortness of breath.

"Maggie, what's going on?"

Gasping for breath, she stammered, "I-I have asthma. I need my puffer. Could you hand it to me? It is in that drawer," she moaned, sniffling while pointing at the end table.

Cutter rushed over and opened the drawer. In it was a puffer and a nebulizer, used to treat her COPD. He grabbed the puffer and handed it to her. She quickly shook it three times, and then took two puffs, about fifteen seconds apart. She leaned back on the couch and breathed deeply as Cutter nervously watched her.

He waited another ten seconds, then asked, "Are you okay, Maggie? Are you in respiratory distress? Do I need to call 911?"

"No, no, no, I'll be okay," she reassured him. She took another puff on the inhaler, inhaled a couple deep breaths, then wiped the sweat from her brow. The temperature in the house was eighty degrees, caused by humidity and heat from the stove being on.

"Let's get you out of this hot house. It's too hot in here," Cutter noted, then walked over to the thermostat in the hallway and turned it down several degrees.

He sat silently for another minute to ensure she could compose herself.

"I'm okay, now," she said. "My asthma acts up when I get stressed. What was the date when this happened?" she asked him, tearfully.

"The twenty-first."

He insisted on moving from the house to a covered patio outside the kitchen.

She did not resist and let him guide her. When seated, she continued, "I had a bad feeling that day. It was the day I had an appointment with my hairdresser, but I woke up feeling bad, like I was having a heart attack. I cancelled my appointment and had Hannah drive me to an urgent care clinic. The doctor said it was angina, but I knew it was having a premonition that someone close to me was about die."

Cutter didn't believe in premonitions. He questioned, "Are you saying you were about to lose a daughter you hadn't seen her since she was a baby?"

She stared at him with a look of indignation. "A mother's instinct never fails her."

He reacted stammering," I-I'm sorry. I did not mean it the way it sounded. Let's continue this at another time," he suggested.

"No. I'm okay," she insisted. "I want to know how she died."

Cutter stood and paced for a moment, a nervous habit of his. "She was involved with some bad people and a lot of terrible things happened to her. I'm afraid I can't tell you anymore because there is an ongoing investigation into her death." Cutter suddenly found himself hoping the news of her daughter's death would overwhelm her enough so she would not ask more questions. He wasn't about to further shock her with the news when he told her he no longer a cop and was actively involved with Penelope.

Shifting the conversation, Cutter asked, "Did you ever get to meet her adoptive parents?"

"I never met them and was never told who they were. Years later, a social services worker told us she was adopted by a family here in Indiana. But because of some ongoing court case, we were kept out of the picture."

"How did you get that information?" he asked in a much softer tone to ensure she did not feel interrogated or criticized by the question. "I'm surprised that anyone was allowed to even tell you those details. I want to you know everything you know."

"I can't tell you anything else, Blake. It broke an ISDH rule by having a close friend tell he what she knew. I won't break our confidentiality trust, especially since it could get her into trouble."

"I wouldn't ask you too, Maggie," he consoled. He shifted, by asking, "You weren't notified about her death from anyone?"

She lamented, "When you sign away your rights to your child, you're not entitled to notification about an adopted child's death or their adoptive parent's death."

Cutter was tempted to reveal all of Penelope's sordid life; her parents' drowning followed by Penelope's disappearance and assuming a new identity. But he decided against it, realizing Maggie had already been overwhelmed by the revelation of a second daughter's death at a young age.

"Are you sure you are alright? I should call a doctor just to be safe and have them check you."

Her voice raised as she argued, "Don't make a big deal about this Blake. If I would change my activity every time, I have an asthma issue, I would never get anything done. This is what happens with old age."

Cutter nodded and decided to leave the issue alone. Margaret was a proud woman, who didn't like anyone making a fuss over her. Jenni had exhibited those same qualities. It is one of the things he loved about her, and he knew he couldn't win that debate.

With the subtle acrimony she held against him for the location of Jenni's burial, Cutter knew there was nothing else to talk about. He could not disclose any more information about Penelope's life either or his personal involvement with her. It was surreal enough for Margaret to be in the presence of the man who had witnessed both her daughters' deaths. Moreover, Cutter was not sure what information regarding Penelope Lane was now a matter of police authorized release in both Terre Haute and Bullet. He knew any unauthorized disclosure of information could jeopardize any chance he would be reinstated back at the bureau and could even result in a civil lawsuit.

They concluded their talk as they walked back inside and sat back on the couch and finished their tea.

For the next few moments, they changed the subject and chatted about happenings in Miami. Cutter attempted again to apologize and explain his reasoning for burying Jenni in Miami rather than bring her body back to her hometown. Margaret remained steadfast, unforgiving, but civil. She then made it clear by politely asking him to leave by pretending she had to make it to an appointment.

As Cutter reached the door, he looked back at Margaret and said, "I don't know when I will see you again, Maggie but I would like for us to separate now on good terms. I can't bring Jenni home to you. But is there anything else I can do to make it up to you."

Margaret stared at him momentarily as tears again welled in her eyes. Then, she said in a shaky tone, "Just bring justice to the people responsible for my twin's deaths. I need closure and peace."

Cutter replied firmly, "You have my promise, Maggie. When we meet again, you will have closure."

With those words, she stepped towards him and gave him a subtle hug and wished him well.

Despite his hope to reconcile their relationship, Cutter had completed his primary purpose for visiting his late wife's mother…to verify that Penelope Lane was indeed the twin sister of his late wife, Jennifer Sullivan Cutter.

Chapter 87

Cutter trudged down the sidewalk towards Alex, sidestepping a tricycle but then kicking a basketball back into the yard. It helped relieve the tension from the issues his visit with Margaret had rekindled.

Alex flicked the butt of his cigarette out the window, exited the driver's seat and eased to the front fender to greet Cutter.

"Are you still intact, chap? McBain asked.

"Yeah, I'm good," he said solemnly. But his somber expression told a different story. He was affected by the notification to Maggie about the death of the younger of her twin daughters.

Cutter slipped into the front passenger's seat and dropped his head against both palms. McBain started the engine but let it idle. He delayed pulling from the curb and delayed the initiation of conversation to give Cutter a moment to compose himself.

Moments later, Cutter finally spoke, "She confirmed it, Alex. They were twins and now they are both dead with two people in common who are responsible, me and Ransom Oliver."

McBain remained silent momentarily in empathy, realizing Cutter needed a moment to vent. But then he felt he had to counter Cutter's guilt.

After several minutes McBain spoke. "Don't be so hard on yourself, my friend," McBain consoled. "You're not culpable for either of these deaths."

McBain had not called Cutter his friend since before the courthouse incident where he was forced to shoot him and prevent him from freeing her during her trip to Watkins.

Cutter turned his head and stared into McBain's eyes. "I appreciate your sympathy and your friendship, Alex. But I must get justice for Maggie's daughters, or I'll forever live with the guilt."

"A lot for you to take on, chap," McBain commented, solemnly. "Where are you gonna get guys to stick there neck out again."

Cutter replied, "I'll get justice if I have to do it alone."

Alex sighed heavily, then turned the engine off and decided to discuss something he had intended to broach until they arrived back at the hotel. But he knew Cutter needed something different to think about at that moment.

"Blake, while you were with Maggie, I got a call from Ryker. Penelope's remains are at the morgue but there is no next of kin notification in the county records. They cannot release it to a funeral home without someone taking responsibility for her body."

Cutter sat and thought for a moment. "Maybe I can do it."

McBain reminded him, "You can't go there, Blake. You know you need to be laying low."

"Then we need to locate someone in Terre Haute who may be related to her deceased parents."

"What about her birth mother? You just spoke to her," McBain hinted.

"That would be a last resort," Cutter countered. "She's already on edge. Going through something like that might break her. Plus, she hasn't seen her since she was an infant and gave her away. There's no way to know what emotions it would trigger."

McBain spoke strongly, "Since you need to maintain discretion, I wouldn't suggest you go nosing around in Terre Haute. But I got an idea."

Cutter perked up, looking attentive.

McBain suggested, "You can have her genealogy traced. We can search the internet and see if there is a genealogist in her home county. Let someone with that background do the tracing and you stay in the shadows."

Cutter broke a wide grin, "It's worth a try."

McBain went on, "I need to get back to headquarters before Ryker finds out I'm here, but I'll leave my rental with you."

They departed the area, grabbed lunch at a downtown diner and then made it back to the hotel in the early afternoon.

After McBain used his phone to change his return flight to Atlanta, he and Cutter did a local internet search for a genealogist. They found three possibilities and settled on contacting the one linked to the local government. It was a genealogist who had an office located in the Special Collections Department of the Vigo County Library in Terre Haute.

The plan was now for Cutter to stay in the hotel overnight after driving McBain to the airport. He would check out the next morning, drive to Terre Haute, find a hotel, and spend Sunday locating the library. Then, he would visit the genealogist at the library early Monday morning.

Chapter 88

After Cutter dropped McBain off at the departure terminal of the Indianapolis International Airport, he was eager to get back to his hotel room and peruse the remaining photos in the Bei'an folder on the tablet. He resisted the temptation to confront McBain before he departed about his appearance in the Bei'an Mining site in the Manchuria, China photo. Yet he had a strong suspicion McBain was hiding something. But like a seasoned poker player, he was not about to show his hand prematurely.

He wanted to stay focused on his mission of locating a relative of Penelope Lane and convincing them to travel to Miami to identify the body for release. It was a tall order upon meeting a person for the first time. He figured he would have to fight suspicion of a fraud or that he could be a threat to a person's safety, especially if the relative he'd contact would be a female.

It was dark when he returned to the hotel Saturday night. He ate dinner in the hotel restaurant, then returned to his room. He showered, grabbed a beer out of the mini-fridge and took it and the tablet to the writing desk. Scrolling down the file where he left off before, he saw various photos of mining areas with Asian laborers and men driving construction trucks around the mine site.

After clicking on the bottom photo in the file, his heart nearly skipped a beat. In the photo were four men posing in front of a mine shaft opening. The furthest man to the left he recognized as Alex McBain. Since the photo was noticeably clearer than the one in the other file, he had no remaining doubt it was McBain even with a heavy shadow obscuring the top of his head above the hairline.

In the photo, McBain had a full beard, different from the previous photo in which he was clean shaven and more resembled his current appearance. Cutter drew the conclusion that the two photos were from different time periods but during the same trip.

Second from the left was a middle-aged unknown man who looked Asian. After a closer, prolonged look, he did not recognize the man. But he instantly recognized the second man from the right. Cutter's mouth gaped open. He could not believe his eyes.

Son-of-a-bitch! he muttered under his breath.

Ransom Oliver, reputed mob boss of the east coast syndicate, was smiling at a camera.

The man to the far right was another man who looked familiar. It was a younger Asian man who was in his late thirties or early forties. Unless a doppelganger, Cutter believed he had passed by this man in the hallway during his visit to Dorothy Drummond's real estate office during the Phillip Drummond drowning investigation.

If he hadn't recognized Ransom Oliver in the photo, he would have dismissed the thought.

What was the connection between all four figures?

He knew Phillip Drummond was directly involved with Bennie DeSalvo and indirectly involved with Ransom Oliver's drug and weapons smuggling operation prior to his murder.

Several questions entered Cutter's mind. *What was a US federal agent, a top US syndicate head and an associate of Dorothy Drummond doing in a photo together at a mining site in Bei'an, Manchuria? Was McBain there acting undercover on an international case? Or was something darker and more sinister taking place?*

A myriad of questions suddenly rocketed through Cutter's mind as he swigged the entire beer in three gulps. *Has Ransom Oliver expanded his criminal network to other countries? There is no information in bureau files about Ransom Oliver having any foreign business ventures. Is overseas mining a front for drug and weapons smuggling? How is Alex McBain involved and why hasn't he disclosed undercover work with Interpol, if that is what he was doing? When were these photos taken?* The only person, besides McBain, who could answer those questions was Penelope Lane who owned the tablet…and she was dead.

Because he had opened the file at his Bullet apartment without checking the date, there was no way of knowing when the file was last accessed and who opened it before he took the tablet from Penelope's hospital room.

He glanced at his watch and noticed it was nearing eleven p.m. He wisely decided it would be better to forego further scrutiny and settle on a good night's sleep. He copied the sub-folder onto the desktop and then opened his personal email account, composed a message, and attached the photo with Alex McBain at the mining site to the email and sent it to himself so he could access it on his cell phone. He then did a google search of the Bullet Herald newspaper and searched the online edition for a story regarding the homicide at the Watkins Psychiatric Hospital. His search of the headlines revealed a two-column article covering the murders of three people at the Watkins Psychiatric Hospital.

Security cameras captured images of three males at the late morning shooting scene. The men believed to have been involved in the shooting of a female patient were observed being shot by the third individual. Police sources revealed two of the males have been identified and a search was currently underway for the third.

Cutter skipped through the rest of the background filler until he read where Penelope Lane had been identified as the murdered patient. The obituary posting had no information besides her name—no names of surviving relatives.

A related article stated *a night receptionist at the hospital identified the two men who shot a hospital employee as the same men who murdered a female patient later the same morning.*

He started to shut down the tablet. But then, he decided to return to the Terre Haute Genealogy page. He located the Vigo County Library page again and wrote in his pocket memo book the name Meredith Shaw. Miss Shaw was listed as the Special Collections Department point of contact. Her biography noted she specialized in not only family heraldry but locating current relatives of deceased persons.

After putting the memo pad into the pocket of the blazer he would wear the next day, he grabbed another beer can out of the mini fridge, drank about half of its contents and dozed off on the bed. The traumatic events of the past week had finally taken their toll. Between exhaustion and the two beers, he was primed to get his first good night's sleep in several days.

Chapter 89

Due to Monday morning rush hour traffic and stops, it took two hours for Cutter to reach the Vigo County Library at 1 Library Square in Terre Haute. The drive gave him time to reflect on the events of the past week. His stomach was unsettled. There were suspicious circumstances surrounding Penelope's murder by Ransom Oliver's henchmen. Then he had the new mystery of his former partner captured in photos at a remote mining site in Southern Manchuria.

To relieve his anxiety, he made two stops along the interstate route: one at a diner where he ate a hearty breakfast, and another stop at a truck stop convenience store to buy a package of antacid tablets and a bottle of aspirin.

He pulled into the library parking lot at nine thirty, entered the building and checked in at the front desk.

The desk clerk confirmed Meredith Shaw was in her office. She directed him to a hallway in the back of the building where the offices for the Special Collections Department were located down the hallway and third door on the left.

When he reached an open door with a placard, *Meredith Shaw, Genealogist* affixed to it, he was surprised by her appearance. He had anticipated an unattractive, middle-aged, conservatively dressed woman with black-rimmed glasses who would look like a librarian. Instead, he was staring in at a cute, athletic, slender brunette with rosy cheeks, full lips, and a wide smile. She looked more like a college graduate assistant than his stereotypical view of a woman who would work in a library facility, such as a retired matriarchs with excess time on their hands.

She wore a red, double-breasted, six button business jacket and matching skirt and high heels.

From the internet, he had learned the Terre Haute native was a Brigham Young University graduate with a Bachelor of Arts Degree in Family History/Genealogy. But there was no picture or a listing of her age in the short bio.

"Can I help you, sir," she greeted him warmly as she moved from behind her desk.

"I hope so," Cutter answered with an eager look. "Are you in the Special Collections Department?" he asked for confirmation.

"Yes, I'm Meredith Shaw, head of the department. What can I do for you?" she replied with a warm smile.

"My name is Blake Cutter." His disingenuous introduction was the first credible-sounding connection coming to mind. "I found your contact information online and I'm sorry I didn't call for an appointment, but I'm on a tight schedule."

She smiled widely, chucked, and said, "It is no problem, sir. It's a good thing you came this morning. I'll be out of the office this afternoon. How can I do for you?"

He continued, "I flew in from Bullet, Georgia to request help in locating any surviving relatives of a woman who grew up in Terre Haute but died in Georgia four days ago. Her name at the time of death was Penelope Lane but her adopted name was Ana Oden."

Her eyebrows rose. "Please sit." she said, directing him to a sofa stationed next to the door. She then walked to the door and closed it.

"Do you know the name of her birth parents?" she asked.

"The birth parents were Ross and Margaret Sullivan from Indianapolis. Ross Sullivan passed away, but Margaret still lives in Indy.

"Hang on a minute." Cutter pulled out his cell phone, opened his notepad app and scrolled through his entries. He found a note he had put in the app two months ago when Alex McBain first emailed him from Terre Haute. "Her deceased adoptive parents' names were Henry and Mable Oden."

She suddenly stood and responded with a solemn voice, "I actually know about her on a personal basis."

Cutter remained silent as she cupped her chin with her right hand.

"Mister Cutter, I would love to help you but I —"

"But—what?" Cutter injected. He had not anticipated a shocking surprise but felt one coming.

She took a deep breath, sat stiffly on the couch beside him, eyed him cautiously, and said, "The reason I will be out this afternoon and evening is because I have a television interview to announce my partnership with the

Terre Haute Police Department to assist them in reopening and investigating cold case homicides. We can now use genetic genealogy to investigate cases previously closed before DNA analysis was developed. It will help us solve a myriad of cold missing person cases.

Cutter could tell by the grim look on her face what was coming next. "And you're about to tell me one of your first cases will be investigating the drowning deaths of Mable and Henry Oden that occurred years ago."

She nodded in acknowledgement. She was reluctant, but she suspected he would back her into a corner. She would have to talk about it.

Cutter let out a deep exhale. "I've been having a lot of shocking coincidences these last few weeks, but this is at the top of the list."

She informed him. "Mister Cutter, my grandmother died from cancer about a year ago. She was a longtime friend of Mable Oden. Grandma was in a nursing home for several years where I visited her quite frequently. She talked a lot about Mabel's death and how much it hurt her when the case was closed, and no one was brought to justice. She didn't believe it was a simple accidental drowning. I'm aware of her adopted daughter's disappearance. I didn't hear anything more until you mentioned her name."

Cutter sat pensively for a moment, then asked, "And you're sure we're talking about the same Mabel Oden?"

She reminded him, "You did say her husband's name was Henry Oden. Need I say more?"

"I guess not," he answered resignedly and dropped his gaze to the floor. "I came a long way, Miss Shaw. I just need you to investigate it for me."

She learned back in her chair, thought for a moment, then said, "I am sorry, Mister Cutter, but I would prefer you find another genealogist to help you. I would like to avoid any potential conflict of interest with my new association with the police."

He argued, "I don't see how it could be. I am only asking for your help to find a relative so they can identify her corpse and release her body for burial. Her birth mother has not had contact with her, so she couldn't identify her; and DNA testing will take too long."

She repeated, "I'm sorry, but I can refer you to another competent person who can help." She grabbed her cell phone off the desk, began scrolling through her contacts list, but came up empty on names.

Frustrated, Cutter replied, "No, it is okay. I will find another way. Thank you for your time."

Cutter turned to walk down the hallway but then turned back to her and pulled out a blank personal business card with only his name and phone number on it.

"Please take this with my phone number. It's not listed, so if you change your mind or decide there's something you can tell me without jeopardizing your case, I'd love to hear from you."

She extended her hand and accepted the card as he left her office before she could offer a conciliatory farewell. He was proceeding towards the front of the library when he heard his name called.

"Mister Cutter, wait a minute, please."

He stopped at the door, and she briskly approached him with his card in her hand.

"Let's step outside. I have something to tell you, but not in here."

CHAPTER 90

Cutter and Meredith Shaw walked to the side of the building near his car.

"Listen," she glanced around the corner and back to the front door to ensure they weren't being observed. "You have to keep my source confidential."

"Of course, "he confirmed to her.

"There is a woman who is an exotic dancer at a strip club in Indy. She was Mabel and Henry's only biological daughter. She ended up in a foster home after they drowned, but she left there seven years ago. I heard she ended up on the streets until two years ago when she started exotic dancing for a living. I didn't want anyone else involved in this case, but you have a legitimate reason."

He broke a wide grin and touched her shoulder, "Thank you. Can you give me a name and where I can reach her?"

She stood in deep thought for a moment and then said, "Look, the only thing I know is her stage name. It's Lavender Jones."

"What's the name of the club?"

"I do not know, but she works in one of those adult clubs downtown. I've done some preliminary work on this, so please don't let anyone know I gave you this information. I owe it to my grandmother to find out the truth about the Odens' drownings. I do not want anything to screw it up."

His final words were, "Trust me Miss Shaw. I just want to get someone to come to Georgia to take care of the remains. It will be the last she or you will see or hear from me."

They shook hands before she walked back to the entrance without another word.

Cutter started the engine, let it idle, and grabbed his cell phone to click the Safari search engine. He punched in *Adult Clubs in Downtown Indianapolis*, saved the link as a bookmark, tossed the phone onto the passenger's seat, and set the car in gear to begin his drive back to Indianapolis.

From experience he knew Monday nights were not normally busy times for strip clubs. He realized there was a chance several might not be open, or the listing might not be accurate. Strip club owners who went out of business rarely deleted their web listing.

But since he was already staying in Indy and he had extended the hotel reservation until Wednesday morning, he figured it would be worth his time to check out several in proximity of each other. He had no other options without a phone number or address. He still hoped before the evening was over, he would get a call from Meredith Shaw with more information about Ana Oden's stepsister, aka exotic dancer Lavender Jones.

CHAPTER 91

Of Indiana's sixty registered strip clubs, twelve were in the greater Indianapolis metropolitan area. Bars and strip clubs had taken stake near former residential neighborhoods in the downtown district and in the former industrial and residential districts surrounding downtown.

Cutter didn't foresee visiting all twelve in his search for Lavender Jones, so he narrowed his search to the clubs within five blocks of downtown. His abbreviated online search revealed seven downtown strip clubs: The Red Garter, Patty's Show Club, Classy Chassis, Lenny's Strip Club, the Cherry Picker Lounge, the Harem House, and the Sunset Strip. Opening times varied from four until ten-thirty p.m. He felt it was feasible to pop in to all seven in two days starting on Monday afternoon through noon Wednesday.

The only information Meredith Shaw told him was Lavender Jones worked at a downtown strip club, which meant he could have to inquire at all seven to ascertain which one she worked at. It didn't guarantee she would be working one of the next two days or was even still employed at one. He hoped he would get extremely lucky and discover she was employed at the first one he visited.

That evening, he had dinner delivered to his room. Afterwards, he thought deeply about how to approach his search for Lavender Jones. He decided to send a text message to Meredith Shaw to inquire about Lavender's real first name. He didn't expect a response based on her reluctance to reveal information due to her concerns of conflict of interest.

Ten minutes after sending it, he discovered he had jumped to the wrong conclusion.

His cell phone buzzed at ten p.m.

"Mister Cutter?"

"Yes," he responded, withholding excitement.

"It's Meredith Shaw. I got your text message and decided to call you instead."

"Thank you for calling Miss Shaw. How was your television interview?" he asked.

"It went well. Thank you for asking. It's the reason I decided to call you."

"I'm listening," Cutter prodded, softly.

"I need your help to get Miss Oden out of the exotic dancer business and start a new life somewhere else before she's hurt. If we accomplish what we expect to happen in this reopened case, it could be so painful, her life could spiral further out of control."

"So, why do you care?" Cutter asked her.

"My mother told me her friend Mabel talked about her all the time. She claimed the girl was highly intelligent and mature before the parents died. If she has any chance to one day find a better life, she doesn't need to relive the nightmare this case will bring back and find out about her stepsister's death at the same time."

Cutter paused and took a deep breath. "A tall order, Miss Shaw. As you surely know, exotic dancers make a lot more money than working at McDonalds or Target, especially if she is worked her way into becoming a high-end call girl, which many do. Many of those girls make enough to afford college or night school. If it's the life she chose for herself, it's extremely hard to get women out of that profession unless they want to. I don't even know her, and rehab is not my line of work."

In a strong tone, she demanded, "You must promise to do what you can to help her start a new life, or you don't get a name or any other assistance from me. I'll deny I ever met you."

Cutter sensed the trembling desperation in her voice. He believed she was being sincere and caring.

"Okay," he relented. "You have my word. If I can find her, I'll do what I can do to encourage her to change. First, I must get her to take custody of her stepsister's remains. I've only got another day here to find her. That's hardly enough time to convince anyone to make a career change."

There was a brief pause, then she said, "Your commitment to try is more than I have now."

"You have it, Miss Shaw. I'll try."

She sighed deeply, then said, "Okay, her birthname is Carrie Marie Oden."

E.T. MILLIGAN

E.T. Milligan is a published author, award-winning poet, and inspirational speaker. He has published two fiction novels; *The Looking Glass Self* and *Inclinations of Fear*, a non-fictional biographical novel, *On Linda: Love, Loss, and Renewal: The Case for Human Organ Sharing* and a poetry book entitled *Images of Life*. He is the recipient of two national poetry awards; The International Pen Award and Poet of Merit for *I'll Never Die* and the Editor's Preference Award for *If I Was a Tree*. He has conducted book signing tours, lectures, and speeches in both the U.S. and Europe. *Past the Line* is his first novel in the thrilling Blake Cutter Detective Series.

FORBIDDEN RESCUE

The Blake Cutter Detective Series (3-book series)

'A good cop never crosses the line in pursuit of justice.' But when Detective Blake Cutter's wife gets killed in a car bomb meant for him, grief and desperation will take him 'past the line.' His obsession with tracking down his wife's killers leads him to an encounter with a doppelganger of his late wife, into a tangled web of intrigue and deceit, and into the dark world of international crime.

What book reviewers said about Past the Line - Book #1

I have found Past the Line to be as entertaining as any book I have read. It captures your attention from page one and manages to keep it there until the very end. **Bookmasters Inc.**

Past the Line is as exciting and suspenseful as those from James Patterson, Faye Kellerman, Nora Roberts, and John Sanford. The first book is a must-read for lovers of romance, suspense, and action. **IP Book Reviewers**

Drama and tension take over the book right from the start. I recommend this book to readers who wish an edge to their fiction. **Bookreview.com**

To download the series onto your Kindle, click the Amazon.com link below:

The Blake Cutter Detective Series (3 book series) Kindle Edition (amazon.com)

Other Books by E.T. Milligan
Images of Life: A Book of Poetry

E.T. Milligan examines subjects that are pertinent today, offering sharp insights into the virtue that binds humans together and the vice that tears them apart. Images of Life is a creative compilation of poetry exploring themes as poignant as nature, devotion, love, equality, and spirituality. The collection includes the award-winning works "I'll Never Die", winner of the International Pen Award and Poet of Merit, and "If I Were a Tree", winner of the Editor's Preference Award for Poetry.

On Linda: Love, Loss, and Renewal: The Case for Human Organ Sharing (1992)

This novel is especially important for minorities. Milligan shows how a shortage of blood and organ donations from Black people, Hispanics and other minorities has led to a health crisis that causes thousands of needless deaths each year. Although written with the awareness of this medical emergency for minorities and the personal story of his wife's tragic death while waiting on a transplant, Milligan's ultimate message is one of hope and inspiration for all of us.

For more information, contact E.T. Milligan

at email: etmilligan9581@gmail.com

Phone: 1-800-551-9671

or

visit his website at

https://www.etmilliganpublishing.com

Facebook page link: https://www.facebook.com/tiger.mill.14

Made in the USA
Columbia, SC
16 February 2024

00f1d807-ccfb-4a8f-bc3d-323d7877674dR01